KANCHHI

Praise for the book

'*Kanchhi* is a tender swirl of a novel, a rich multisensory immersion into the world of rural Nepal. As the Maoist uprising stirs up political rebellion, the novel follows the coming-of-age of the high-spirited protagonist as she and her single mother negotiate the myriad limitations enforced on them by their society. Weena Pun writes with exceptional intimacy and grace about the emotional and intellectual quests of girls and women. *Kanchhi* is a major work – a gem.' – **Manjushree Thapa, author of *Forget Kathmandu***

'A brilliant novel by Weena Pun, where words are chosen with love. The poetic language shakes you to the core. This is not just the story of one Kanchhi; as you read, many Kanchhis begin chasing you. In the end, the story rips your heart apart like a razor blade.' – **Buddhisagar, author of *Karnali Blues***

'What lovely and lively characters from a lonely village by the millet fields. A new and authentic voice from a western mountainside!' – **Narayan Wagle, author of *Palpasa Café***

KANCHHI

WEENA PUN

hachette
INDIA

First published in 2024 by Hachette India
(Registered name: Hachette Book Publishing India Pvt. Ltd)
An Hachette UK company
www.hachetteindia.com

1

Cover design and illustration by Pia Alizé Hazarika
Author photograph by Porter Brown Jr. (2024)

Hardback ISBN 978-93-5731-630-9
eBook ISBN 978-93-5731-798-6

For sale in the Indian Subcontinent, Singapore and Malaysia only

Hachette Book Publishing India Pvt. Ltd
4th & 5th Floors, Corporate Centre,
Plot No. 94, Sector 44, Gurugram 122003, India

Typeset in ITC Galliard Pro 11/15.5
by R. Ajith Kumar, New Delhi

Printed and bound in India
by Manipal Technologies Limited

MIX
Paper | Supporting responsible forestry
FSC™ C043100

To Mom and Mau
G and Bubuli

Prologue

KANCHHI WAS SIXTEEN WHEN SHE DISAPPEARED. Sixteen. The age *apsaras* are when gods send them to lure *sanyasis* out of their deep, meditative state. *Sanyasis* who are supposed to be old and wise and beyond the pettiness of love, lust and seduction. A knock on the window. A romp in the hay. A dance in the millet fields.

A *sanyasi*.

A future a Nepali teacher once read on her fingers. That or a king, he had said. Both were extremes. One gives up everything that is power and pleasure, the other hoards them in abundance. Both of whom Kanchhi had weighed the possibilities of becoming. Neither, she wanted to become – especially not a *sanyasi*. A *sanyasi* was forged out of tragedies. Tragedies that Maiju, her mother, had hoped an old, rusty razor blade would forestall. A chipped and blunt, handleless barber's blade that once belonged to Kanchhi's grandfather. Maiju had left it out all night outside Kanchhi's room, out by the pillar supporting the porch roof. Its job was to stand guard and ward off evil. When Kanchhi left, she had taken it with her, along with a clear instruction from Maiju to leave it in the bag until she reached Pokhara. It did not work. Kanchhi disappeared.

That was the year 1995. Month: mid-November. A Monday. Two days after incessant rainfall wreaked havoc across Nepal, killing more than sixty people. In Torikhola too, a tiny hamlet in the district of Parbat, it caused a side of a slope and a wall of an abandoned house to cave in. Fields were waterlogged, millet plants flattened and trees uprooted. Maiju's front yard was littered with broken branches and tiny puddles where swarms of earthworms floated dead.

Otherwise, it was a beautiful, moonlit morning. A little past three. No fog. Just crisp and dark, vast mountains with their own noises. The moon, waning and gibbous, hung low on the horizon. Both Maiju and Kanchhi could see its light, a dim white floating in the space between the yard and the porch roof. Kanchhi from her room, Maiju from inside the kitchen, where a fire burned on the floor in front and within a small brass lamp on a shelf behind her. Some of the firewood was still damp from the rainfall. The logs hissed and dripped water as Maiju pushed them into the fire.

In Kanchhi's room, Kanchhi sat at the edge of her bed, ready and packed for the journey. In front of her, a lamp fashioned out of an ink bottle burned on the windowsill. The bed was already made – the sheet was straightened, the quilt was folded lengthwise and the two pillows, one without a cover, both dark and dirty, were on top of the quilt like stones on a shrine. When Maiju walked in with five pieces of millet bread wrapped in a rag and a glass of tea, Kanchhi was wrapping herself in a grey woollen *chadar*.

'Here.' Maiju gave her the bread. Kanchhi lifted the flap of an orange cloth bag sitting next to her and tried to cram it in.

'Gently,' Maiju said. 'Did you pack some tangerines too?'

'No.'

'Why not? I told you to pack some.'

'There's no space left.' Kanchhi showed her the orange bag. It bulged with her clothes. Another bag, a checkered plastic one on the floor, was full of her textbooks.

'That's not an excuse,' Maiju said. 'You have to take something for your aunt. You have to always take something whenever you go see someone, understand? Finish drinking the tea and get some from the attic.' Maiju placed the tea on the windowsill and headed towards the door.

'Where are you going?' Kanchhi asked.

'To the latrine,' Maiju said.

Kanchhi got up and followed her outside.

'You don't have to go now,' Maiju said. 'Drink your tea first.'

'No, I'll get it done. How many should I bring down?'

'Fifteen–twenty.'

'Fifteen, twenty? That's too many.'

'Just do as I say,' Maiju said and began to cross the yard. The latrine was two terrace fields below, on her right.

Maiju walked Kanchhi all the way down to the Setikhola river, past a small bazaar on its bank called Bagar and up to a point where a monsoon creek, now flowing because of the recent rainfall, met the river. It took them forty minutes – slightly longer than usual – because it was still dark, and the path was still muddy and slippery in places. Kanchhi showed the way with a flashlight. Maiju followed behind, carrying the checkered bag on her back with a tumpline. Both relied on walking sticks. Both remained quiet. The mountains were still sleeping, except for the crickets and cicadas, the brooks and the creeks and the occasional whimpers and barks of dogs far away. Sometimes, when they passed by houses, they could hear people sleeping, snoring, coughing or just breathing. A few times, they heard them clearing their throats. Both Maiju and Kanchhi whispered when needed, like when a section of a path was particularly slippery or when they had to fill up a canteen or when a door of a police station creaked and Maiju had to shush at Kanchhi to stop. Only after they crossed the bazaar and reached an isolated riverbed of the monsoon creek did they let their guard down.

'Listen, Kanchhi,' Maiju said, resting on a boulder. 'Don't buy street food or water, understand? Eat the bread and the tangerines instead. Don't talk to any strangers. Don't dawdle. Call your aunt as soon as you reach Pokhara. Ask her to come pick you up. If she does not, use the directions to her place. Remind her you are Kal's daughter. Once you reach her house, call the bazaar here and leave a message. If the line is broken, write a letter. Send two copies in case one gets lost. Just say you're well, and I'll understand. Now, don't be a nuisance to your aunt. Help her with the household chores and the kids. Tolerate her for a few months. No matter what she says, don't raise your voice at her. Don't do what you did here. Come back for the SLC exams. When are they again?'

'In two months.'

'Good. Once you are done with the exams, you can go back again, this time for jobs. No matter how hard life gets, don't come back until the exams, understand? Are you scared?'

'No.'

'No need to. Just keep to yourself. And throw the blade away after you get to her house.'

Maiju reached inside a fold in her *patuka* and took out a note. One thousand rupees.

'Where did you get it?' Kanchhi asked.

'Doesn't matter. Don't lose it.'

'Why would I?' Kanchhi took a pouch out of her *cholo* pocket and tucked the note in.

'What time is it?' Maiju asked.

Kanchhi flipped her wrist to look at her watch. A second-hand HMT watch given to her as a gift. 'A little past four,' she said.

'*Eh. Eh.*' Bayarghari by noon, Pokhara by three, Maiju calculated. 'Leave a message by five,' she said. 'Someone will get it.'

'Okay,' Kanchhi said and adjusted the tumpline around the checkered bag. 'Don't you need this? I can use my shawl.'

'No, take it. Bring it back with you,' Maiju said.

Kanchhi lifted the checkered bag on her back. Maiju threw the other one on top.

'Don't forget the stick,' she said.

Kanchhi yawned.

'Don't fall asleep on the way either,' Maiju said. 'You've got to look after the bags.'

'All right, all right. I'm leaving now. Don't let anyone use my room.'

'Who'll want to use it?'

'I don't know.' Kanchhi turned around and began walking up the riverbed. In the distance, the path turned left and disappeared up the mountain.

'Walk carefully.' Maiju raised her voice a little.

'Okay,' Kanchhi said and plodded on. Soon, she reached the bend and turned around. The flashlight was the giveaway. It was directed at Maiju and glowed like the tail of a glowworm. Then, it was gone.

That was the last Maiju saw of Kanchhi.

1

TORIKHOLA IS A MISNOMER. IT HAS NEITHER *TORI* (mustard) nor *khola* (river). Not anymore. Once upon a time, it was a lake. Perhaps the Tethys Sea, people meant to say, but they do not recall events that far back in time. The story is more recent and at once more ancient. A god drained it, they say. The lake. He had taken the form of a farmer and was on a mission to plough the whole earth flat in one night when he encountered a woman washing a blood-soaked petticoat by its shore. The woman was young, about twenty to twenty-two years of age, and the blood came from her period, the story goes, but the god did not know that for sure. He was standing behind a boulder and only saw the woman dipping in the petticoat and wringing it, colouring the water red as she did so. The red could have been from red mud or red juice or, if indeed blood, then from a chicken, a goat or childbirth. The god did not ask. He conjured a hoe and roared, 'You—'

The woman, startled by the noise, turned around. The god had sent the boulder tumbling towards her, and it missed her by an inch, crashing into the lake instead with a big splash. The water it displaced almost swept the woman off her feet.

'What's going on?' the woman wondered as the god ballooned as big as a tree and began slashing the slopes around him. His form was still that of a farmer.

'I'll show you—' the god muttered in anger and continued to attack the slopes left and right. The lake's outlet widened, and soon enough water cascaded out like a herd of sheep freed from a pen. It roiled and rumbled and swept along everything that could be swept along – trees, fields, hamlets, people still deep in their sleep.

The woman looked on. The god continued his rampage. When he was finally done minutes later, she was surrounded by deep rifts, valleys and mountains for as far as she could see. Nothing that was there before was there anymore. The woman herself, for instance, was standing in front of a massive gorge next to a ridge that would later become Torikhola. A newly formed ridge on her left.

There is another story of origin. Less magical, less than a thousand years old, more mundane. According to this story, the Bhusals founded Torikhola. Bhusal Chhetris, the sub-caste/caste of people Maiju married into. A long time ago, the story goes, the Bhusals, believed to be the descendants of Khas Aryans, first settled in the far west of the country and then moved east to Arghakhanchi, where they formed a settlement called

Bhusal Danda. The Bhusals, the story continues, lived there for generations until one day one of the families decided to pack everything up and move again, this time to the north, up along the Kali Gandaki River. When this family reached Parbat, back then its own kingdom, it decided, the story goes on, to follow a much smaller stream called the Setikhola and came to Bagar. Bagar then was nothing but fields, wild ones, and this family, believing it had come far enough, climbed up a mountain and founded Torikhola.

Maiju remembers the morning she arrived at Torikhola. It was almost winter. She was twenty-five and exhausted from a night-long walk from her first husband's house in Baglung, a district to the immediate west of Parbat, where she was also born and raised. With her was Saili *didi*, her fifth cousin and the reason she was in Torikhola. On her suggestion, or rather light prodding, Maiju was leaving her first husband and marrying Kal Bahadur Bhusal Chhetri, a man Saili *didi* said might not be any different from the rest but was at least willing to marry her despite her reputation as a childless woman.

By then, ten years had gone by since Maiju's marriage to her first husband, Dil Bahadur Karki, a big, muscular man with shoulders robust enough to father a whole volleyball team. He was a gentle giant, an ox, built like one and worked like one but in Dibai in the Uttar Pradesh state of India. A bodyguard to a restaurant owner, Dil

Bahadur came home only once every few years, and when he did, nothing happened. While other men's wives got pregnant and gave birth like leaky pots, Maiju continued to change rags and sleep in a corner of the buffalo's shed. She also continued to cut grass, gather wood, cook food, do the dishes and wait, never doubting, not even once, that it might have been Dil Bahadur who could not father a child. Like most women of her generation, she blamed herself and sat in front of shamans looking for a cure, travelled to temples near and far, donated rice, clothes and shoes to ascetics, and even avoided 'slippery,' 'abortion-inducing' foods like bottle gourd and okra. Nothing worked. Dil Bahadur continued to come home every few years, and Maiju continued to remain a *banjh*.

It was Saili *didi* who asked her if she had ever wondered whether it might be his fault.

Maiju had not. There was a rumour that Dil Bahadur had a child somewhere in the plains, and Maiju believed it.

'Why don't we do this?' Saili *didi* whispered, sitting under a gooseberry tree. 'I know a man in Torikhola who's looking for a wife. He lives in Assam, in India, is a car mechanic there, is an only son, all his sisters are already married, and when I told him about you, he said he didn't care that you're already married and childless.'

'How is it going to be any different?' Maiju asked.

'It's not,' Saili *didi* said. 'We're women. It's not going to be any different. But he might give you a child. If he does, great. If not, you'll at least have me there.'

The wedding to Kal Bahadur took place a week later. It was small and informal. Kal was fine, physically at least – five-five, slightly taller than Maiju, and wearing a pair of waist-high brown pants that matched his brown leather shoes. Both were old but not terribly worn out. Maiju herself was in a red nylon sari, a red, shimmering *cholo* and a red veil – all gifts from Kal. When Maiju walked up from Saili *didi*'s house, a few fields below on the left, Kal was standing in front of the stoop that led to the kitchen. His parents, both in their late seventies, were a step above, holding a bowl of curd and a brass tray dotted with a handful of *akshyata*, a pinch of red *sindoor* powder, a few unbloomed hibiscus, and a bunch of sprigs of wild sage. A small number of villagers hung around them, but most squatted along the raised edge of the front yard. Maiju walked past them and joined Kal at the stoop.

'May your marriage be fruitful. May it be successful,' the parents chanted.

The ceremony began. Kal's parents marked Kal's forehead with a dollop of red *akshyata* and then hers, placed a leaf of wild sage and an unbloomed hibiscus in his hands and then hers, made him eat a spoonful of curd and then her, told Kal to line her hair with the red *sindoor* powder, he did, and they were married. There was no priest, no *panche baja*, no party. Just a sense of having sat through the rituals and the quiet cassette player Kal had brought with him. Maiju reckoned they did not want to waste money on a second-hand bride.

That Kal too was a second-hand groom would be confirmed four years later. That night, however, Maiju only prayed for a child. As Kal lay asleep next to her on a tiny bed strewn with hibiscus, she only wondered whether their child would have his thick hair and small ears or his quiet nature and left-handedness. Unlike Dil Bahadur, Kal was a messy sleeper. He slept with his arms above his head and drooled on his own shoulders – a trait Kanchhi would later inherit. But not that night. Maiju did not get pregnant then. Or the night after. On the third day, Kal left, saying he would be back in a few months on a longer break.

Months turned into a year. Kal's father suffered from a stroke and sat still, staring into the distance, shitting wherever he was. Soon afterwards, his mother began asking to speak to people long dead. Messages were dispatched. Letters were written. But Kal did not return. He did not even reply. Neither did his seven sisters, all married and scattered around the mountains like *simal* seeds. One day, Maiju made a small urn of ghee and went to see a shaman in Bayarghari. The shaman, a petite Bahun woman as old as Maiju with a tattoo of a snake on her inner wrist, told her that a spirit was in pain and blocking Kal's way home. Maiju should use some of the ghee she had brought with her and light two candles in two corners of the house, the corners where the yard met the paths. 'Show Kal the way home,' she said.

It took three more years and the death of both of his parents for Kal to find his way back. His father died first. A week later, his mother. Maiju confined herself in the same room they had died in and mourned as the ritual demanded, eating nothing but plain rice for thirteen days. Kal returned just before the *Dashain* festival ended. He disposed of the dead's ashes in the Kali Gandaki River, allowed their spirits to cross to paradise and then fell ill before he could catch the bus back to India. Cholera nearly killed him.

It was an October afternoon. Kal, stricken with the disease, lay dried and shrivelled on a mat on the porch. Covering him was a thick and lumpy cotton quilt. Underneath it, Kal seemed like a little twig, ready to snap at the slightest force. Maiju herself was in the kitchen garden, on a small patch of land right off the front yard, digging for taro roots. When Kal woke up, she was rubbing mud off of one of the roots.

'*Maiya, Maiya,*' Kal cried. He never called Maiju '*maiya*.'

'What happened?' Maiju asked.

'*Maiya*,' Kal cried again.

Maiju walked up to the porch with a mattock in one hand and a few taro roots in the other. Kal had raised himself off the floor and was leaning against the wall. Maiju helped him pull up the quilt and tucked it around him.

Kal began to cry.

'What happened?' Maiju asked again.

'I'm going to die too' Kal said.

'Nonsense. Are you hungry?' she asked.

'No,' Kal said and wiped his lips. They were heavily chapped. A deep gash had formed in the middle of his lower lip, and it was bleeding.

'Did you have any more *dal*?' Maiju reached for a bowl at the edge of the porch and lifted the plate covering the lentils. He had not touched it.

'Want me to heat this up?' Maiju asked.

Kal shook his head.

'You need to eat something,' Maiju said. 'Want me to warm you up some milk instead?'

'No,' Kal said.

'Well, wait then. I'm making some taro soup tonight. It'll be good for you. Anything you would like me to add to it? What does your stomach say?'

'No, listen to me,' Kal urged. 'I saw my father in my dream just now. I know I'm going to die too.'

'No, you're not. Stop saying the same thing.'

'Listen to me.' Kal raised his voice a little.

Maiju paused.

'I have to tell you something, everything. You've been such a good wife to me, and all I've done is mistreat you.'

'Don't worry about it now,' Maiju said. She thought he was talking about his long absence from the hamlet.

Kal pulled the quilt closer to his chest.

'The wall's cold. Lie back down,' Maiju said. 'Or put this pillow behind you.'

Kal put his hand on the pillow. 'Forgive me, Syani,' he said. 'I didn't want to hurt you, but she wouldn't come to the hills.'

'Who?'

'My parents were getting old. I had to find someone for them. You understand, don't you? I have a wife and two daughters in Assam. They have no one but me. If I die, find them and bring them here.'

The truth was it was different. Maiju had hoped it would be different. If not love, then mutual exhaustion would bring them together. Her being tired of the mountains and the drudgery, him being tired of the cities of India. That first night when she had watched him sleep in a white vest turned yellow from sweat, smelling like the bidi he had just snuffed out, his face down on the pillow, squished as he drooled, she had not been able to help but fall for him. She thought she understood him. He was a struggler like her. An outsider. Desperate and devoid of swagger, someone who hid his shame in cassette players and worn-out brown leather shoes. An unbloomed hibiscus. She understood him, she had thought, and had allowed this feeling to grow and morph into love even in his absence.

Guleli jhika, Saila
Pinjada buna, Saila
Salaijo ma chari bani aunchhu

(Get the slingshot out, Saila
Build a cage, Saila
I'll turn into a bird and come to you)

A week after the delirious confession, Kal left. As soon as he could stand, he packed his duffle bag and walked out. He did not even wait until the *Tihar* festival was over. All he said, standing under the jackfruit tree that his father had planted, was that Maiju should take care of herself. He did not say he would never return, but as he walked by the millet fields and briefly vanished behind a hedge of Malabar nut plants, Maiju knew she would never see him again. A last bit of love surged up to cloud her eyes, to force her to run after him and beg him to stay, but she stayed put under the jackfruit tree, fighting its sweet scent and the bitter separation.

That night, Maiju too dreamt of Kal's father. He was blind in one eye and crawled around a room with a bowl in his hand. Kal's mother screamed from the kitchen, asking him to stop dragging the bowl like that. She could not hear who she was talking to. Kal himself was asleep on the porch, cured of cholera, and Maiju stood by him with a mattock in her hands, still shocked at what he had revealed.

In the distance, a forest below the village temple caught fire. A bird, with its tail alight, flew to the house and landed on the roof. It rolled around, trying to extinguish the flame, but its desperation only lit up the thatch. Within seconds, the whole roof was ablaze. Maiju tried to run to the yard, but her legs would not move. They were heavy like pillars, as if under the influence of *dhaturo* seeds.

'This way, this way,' Kal shouted to his parents. He was no longer on the porch but in the yard, waiting for them.

'Get me a hoe or something,' Maiju too shouted. She had been using the mattock to try to chip away at the clay around her, but the mattock was too small and the plaster too hard. It did not even create a dent.

'Get me a hoe,' Maiju shouted again. Her voice only came out as a mumble. No one heard it. In the meantime, the fire kept raging. It burnt everything around her – the mats, the quilt, the baskets, the beams – and the smoke engulfed her. When she looked up again, there were three more people in the yard – Kal's first wife and his two daughters.

Maiju let go and knelt, exhausted, defeated, ready to be burnt.

That was when she saw the pumpkin, golden like the lines on a *yogi*'s forehead, squatting in the middle of the porch where Kal had been. The biggest, the fullest and the most reverential pumpkin she had ever seen in her life. Its leaves were equally astonishing. They spread above the fruit like an umbrella and twinkled as bright as a thousand fireflies.

Maiju was pregnant.

2

November 13, 2005

'SYANI, *EH* SYANI.'

'Hoi, hoi.'

'Syani. Syani, *ho*,' Saili *didi* calls again.

Maiju, standing in her front yard, picking up a bundle of rice-bean shrubs, throws them on the porch and walks all the way to the edge of a small terrace field. Then, she looks down.

'What happened, *Didi*?' Maiju asks.

Saili *didi* looks up. She is a sight – a small, frail woman enveloped in a thick fog and a blouse too big for her. She is hurling fresh buffalo dung down to a manure heap.

'Connect the pipes for a bit, Syani,' Saili *didi* says. 'He needs to leave right away.'

By 'he,' she means her husband, Bir Bahadur *dai*, a retired Indian army veteran and Kal's second cousin. He is standing behind Saili *didi*, brushing his teeth in his usual clothes – a faded green vest and green shorts. He does not look up at Maiju.

'Going far, *Dai*?' Maiju shouts.

'Yes,' Saili *didi* answers for him.

'Bayarghari or all the way to Pokhara?'

'Pokhara,' Saili *didi* says.

Bir Bahadur *dai* still does not look up at Maiju. Instead, he continues to peer through the fog as if he can see the mountains far away and on them a jeep waddling down to Bagar Bazaar. For a while now, jeeps have been ferrying passengers from Bagar to Bayarghari and back.

'Why, what happened?' Maiju asks Bir Bahadur *dai*. She can tell he and Saili *didi* have fought again, and whenever they fight, his anger automatically extends to Maiju. 'Won't you stay for the *ratyauli* party tonight?' she adds.

Bir Bahadur *dai* spits out the toothpaste.

'Syani,' he shouts. He has a faint Indian accent that he never let go of. 'Don't just stand there and ask questions. Connect the pipes. I'll miss the jeep otherwise.'

Maiju chuckles, a little startled. Saili *didi* lifts her hand up in the air and signals Maiju to restrain herself. She will come up and explain things later, the gesture says.

Maiju shakes her head and turns around. Right before the yard, just off and adjacent to it, is an outdoor sink, a cobbled space where Maiju washes dishes and sometimes clothes. Maiju stops by it and lets water flowing out of a black PVC pipe collect in a big copper cauldron. Then, she fills up a water pot, washes her hands and face and squirts water at the base of two tangerine trees. The pipe is threaded through one of them. When she finally does as asked – connecting the pipe coming down from Thapa Nani *didi*'s house to the one going down to Saili *didi*'s – a jeep honks from the mountains far across the Setikhola gorge. It is a signal that the vehicle has left its parking spot and is on its way down to Bagar Bazaar. From there, it will leave for Bayarghari in exactly an hour, at 6:30 a.m. On a clear morning, the jeep can be spotted as a tiny, moving speck. Today, the fog is too dense.

3

PREGNANCY WAS TERRIBLY DEPRESSING. THE SURGE of hormones carried with it a sense of foreboding that hung over Maiju like a thick cloud. In the beginning, it numbed the pain and humiliation that Kal's confession had left. All Maiju could do was sleep. The body demanded rest, and Maiju gave in. She slept for fourteen hours a day, eating nothing but a thyme–fennel concoction that Saili *didi* would force her to swallow. There were no dreams to dream then, just exacting fatigue that took her far away from the world that spun around as if it would collapse upon itself.

'Saili *didi*,' Maiju would ask once she was able to pull herself out of the haze. 'Are we sinners or is the world like that?'

'It's the world, Syani,' Saili *didi* would reply. 'Always the world.'

The world trundled on. Autumn gave way to winter, and Maiju reared her head up a little. She dumped manure in the fields, racked straws on a rick and wove a swinging basket for the unborn child. She also tore up rags and sewed it *bhoto*s and trousers. Fatigue still hounded her, and whenever, wherever sleep possessed her, she slept, sometimes on a bed of fodder in the middle of a field, sometimes in the middle of the yard in the middle of a task. Oftentimes, she drifted in and out of consciousness, seeing visions and hearing voices that were not there. Occasionally, she woke up to unbearable cravings and nibbled on earth like an earthworm.

In the spring, Maiju planted corn and beans in the fields she had fertilized all winter. Then, she weeded them, pulling the unwanted by their ears and burying them a lump at a time. Through it all, Saili *didi* helped. She brought Maiju kettles of tea and jugs of buttermilk, and when Maiju became too large to climb trees, she lopped branches for her. She also carried Maiju's *doko*s from the fields to the house and from the house to the watermill. She took her animals out to graze.

Then came the monsoon. The first drops fell, and the corn produced tassels. The beans crept up the stalks and flowered white, some purple. Maiju weeded the fields again and tilled them, hoed the soil upside down and planted millet. She tucked the saplings under the earth, challenged them to dig deep and will themselves up. When they did, it was the midst of the monsoon in mid-July. The day: *Shrawan Sankranti*, when people chewed on sugarcanes and thanked god for helping them survive the monsoon, even though the season was not over yet. In the evening, they threatened measles by burning wood. They burned two pieces. One, they threw over the roof, the other, across the yard. Ironically, the being they invoked was a king. An ancient king of Galkot. *'Galkote raja, luto laija,'* they said. 'Run, measles, run,' they shouted. It was an irony because the year was 1979 and anti-king sentiments were at their peak. Youths met in buffalo sheds and took out protest rallies at night. They burned torches made of corn stalks and rags and demanded the fall of the monarchy. Even a tiny hamlet like Torikhola was steeped in the spirit of revolution.

> '*Rajtantra.*' '*Chahidaina.*'
> '*Janatalai marna.*' '*Paidaina.*'
> '*Paisa sabai?*' '*Switzerland.*'
> '*Desh banayo?*' '*Jhingaland.*'

> ('The reign of king.' 'We don't need it.'
> 'Murdering people.' 'You can't do it.'
> 'Where's the money?' 'Switzerland.'
> 'What about Nepal?' 'Fly-land.')

It was as they passed by the house that Maiju went into labour.

'It's begun,' she said, and Saili *didi*, who was at the outdoor sink washing dishes, walked her to the kitchen. The space between the hearth and the window was prepared for delivery. A thin mattress lay on top of a straw mat and an old *lungi* on top of it all.

It was a difficult labour. Kanchhi's hand slipped out first.

'Lau na ni,' Saili *didi* gasped. Gathered around her were her two sisters-in-law and three other women from the hamlet: Thapa Nani *didi*, Saru *didi* and Poudel *didi*.

'Where's the midwife?' Thapa Nani *didi* asked.

'Where are the boys?' Saru *didi* asked.

The boys – Saili *didi*'s two sons, first and third born – were up the mountain to fetch a midwife. The midwife lived in a Gurung hamlet in Balakot – about an hour's walk away.

'They should be here soon,' Saili *didi* said. On the hearth was a thin stainless-steel blade submerged in a pot of boiling water.

'Is everything ready?' the midwife asked when she walked in just before midnight, soaked in rain and covered in leeches. Had she been a minute late, it would have been all over, she would later say. In the dim light of the fire, she could see that Maiju's head lolled like dough and Kanchhi's hand was turning blue.

'Yes, it is,' Saili *didi* answered, pouring the midwife a jug of warm water to wash her hands.

The midwife did so over a cauldron and took her position by the foot of the bed. 'It's okay now,' she whispered to Maiju. 'I'm here. One more push and it's done.'

The midwife then inserted her whole hand in and pulled Kanchhi out alive.

Ek din, eh Maiju, dukhaka dina ferinchhan
Ferinelai bido mala deu
Haaaaa, manama maya sanglina deu

(One day, my dear aunt, the winds will turn
Bid farewell to those who're already gone
Let love pool again in your soul)

4

KANCHHI PLAYED HOUSE IN A CORNER OF THE PORCH. There, she kept a short straw mat as her bedding, a wooden log as her baby and a collection of discarded items, such as snuffboxes, cigarette packs and matchbox trays, as kitchen appliances. The snuffboxes (her pots) had wild burs (rice) in them, the cigarette packs (sacks) had dirt (millet) and the matchbox trays (plates) had pebbles (corn). She had a buffalo too – a small, pointed gourd on four little twigs. Although the buffalo, with its legs awkward and akimbo, looked more like a newborn calf, it had just been 'milked.' An aluminium bottle cap, almost as big as the buffalo itself, stood by it as a milk pail. Kanchhi, five years old, 'emptied' the pail into a broken spoon (her wok) and set the wok on top of three pebbles (her stove). Then, she pretended to light a fire and blow on it using the shell of a pen.

Usually, Laxmi played with her. Laxmi – Saili didi's youngest daughter, who was two years older than Kanchhi but followed her around like a younger sister. She would pretend to be her own mother, sometimes her father, albeit a quiet, shy one with dark black hair tightly plaited and folded onto themselves over each temple. That afternoon, however, Laxmi was in school (she had just begun first grade) and so it was Ramesh, Poudel *didi*'s son and a Bahun boy of Kanchhi's age, who played with Kanchhi. He was her husband, a lousy one – did nothing but stand in the yard and spin his top, and when bored with that, kept pleading with Kanchhi to join him in getting crabs from the spring. The crabs could be found hidden under rocks, and, if patient and lucky, they could also be seen walking along the floor of a shallow puddle.

'Kanchhi, please,' Ramesh pleaded.

'Later,' Kanchhi said and served him burs on a rind of a tangerine. Ramesh brought the rind to his chin, pretended to chew the burs and threw them away.

'Now, we sleep,' Kanchhi said and made room for Ramesh on the mat. Their daughter, the log wrapped in a shawl, was already 'asleep' on it.

The second Ramesh lay down, Kanchhi crowed like a rooster and said, 'Up, up, it's morning.'

Just then, another Kanchhi, Ramesh's younger sister, walked down and Ramesh gave up the act altogether.

'Kanchhi kanchhi bhet bhako ghyampo jatro pet bhako / babari phulko bot,' he sang and hopped in the yard, ready to head to the spring.

'Listen, Kanchhi,' he said, slipping into his flip-flops. 'If you want to come with us, come, but I'm leaving.'

His sister followed him.

Kanchhi watched the two walk towards the buffalo shed for a while and then grabbed the shawl off her log daughter and sprinted after them.

'Don't go too far,' Maiju shouted as the three passed the shed.

The spring was not far. At most, it took them fifteen minutes – past the shed and a long stretch of a millet field, past the Chiuridanda bend, where a lone butter tree flowered white, and down a slope and across a rift. There were no other houses in between, just rows and rows of fields flanked by trees, fields then yellow with millet and ripening beans. But the three dilly-dallied for a bit, catching grasshoppers flitting between millet plants first and then picking up *chiuri* flowers fallen on the ground. At the bend, they also encountered Ramesh's mother cutting grass on a field below. Ramesh's mother told them to come and get the *khaneu* figs she had collected. The figs were late bloomers and a little hard to the touch but still reddish and tasty. Afterwards, the three came across a wasp nest built in a hole on the slope and almost forgot about the crabs, talking about smoking the wasps out instead and taking the larva home to eat. Ramesh's mother shouted them out of it. When they finally made it to the spring, their bellies full of figs and their little legs a little tired, it was late afternoon, and Kanchhi wondered if they should just head home. The other Kanchhi had already thought the same and was beginning to cry. She even turned around towards her mother when her brother exclaimed, 'Look, a crab!' He had noticed a little brown one crawling at the bottom of a puddle.

The puddle was in between two wide slabs of stone. Ramesh quietly stepped on one of them and bent down to pin the crab. Then, he picked it up by its shell. The crab fought to be free right away. It clawed at the air in front and kicked with its legs. When it got hold of nothing, it splayed its pincers out, waiting for Ramesh to make a mistake. Ramesh laughed and presented a twig to the crab to nip at. The crab did not fall for it. It did not even move. The torture had begun, and the two Kanchhis waited for it to get ugly before it ended. There had been times when Ramesh would rip a crab's shell off to neutralize it. And once, he had gouged its eyes out with its own pincers. Surprisingly, this time, Ramesh only stroked the crab's back and put it down in the puddle exactly where he had found it. The crab scurried towards a hole in the wall and disappeared.

'What happened?' Kanchhi asked.

'It's too small,' Ramesh said and hopped across the puddle. 'Let's go look in the other spring instead.'

The other spring was another fifteen minutes away, in the midst of a wooded slope. *Sal*, *chilaune*, *uttis*, *simal*, *amaro* – all kinds of trees that nodded in the breeze as if to a piece of gossip. Ramesh picked up a stick and began thrashing the bushes lining the path. Kanchhi hopped across and did the same.

Up ahead, there was a bend, and around the bend, a chestnut tree that had just fruited. The three got distracted again and began gathering the nuts that were scattered on the ground. Some were just husks and tasted burnt, but most were edible. Still, it was a lot of work for a little bit of nothing. Ramesh soon gave up and began collecting acorns instead. He then threw them against a tree that was below the path and listened to them roll down.

'Wait a minute here,' he said and walked into the woods below. The two Kanchhis continued gathering chestnuts in their shawls. A while later, Ramesh walked up with a days-old hatchling in his hand. The chick was pink and blue, slightly bigger than the crab they had found, and bald. It also had a startling yellow beak. Kanchhi remarked on it.

'Do you want it?' Ramesh asked.

'To eat? No,' Kanchhi said.

'No, no, not to eat – to play house later,' Ramesh said. 'You can be its mother, and I can be its father.'

Kanchhi looked at the hatchling again. It craned its neck up, as if in hunger, and chirped loudly. The inside of its mouth was as yellow as its beak.

'Okay,' she said and took the bird in her hands.

At home, Maiju shrieked when she saw the hatchling.

'Where did you get it from?' she asked. 'Go back and leave it exactly where you found it.'

'It didn't have its parents,' Kanchhi said.

'How do you know?' Maiju asked. 'Maybe they went off to get food. Maybe they are now looking for it. Go back and put it right where you found it.'

'There's another one there,' Kanchhi said.

'Just go and put it back,' Maiju shouted.

By then, Ramesh and his sister had already run up to their house at the top of the hamlet. Kanchhi looked at the hatchling in her hand and then at Maiju, now dusting a straw mat at the edge of the yard. She would not allow Kanchhi to keep it, that was for sure. Kanchhi turned around to walk back to the bend with the chestnut tree.

'Leave it exactly as you found it,' Maiju shouted again, as Kanchhi walked away.

Back by the chestnut tree, Kanchhi surveyed the woods below the path, but she could not remember which tree it was that Ramesh had climbed. She had not seen him do so. Besides, the trees now all looked the same, and the canopy had tens of birds gathered above, some circling the trees, some sitting on their perches and ruffling their feathers, and some flapping their wings and trilling hello to each other. Their trills, together with the sloshing of the streams and the silhouettes of the mountains, now appearing ghostly against the darkening sky, began to scare Kanchhi, and she hastily placed the hatchling down by the base of the chestnut tree and ran. A moment later, she ran back. The hatchling, cold, weak and its beak no longer gawking, had crawled a little after her and stopped. Kanchhi picked the chick up and took it to the spring, leaving it on a stone bench cut on the slope instead, hoping that someone would find it and take it to its nest.

The next morning, Maiju found the hatchling dead, with its neck and wings outstretched, as if it was trying to fly home. Maiju took it back to the house, woke Kanchhi up and told her that since she had killed it, she would have to eat it. Maiju even started a fire out by the sink and began roasting the hatchling, turning it on its side every few seconds. Kanchhi, wrapped in a green *chadar*, sat on the porch and pecked the floor with her fingernails. The air was heavy with the smell of burnt skin and her guilt.

'You killed it, you eat it,' Maiju kept saying.

Two months later, Kanchhi, Ramesh and the other Kanchhi went on another excursion. This time, Laxmi too joined the troupe, and Kanchhi led the charge. Their plan was to go to India and live with Kanchhi's father in Assam. They walked all the way down to Bagar, crossed the bridge over the Setikhola River and sauntered their way towards a teashop. The teashop was a room in a house converted to sell a little bit of everything – tea, doughnuts, noodles, biscuits, notebooks, used textbooks, pens, pencils, tobacco, soap, sandals, socks, handkerchiefs and even yards of unstitched clothes. It was what made Bagar a bazaar, for Bagar had nothing then but that shop and two buildings of a public high school. The rest was just rice fields, one after another, up and down the river.

'Where are you going?' Thapa Maila *dai* asked. He was Thapa Nani *didi*'s husband and the secretary of the Torikhola Village Development Committee. Sitting on a bench outside the shop, he was drinking tea.

'Assam,' Kanchhi said.

'Assam? Assam or Achham?' Thapa Maila *dai* asked.

'Assam,' Kanchhi said again.

'*Lau na ni.*' Thapa Maila *dai* laughed. The shopkeeper, a man with a hole in the bridge of his nose, laughed as well.

'Turn around right away or else I'll tell your folks what you've been up to,' Thapa Maila *dai* said.

Kanchhi looked at the other Kanchhi, and the other Kanchhi at Ramesh and Laxmi. The four were suddenly fearful of being caught.

'I said, right now.' Thapa Maila *dai* stamped his foot to stress his point.

Kanchhi and the other children turned around. Soon, Thapa Maila *dai* finished his tea and joined them, corralling them like goats if they lingered around at a spot for longer than he liked.

'*Rakshasni, kukurni,*' Maiju screamed as soon as she saw Kanchhi. The whole village had descended on their front yard, exhausted from the search for the four everywhere. Thapa Maila *dai*, despite his promise, told everyone where he had found them.

That evening, Maiju tied Kanchhi to a pillar on the porch and whipped her with nettles soaked in water. The villagers demanded it. 'She has gotten out of hand,' they said.

The shenanigans continued for two more years. One day, Kanchhi threw a stone at a boy, splitting his head open. Maiju had to sell a chicken to pay for his treatment. Another day, she 'wrote' pussy on an agave leaf and went around calling *'bakulla'* (fava beans) *'bauko gula'* (father's dick) even though she knew how to say *bakulla* and knew what *bauko gula* meant. The following autumn, she assembled a group of village children and walked them down into a bamboo grove far below the house. Each of the children had stolen a bulb of onion and a handful of salt from their kitchens. They were holding a picnic, Kanchhi later said when Maiju found them all asleep on dried bamboo leaves, listless as if poisoned. One of them had even shat in his pants, but none had woken up.

Things changed in 1986 when the primary school below the hamlet finally opened after years of being under construction and Kanchhi was enrolled in grade one. As if overnight, she became quiet and 'nice,' turned into a non-threatening, non-rebellious little girl. No roaming around villages after school. Okay, *Ama*. No playing after dark. *Hus, Ama*. No stretching your legs in front of the fire. *Hunchha, Ama*. She did as asked.

Later, Kanchhi would often wonder if the changes were because she was tired of doing what she had been doing until then or if it was because the school had opened a whole new world and she had to focus on mastering it. In particular, there was a certain male teacher who demanded all her energy. This teacher loved to punish children by dunking them in a metal barrel full of cold water, regardless of the weather, sometimes with their clothes on. Often, by the end of his class, there would be a long line of students shivering in cold and in fear. Kanchhi hated to see them like that, but when she told Maiju about it, Maiju said the kids probably deserved it – a punishment like that would bring them in line. Thapa Nani *didi*, who taught Kanchhi Nepali then, laughed at her and then told the teacher what Kanchhi had told her.

'Today, Deepa's going to name all the months in a year,' the teacher said in the next class. 'If she fails, she's going to take a bath.'

Deepa was Kanchhi's school name, and she had a hard time remembering the fifth month of *Bhadra*. For some reason, she kept skipping it when asked to recall it.

'*Baisakh, Jesth, Ashadh, Shrawan…*' Kanchhi began.

Fortunately, Maiju had just begun to work in the school as a sweeper, and the 'sir' only struck Kanchhi with a long bamboo pipe when she stumbled on the fifth month.

That first year came to an end in mid-December, in the month of *Mangshir*. To her surprise, Kanchhi came first,

first out of seven students, first with a 60 per cent, still a first, and that cemented the change that had begun a year ago. On the results distribution day, Thapa Nani *didi* told Maiju that Kanchhi was a pearl. 'What takes others days to comprehend, she does so in a few hours. What takes others hours, a mere minutes. Kanchhi's going to make us all proud someday, *Bhauju*,' Thapa Nani *didi* said. 'She's going to make us all proud someday.'

5

November 13, 2005

THE JEEP CONTINUES TO HONK IN THE FAR DISTANCE. Maiju gathers in a *doko* a gallon can, a towel, a *lungi*, a T-shirt and a *puja* tray and leaves for the spring. An important part of the anniversary ritual is taking a bath there. The anniversary of Kanchhi's departure. Maiju considers the water here purer and fresher compared to that stored in a tank and then distributed through pipes. The water here is also warmer. It flows out of a bamboo pipe in a thick and loud hypnotizing stream and collects in a puddle that drains down a small channel dense with wild vegetation – mint, watercress, wild yam, ferns. When she is ready, Maiju stands by the puddle and bends forward. '*Harhar Gange*,' she chants as the water hits her head. Ganga, the water goddess, resides above the bamboo pipe under a cover of ferns. A small rock no bigger than Maiju's fist. After her bath, Maiju touches the rock and offers it a sprig of wild sage. One leaf touches the stone, the other the stream.

6

IN SECOND GRADE, ONE OF KANCHHI'S CLOSE friends was a girl named Jharana. She lived in a Thakuri hamlet below Torikhola, on the left, and the two were close because both were short and stout, while the third girl in their class was tall and lanky. All three loved to play ghost. They would put a shawl over their heads or just let their hair fall in front and growl. Kanchhi usually played the ghost. Her growls sent Jharana and Samjhana, the tall girl, shrieking in joy and horror. Kanchhi never understood what exactly was so funny or scary about it, but she enjoyed doing it for their laughs.

Of the three, Jharana was the 'girly' girl. She had pink, puffy cheeks that the grown-ups loved, and she flashed a cute, innocent smile whenever they pulled on them. Samjhana was the opposite. She carried a scowl on her face and scrunched up her nose while talking, as if she could sniff what the world was up to. Kanchhi fell in the middle. A teacher's pet but a quiet, confused one.

Jharana was also fragile. She was prone to sudden bursts of headaches. Sometimes, in the middle of a class or during playtime, she would clutch her temples with both hands and say that her brain hurt. One day, she fainted. Thapa Nani *didi*, who was now their class teacher, had just entered the room and was writing the date on the blackboard when Jharana's head flopped and hit the table.

'Miss, miss, Jharana's fainted,' Samjhana said, standing from her bench.

Thapa Nani *didi* walked over and gently tapped Jharana's head. 'Jharana,' she said.

Jharana did not respond.

Kanchhi stepped out of her seat. Thapa Nani *didi* slid in behind the table and stretched Jharana on her back on the bench.

'Go get some water, Kanchhi,' Thapa Nani *didi* said.

Kanchhi ran to the tank outside and got a jug of water. Thapa Nani *didi* was now fanning Jharana with a notebook. If Jharana felt the air, she did not show it. Thapa Nani *didi* passed the notebook to Kanchhi and sprinkled some water on Jharana's face. After a few tentative blinks, Jharana opened her eyes.

'Are you okay? What happened?' Thapa Nani *didi* asked.

'I don't know. My brain hurts,' Jharana said.

'Your brain?'

The boys laughed.

'Acting, acting,' someone said.

'Shh.' Thapa Nani *didi* turned around and scowled at the boys. Then, she told Kanchhi to walk Jharana home.

'Samjhana, go with them,' she added.

The walk to the Thakuri hamlet was straight, no ups or downs. It was to the left of the school, and most of the walk was under the cool shade of the trees that lined a side of the path. At first, Jharana walked, but as soon as the school, a long, one-story building, disappeared from view, she leaned against a slope and said that her legs were too weak, that someone should carry her. Neither Samjhana nor Kanchhi wanted to, but they could not force Jharana to walk. So, Samjhana carried Jharana half the way and Kanchhi the rest.

On the way back, Samjhana too fainted. Kanchhi immediately ran to Thapa Nani *didi*.

'Hey, *Bhagwan*, what's going on with these girls?' Thapa Nani *didi* said and asked one of the boys to go get a male teacher who could carry Samjhana back. Samjhana had fainted in the middle of a path closer to the hamlet. When Kanchhi and Thapa Nani *didi* reached her, a goat had discovered her, and it was sniffing her slippers.

Thapa Nani *didi* shooed the goat away and did as she had done with Jharana, but this time, she sounded and looked a little irritated.

'What happened?' the male teacher asked. He was the third-grade class teacher, Madhav sir.

'I don't know,' Thapa Nani *didi* said. 'Another of the girls had just fainted too.'

'It must be the heat,' Madhav sir said, picking Samjhana up. Madhav sir was a kind man, with jet-black hair and a jet-black moustache. He also smiled all the time, as if everything was ticklish.

'Kanchhi, are you going to faint too?' Thapa Nani *didi* asked.

'No.' Kanchhi shook her head.

Madhav sir carried Samjhana to the staffroom. There, he laid her on their much wider table and patted her cheeks. Samjhana did not get up. The teacher then sprinkled water on her. No response.

'You all, go back to your class,' Thapa Nani *didi* shouted to the students. They were all huddled at the doorway. Both the second and third graders. None of them moved.

'I said, go,' Thapa Nani *didi* said again.

The students turned around. Kanchhi, who was inside the room by Thapa Nani *didi*, began to make her way out as well. As she reached the door, the strict teacher from her first grade suggested making Samjhana sniff a worn sock. Madhav sir dismissed it and said Samjhana probably needed some rest. 'The sun's fierce,' he added.

The next day, Kanchhi was at home playing with Laxmi. They usually played hopscotch or made fans out of bamboo sheaths and ran from one end of the yard to another, trying to get them to spin. That day, they decided to whip each other with a rolled-up T-shirt and note where it hurt the most. They started at the bottom, at the shins, and made their way up to the upper back. Up next was the face. So far, the verdict was: it hurt the most wherever the skin was bare.

Kanchhi decided to be the test case for the face. She closed her eyes and pursed her lips.

'Ready?' Laxmi asked.

'Ready,' Kanchhi said.

Laxmi flicked her wrist and let go of one end of the T-shirt. It hit Kanchhi smack in the middle of her right cheek.

'Aiya.' Kanchhi clutched her face and hid it.

'What happened? Did it hurt?' Laxmi asked.

Kanchhi could not say anything. She was reeling both from pain and anger. When Laxmi asked again if it hurt, Kanchhi lay down in the yard, with her knees bent under her and her face buried in her hands.

'Where did it hurt? Let me see,' Laxmi said. She tried to turn Kanchhi over, but Kanchhi resisted and stayed bent down. The cheek hurt as if a bee had stung it.

After a while, the pain faded, and Kanchhi's heart slowed down. She relaxed and opened her eyes. The darkness in her palms was soothing, and it was while focusing on it that she began to wonder what it was like to faint, whether it was like sleep or paralysis, whether the girls were faking it and whether she herself could do it too – faint, block everything out and scare Laxmi a little.

'Kanchhi,' Laxmi called. 'Kanchhi. What's wrong?'

Kanchhi did not move. Laxmi poked Kanchhi and again tried to turn her over. This time, Kanchhi let her, but she turned over limply. Laxmi saw a bruise on her cheek.

'*Abui*, it's very red,' she said.

Kanchhi almost opened her eyes to ask what she was talking about.

'Kanchhi, did you hear me? You have a bruise.'

Kanchhi did not say anything. The sun was bright on her face, and she concentrated on the orange glow inside her eyelids.

'Kanchhi,' Laxmi called again. Then, she called Maiju, '*Chhyama*.'

Maiju was on a tree two fields below the yard, lopping its branches. When she did not holler back right away, Laxmi got up and walked over to the edge of the yard.

'*Chhyama*,' she called again.

'*Hoi*,' Maiju answered this time.

'*Chhyama*, Kanchhi's fainted.'

'Huh? What are you saying?'

Kanchhi chuckled a little and then went back to pretend fainting. Within minutes, Maiju was by her side, patting her unbruised cheek a little too hard.

'What happened? What were you two doing?' Maiju asked. 'What happened here to her cheek?'

'I don't know. We were just playing,' Laxmi said.

'Go get your father,' Maiju said.

By then, Bir Bahadur *dai* had already been retired from the Indian army for four years and spent most of his days sunbathing either at home while listening to the radio or on the fields grazing goats. He was home that day. Laxmi ran down and fetched him.

'What happened?' he too asked, but instead of patting Kanchhi's unbruised cheek or rubbing her hands for heat or sprinkling water on her face, Bir Bahadur *dai* decided to carry Kanchhi over to Ramesh's father, a self-taught Vedic astrologer and a part-time shaman. Maiju flung Kanchhi on Bir Bahadur *dai*'s back, and the four left. On the way, Bir Bahadur *dai* stumbled on a rock and nearly ended Kanchhi's act. It took everything in her to not burst into giggles. Kanchhi was also holding on to Bir Bahadur *dai* a little too tightly, but nobody seemed to notice it.

At Ramesh's, his father threw a pinch of ash in a bowl of water and sprinkled some of that water on Kanchhi's face. That made her blink involuntarily, and Kanchhi understood why it worked on Jharana. But she did not get up. Ramesh's father then rested the tip of a sickle on Kanchhi's wrist and chanted a mantra. In the end, he blew air on her face. That too did not work.

'It's the wild,' Ramesh's father told Maiju.

'The wild? What are we to do now?' Maiju said.

'I heard a few other students fainted the other day too,' Bir Bahadur *dai* said.

'Well, I've done what I can,' Ramesh's father said. 'Let's keep her here for a while. If she doesn't get up, we'll have to take her to the health post.'

The health post was in Hatiya Bazaar, about a two-hour walk down south. Kanchhi did not want that.

'Her eyes are blinking,' Ramesh's father said. 'Ramesh, go get the flashlight.'

Kanchhi immediately regretted the whole thing. She had not realized that Ramesh was around. He would now tell everyone in her class about what had happened.

Ramesh brought the flashlight to his father. His father peeled one of Kanchhi's eyes open and shone the light right on it. It was so bright Kanchhi had to squirm.

'She's up now,' Ramesh's father said and turned off the light.

It took a minute more for Kanchhi to fully 'regain' consciousness, and for a second there, she was truly confused about where she was. They had her lying down on the porch, and a picture frame high on the wall was the first thing Kanchhi saw.

'*Dhanya prabhu*,' Maiju said.

Kanchhi sat up, relieved as well. With Maiju around, no one would dare say anything.

'Tell me now, did you really faint or were you only acting?' Bir Bahadur *dai* asked.

Kanchhi leaned into Maiju and hid her face against her chest.

A few days later, Kanchhi fell ill for real – a dull ache high in her stomach, in the pit just below the ribs, an ache that would not go away. Maiju made her some *simal* bark juice first. She shaved a bark off a *simal* tree, beat it into a pulp and squeezed its juice into a bowl. When that did not work, Maiju baked a ball of mud stuffed with turmeric, cumin, dried red chilli peppers and salt and dropped it in a glass of hot water. Kanchhi drank this concoction as well. The next morning, on Saili *didi*'s advice, she drank a bowl of cow's piss too. None of it worked. The pain remained, sucking her stomach in as if a spirit resided there. On the third day, Maiju took her to a health post in Hatiya and then to a professional shaman in Bayarghari, the same shaman who had once told Maiju to light lamps and show Kal his way home.

At the health post, the health assistant gave Kanchhi one more blend to drink – an oral rehydration solution – and then told her not to eat anything oily, spicy or tangy. He also gave her a pill for intestinal worms. At the shaman's, the woman gave her a herb amulet and told Maiju that Kal's ancestors were angry at them both because Kal had not returned home in years. Maiju should hang a piece of his clothing where the ancestors could see it, the shaman said. 'They want to be assured that their son still lives in the house, that the house still belongs to him,' she added.

Once home, Maiju rummaged through an old trunk full of Kal's old clothes and found a pair of grey, musty pants. 'Look at your son, here,' she said, dangling the pants in front of the room where her in-laws had died. 'He just washed them and wants them dry,' Maiju said and then flung the pants over the porch roof.

The next morning, Kanchhi shat out the worms. A thick rope of them.

The amulet was supposed to remain around Kanchhi's neck for at least six months. It stayed there for much longer, until it turned black from dirt, soot and sweat and disintegrated on its own. The shaman had also given Kanchhi rice grains wrapped in a leaf and blessed by her gods. That stayed with Kanchhi for years, tucked safely under her bedding even after she moved into her own room, the same room where her grandparents had died. Until then, Kanchhi and Maiju shared a bedroom, the room to the right of the kitchen. Kanchhi's bed was at the back, Maiju's by the door. The two beds lay head-to-head along a wall, and sometimes, at bedtime, Kanchhi would ask Maiju for a story. Maiju would always say she did not know any.

'Not even one?' Kanchhi would ask.

'No.'

'Should I tell one?'

'No. Just fall asleep.'

'How about a real one? Tell me how you and father met.'

'The same as others,' Maiju would say.

'What do you mean "the same as others?"'

'It means the same as others.'

'*Hya*. Tell me, is he really in India?'

'Who told you that?'

'Everyone.'

'No, he's not in India.'

'Where is he then?'

'He's dead.'

'Dead? How?'

'I don't know how. Maybe he forgot to breathe.'

'My father's a big man in India,' Kanchhi told Jharana the next day in class.

'How big?' Jharana asked.

'He's a lieutenant in the Indian army.'

'A lieutenant? My father's only a constable,' Jharana said.

'You're lucky,' Kanchhi said. 'A lieutenant never gets to go home. He's a very busy man.'

That morning, Thapa Nani *didi* made the class stand up, close their eyes and recite a Saraswati prayer out loud. While singing the hymn, Kanchhi willed herself to cry. She felt like she should.

7

A FEW DAYS LATER, KANCHHI GOT HER NOSE PIERCED. Maiju grabbed her head tight, one of Saili *didi*'s sisters-in-law held her hands down, and Saili *didi* pushed the needle through. The needle was warm, and it felt as if the muscle in her nose constricted to make room for it. Kanchhi did not cry, just squeezed her eyes shut and held her breath. In return, she got a banana, a doughnut and a red dress donated by the Red Cross. The red dress came down to her knees and was thick. It was made of felt and had a collar and lapels, a tiny breast pocket on the left and two lines that ran parallel at the hem. Kanchhi loved the dress and wore it every day until the lapels tore off, the pocket fell off and the hems looked like the edges of a leaf munched by a caterpillar. She even wanted to wear it at a dance show at the end of that school year. But Thapa Nani *didi*, who was the choreographer, would not allow it. She wanted everyone who was performing to be in a traditional *gunyu cholo* costume.

Kanchhi's first dance was to the song '*Bhooli Gaye Samjhanalai*' from the movie *Kusume Rumal.* She was in a group of six – Samjhana and Jharana from her second grade and three other girls from a year above. One half entered the stage – the ground in front of the school – from the left, and the other from the right. In the middle, they met and swung their handkerchiefs in semi-unison. Thapa Nani *didi* had to go to Pokhara and watch *Kusume Rumal* in a cinema hall just to be able to choreograph that song. As the girls danced, men and women walked up to them and tucked money under their scarves. Maiju gave Kanchhi two rupees.

That was also Kanchhi's last dance. For a while at least because, soon afterwards, Kanchhi got a haircut, so short it made her look like a boy. Maiju cut it. Kanchhi hated it. She even tried to run and hide before the haircut, but Maiju would not have it long. Kanchhi had lice, and most of her afternoons were spent bent on Maiju's lap as Maiju fumbled through her hair looking for the lice that had just gorged on blood. If the lice became too many to pick one by one, Maiju would use a bamboo comb, insert little splinters perpendicular to the teeth and run them through Kanchhi's scalp as if she were ploughing it. It hurt immensely, especially when the comb got entangled in the hair.

'You look like my brother,' Jharana said in class the next day. They were in third grade now. Top dogs. The primary school did not teach beyond that grade.

'I hate it,' Kanchhi said. 'How long does it take for hair to grow back long?

'I don't know. My mother uses special oil in her hair,' Jharana said.

'Really? What's it called?'

'I don't know.'

'Can you ask her?'

'Okay,' Jharana said and took out a new geometry box from her bag. Third graders did not need or use geometry boxes.

'*Waah!*' Kanchhi exclaimed when she saw the Sony box with a picture of a little girl on top. The girl had bangs, and she sat inside a bright blue square painted in a corner on the right. The rest of the lid was in red – a bright, shiny red. When Kanchhi tilted the box a little, the girl seemed to move. Kanchhi even thought her smile shifted. It was fascinating. Kanchhi wanted a box just like that.

Jharana told her she could have it for a day if she wanted to. She would just have to return it in the same condition it was in.

Kanchhi agreed to the condition, and at the end of the day, put her few stationery – a pencil, an eraser, a sharpener and some loose graphite sticks – inside the box. She even made a paper divider/organizer and tucked it in. Then, she trotted home.

On the way, right below Saili *didi*'s house, she had an urge to look at the box again and took it out of her bag. The box was new. No dents, no rusts, no scratch marks, no loose screws. Just clean, glinting lines. Kanchhi opened it and closed it. She turned it up and around, swiped it with her thumb and blew on the impression. It was an admirable piece of manufacturing. Kanchhi had never seen anything like it. Then, she dropped it. Right on top of a piece of stone as sharp as a sickle. The drop was so forceful the box sprang open, and the contents flew around. Kanchhi picked up the scattered stationery one by one and then the box. That was when she noticed that the stone had left a mark. Two, in fact. One at the bottom, the other right above the girl's bangs. Two tiny but clearly visible dents.

The next morning, Jharana demanded a new replacement.

Maiju would never give Kanchhi money for that.

Jharana sulked for a whole period and then suggested that Kanchhi switch boxes with someone else. To Kanchhi, that sounded like a fine idea. She looked around the classroom, wondering who would have a box like that. No one did. They did not need it until the fourth or fifth grade.

At the lunch break then, the three girls – including Samjhana – ran all the way down to Bagar's high school and went through every single empty classroom, peeping inside student bags for a new-looking geometry box. They found one in the seventh-grade classroom, tucked inside a backpack. It looked new enough. Kanchhi pulled it out.

'No, leave it,' Jharana said.

'What? Why?' Kanchhi asked.

'I'll stick to mine,' Jharana said. She had a change of heart.

Relieved, Kanchhi shoved the box back inside the backpack, and they all bolted out of there. They were twenty minutes late to the next class, and as it turned out, too late to save their skin. As they sat on their bench, Ramesh told them they had been noticed snooping around in Bagar. 'By whom?' Kanchhi asked. 'Who saw us?'

Ramesh only shrugged.

The next morning, Thapa Nani *didi* walked in for the first class with a book in one hand and a *banmara* stick in the other.

'Good morning, miss.' Everyone stood up.

'Sit, sit,' Thapa Nani *didi* said. 'Except you three.' She pointed at the girls. 'Deepa, Jharana and Samjhana, stand in front of the class and hold your ears.'

The three girls scrambled to the front and faced the class.

'Do you know why you're here?' Thapa Nani *didi* asked.

Kanchhi shook her head. Jharana and Samjhana began to cry.

'Put your hands forward,' Thapa Nani *didi* said.

She hit Kanchhi first. Two slaps per hand.

'Why would a good girl like you do this?' Thapa Nani *didi* wondered aloud. 'Now, stand here for the rest of the class.'

By the time the girls walked back to their bench, their friendship as they knew it had ended. Kanchhi blamed Jharana, and Jharana blamed Kanchhi. The two did not speak to each other for the rest of that day. When they finally did, there was a clear strain. They began to drift apart. Jharana hung out with Samjhana more. Kanchhi kept to herself.

At the end of that grade, Kanchhi had one more reason to dissociate from her peers – that year's end-of-school cultural performance, or rather, what happened during its preparation. Thapa Nani *didi* was directing a song from a musical based on Laxmi Prasad Devkota's epic *Muna Madan*, and Kanchhi was chosen to play the son of a Tibetan man. A Magar girl would play Madan (a Chhetri merchant) and a Thakuri boy would play the Tibetan man. The scene they would enact was the one where Madan falls sick while on a trade trip to Tibet and is rescued and nurtured back to health by the Tibetan man. Kanchhi's role came in when Madan, fully recovered, gets ready to walk back to Nepal. As he sings and bids adieu, Kanchhi was to run and fall on his leg, begging him not to leave. To mimic a Tibetan boy, Kanchhi had to wear a robe over a boy's short-sleeved undershirt and take one arm out of the robe.

A day before the show – at the rehearsal – Thapa Nani *didi* asked Kanchhi to try out her costume, and when she did, Thapa Nani *didi* gasped in horror. Kanchhi's chest was no longer just nipples. A hard mass was forming around them.

'Kanchhi, you can't be seen naked like this anymore, understand?' Thapa Nani *didi* said, taking the vest off Kanchhi and looking for something thicker.

'Why not, miss?' Kanchhi asked.

'Because you have breasts now.'

'No, I don't.'

'Yes, you do.'

Thapa Nani *didi* found a *bhoto* and told Kanchhi to wear that instead.

Kanchhi was only nine.

8

November 13, 2005

'WHERE TO, SYANI *BUHARI*?' AN OLD MAN GREETS Maiju as she walks up a path towards his house. He is her half-uncle-in-law (Kal's father's half-brother) and is sitting on a plastic chair, drinking his morning tea, looking out at the rest of Harichaur through the blanket of fog. Harichaur is to the right of Torikhola – beyond the spring and past in and out several slopes. It is also populated with Chhetris: Bhusals, Karkies, Acharyas, Adhikaries and a few Poudels. Like Bir Bahadur *dai*, Harichaur *buwa* is an Indian army veteran, but he returned to the mountains only a few years ago.

'Temple, *Buwa*,' Maiju says.

'That I can see.' Maiju has a *puja* tray in her hand. 'But what is so special about today? *Ekadashi* was yesterday,' Harichaur *buwa* says.

'It was,' Maiju says.

'Am I forgetting something?' *Buwa* leans back on his chair and tries to read a calendar hanging on the wall of his porch, but the porch is too far. When he looks back, Maiju tells him the reason. 'Today is the day Kanchhi disappeared, *Buwa*.'

'Huh?' *Buwa* groans. 'Today is the day?'

Maiju nods.

Buwa pats his knee as if he is counting. 'How many years has it been?'

'Ten,' Maiju says.

'Ten already?'

Maiju nods again.

'*Eh*, *bafre*. Time. It flies, doesn't it?' Harichaur *buwa* looks at the fog around him and then at Maiju. 'But you can't lose hope. Did you hear about this boy who they thought was killed in the war but turned out to be in Delhi all along?'

Maiju had not.

'He was from Jajarkot or Rukum – one of those districts in the west. I heard it in the news today. A Magar kid. He was only twelve when he had disappeared. They thought he was dead and performed all the rites too, but then he turned up last *Dashain*. He was working in Delhi all along. Poor kid, he must have forgotten his way home.'

'Why did he come back now?' Maiju asks.

'I don't know. Maybe it's the ceasefire. Maybe because ten years have gone by. Don't they say even a river returns to its original course in ten years? Maybe that's what happened. The point is, we should never lose hope. Just do what we can from where we are.'

Maiju nods.

'Are you fasting today?' *Buwa* asks.

'Yes,' Maiju says.

'Can you drink tea?'

'Yes.'

'Go finish your *puja* then. I'll have tea ready for you. *Budhi!*' he calls his wife.

Maiju waits for her aunt-in-law to show up, but she does not.

'I'll be on my way,' Maiju says and walks past Harichaur *buwa*. The temple is beyond the house at the beginning of a *sal* forest.

'Don't forget the key,' *Buwa* shouts. 'It's on a pillar right there.'

9

'*AMA*, WHAT IS *DIWANA*?' KANCHHI ASKED MAIJU ONE day.

'I don't know,' Maiju said.

'Who knows?'

'Ask Bir Bahadur *dai*.'

'Why him?'

'Because he's been to India.'

Kanchhi ran down to Bir Bahadur *dai* and asked him what the word meant. He said it was not time for her to know it yet. She would understand it on her own someday. 'Why do you need to know?' he asked.

'No reason,' Kanchhi said. She was writing a poem, stealing in fact from her cousin in Harichaur. He was the son of Harichaur *buwa*, and when she had gone to their house one day, she had found a notebook with the poem written in Hindi. Kanchhi had memorized the first two lines and later written them down in her own notebook, making no changes to them except in the byline. The lines were about a lovesick heart and a heartless god.

Hey, bhagwan, tu yitna beraham kyu jo mujhko diwana banadiya?
Yeh pagal dil jo tune dhadakna sikadiya?

(Oh god, how can you be so cruel and make me lovesick?
How can you teach this wild heart to beat?)

Kanchhi showed the lines to her classmates – all in fourth grade now, down in Bagar. Janasewa Secondary High School. Her classmates loved the couplet, even though few, including Kanchhi, understood Hindi well. But that praise encouraged Kanchhi, and she decided to try writing her own poems. She wrote about herself first.

Deepa Chhetri mero nam
Bidhyarthi mero kam
Chungi, gatti, dandi biyo
Khelna sathi jam

(Deepa Chhetri is my name
Student is my trade
Chungi, gatti, dandi biyo
Are my favourite games)

This, she did not show to anyone.
The next poem was about Maiju:

Syani meri ama
Lagauchhin gharma jama
Khetbata farkepachhi
Adesh lauchhin khama

(Syani is my mother
There would be no another
When she gets back from the fields
She leans against a pillar)

Similarly, there was one about Laxmi:

Meri pyari Laxmi
Mero milne sathi
Ekdin nabhetda
Polchha mero chhati

(My dear Laxmi
My best buddy
If I don't see you for one day
My heart will be hurting)

The last one was about Saili *didi*:

Saili didi mero arko ama
Tinka aunla lama lama
Jiu bhane dublo patulo
Tara hidna sakne ukalo woralo

(Saili *didi* is my other mother
She has very long fingers
Her body is thin and tiny
But she can travel up and down alrighty)

Then, she stopped. There was a real poet in class, with much more promise and potential than her – a student named Shiva Shirish, who in just grade four seemed to already buckle under the burden of existence. He even had a pen name – Shiva Shirish, Shishir – which the Nepali teacher had thought of for him. One day, the teacher read out loud one of his poems in class:

Chirera yo chhati hera
Mero balapan koriechha yesma
Setikhola bageko hera
Mero geet sustaechha tyesma

(Tear this heart open and
You'll see my childhood seared there
Listen to the Setikhola swoosh, and
You'll hear my song there)

He also came first at the end of the fourth grade. It was English, introduced in that grade, that did it for Kanchhi. She almost failed it. Received forty out of hundred marks. The language was so new to her that the questions themselves made no sense. 'What is your name?' 'What' meaning '*ke*.' 'Is' meaning '*ho*.' 'Your' meaning '*timro*.' 'Name' meaning '*nam*.' 'Where do you live?' 'Where' meaning '*kaha*.' 'Do' meaning '*garnu*.' 'You' meaning '*timi*.' 'Live' meaning '*basnu*.' Her head spun from all the rote memorizations. How could one remember everything?

Of course, her English teacher, also her class teacher, did not see it that way. When he handed her the report card, he said it was expected. Girls after a certain age could not excel in academics. They were too focused on other things. Boys, he meant. Kanchhi looked down at the mark sheet and said nothing. Both his words and the marks stung like the T-shirt whip. What hurt more was Maiju's reaction. She did not talk to Kanchhi that whole day, took away her blanket at night (it was January), and in the morning, instead of bringing Kanchhi her regular glass of tea, brought her a *doko* and a sickle. 'This is what you get if you can't study,' Maiju said. 'Better get ready for your new future.'

The next day, Kanchhi went and brought all of Laxmi's old fifth-grade textbooks and began reading them from front to back. Laxmi was two grades above her, and all her textbooks were always reserved for Kanchhi. Kanchhi also borrowed Dhan *didi*'s (Laxmi's older sister's) eighth-grade Nepali textbook, *Mahendra Mala*, and read all the tales included in it. This was more for fun. Govinda sir, the Nepali teacher, had told her that that was how one got better in school. He had also just set up a small, informal library in his house, and when it was opened to students that winter break, Kanchhi began frequenting it. Unfortunately, it had only one book in English, a picture book about two children creating a garden in a cardboard box. Kanchhi had never seen or heard of a cardboard box, and with her life spent planting crops and cutting grass, she did not see the point of creating such a garden either. Still, she imitated the children and planted weeds in a section of the kitchen garden at her house. Maiju yanked them out. The garden was not for weeds, she said.

It was true, however, that Kanchhi was getting interested in 'non-academic' things. Like herself. She was growing up. In fifth grade, her height shot up to 4'11", as high as the end of the porch roof, almost as tall as Maiju. Everyone briefly wondered if she was going to be taller. 'Are you going to be a bamboo?' they asked. Others said a tall person looked old sooner than a short one. Her friends came and measured themselves against her. Up to her shoulder. Up to her neck. Up to her forehead.

Kanchhi's face was changing as well. It was getting longer. The jaw looked more square, more like her father's. The nose now had freckles. The cheeks too. And her breasts were 'real' breasts now, still developing but noticeable enough that she stopped playing any games that involved running, jumping or hopping. Instead, Kanchhi danced. By herself. Any moment she found, she began to sway. Her hands wriggled like a vine creeping up for support, her hips swayed as if touched by a breeze, and her eyes glinted with the new-found awareness of the world, of herself in the world. Wherever she was, she began, '*Laijau! Laijau! Laijau!*,' as if goaded on by an invisible force. Like a termite in the monsoon. In the yard, in the fields, in the school, even while in the latrine. Wherever she was. Maiju called her a mad woman.

One day, Kanchhi was dancing in the yard, with a bed sheet wrapped around her waist like a sari and a shawl draping her head like long hair when Thapa Maila *dai* saw her and asked if she wanted to perform for the camera. He said he knew someone who knew someone who was a cameraman behind a children's programme on Nepal Television and that someone he knew said that the crew was looking for fresh talent to showcase in a segment of the programme.

'Do you want to?' Thapa Maila *dai* asked. 'You'll be on TV.'

Kanchhi had never seen a TV, but yes, she said.

A few weeks later, a man in a brown suit came to their school and auditioned five students, including Kanchhi. One of them recited a poem from a textbook. A poem about the life of a farmer entitled '*Kisanko Rahar*.' The other put his hands behind his back and sang an old song, '*Kaha Timro Mayalulai*,' from a Darjeeling-based band. And the last two students, a boy and a girl from the seventh grade, who did not really want to perform but were forced to, danced to a song from the movie *Santan*, '*Chha Bhane Maya Chhapakkai Laideu*,' a song that they had previously performed to. After the first stanza, however, the girl ran away, giggling, and the boy stood scratching his head in embarrassment.

Kanchhi herself did two things. First, she danced to the song '*Laijau! Laijau! Laijau!*' in an orange sleeveless dress with a waistcoat on top, both chosen from a pile of dance clothes in the school's music/culture/arts/entertainment room. Then, she held the microphone attached to the video camera and gave an update on the school, an update Govinda sir had written and she had memorized.

'Namaste, my dear friends,' she began. 'Welcome to your favourite children's programme on Nepal Television. As usual, I, Deepa Chhetri, am here with news and updates about schools across the nation. Today, let's begin with news about a school in the district of Parbat. The school's name is Shree Janasewa Secondary School, and it is located in a small bazaar called Bagar. We are talking about this school today because this school has just finished installing a small library on its premises. Students can now sit in a room and read for news and recreation. Friends, this school has shown us that there is nothing we cannot do if we really want to do it.'

Of course, there was no library in the school. Just a stack of old books locked inside a shelf and never read.

But her delivery, Kanchhi thought, was flawless. So did Govinda sir, Thapa Maila *dai* and the man in the brown suit. The man also thought that Kanchhi and her clip had a high chance of being selected and broadcast because they were always looking for underprivileged, talented children like her – a poor, fatherless little girl from a remote part of the country. He even interviewed Maiju before he left, questioned her about Kanchhi's academic performance and about Kal's absence. 'How long has it been since he left?' he asked.

But nothing happened. Weeks passed. Months passed. Thapa Maila *dai* failed to get in touch with him again. If Kanchhi's clip or that of other students were ever played on TV, Kanchhi did not know. She assumed they were not and wondered if that was because they did not like the dress she wore. Maybe she should have stuck to traditional attire. A *fariya cholo*. Or maybe her school uniform. Then, she wondered if her dancing was too stiff, if her moves harkened back to the days when she danced like the older women who stomped the ground as if it were a grain huller – eyes on the ground and expressionless, with carousel refrains. In the end, Kanchhi wondered if she was just not as cute as they wanted the performer to be. Her hair had grown long, down to her shoulders now, but she had never once smiled during the dance or while giving the news update. It must have been sorely apparent to the cameraman and to anyone watching that the update was all mugged up.

Govinda sir tried to cheer her up. 'See the whorl in your fingers,' he said, opening her palms wide. 'You have only one whorl in ten fingers. You know what that means? You're going to be bigger than a TV performer. You're going to be a king or a *sanyasi*.'

10

A KING WAS OUT OF THE QUESTION. BOTH LITERALLY and figuratively. Literally, because kings were men and married within their own circles. Like the Chhetris. Figuratively, Maiju said, it took three generations for a poor family to be rich, and they were still in the first or maybe zero generation. Besides, Kanchhi was a girl born in the mountains. She should know her limits. A prosperous, powerful life was probably not in her future, although Maiju wished it were.

But a *sanyasi*... there was always a possibility of becoming one. Anyone poor was always on the brink of *sanyasa*, Maiju said. One tragedy and it was tempting to give it all up and go live in a temple. Kalighat *dai*, for instance, who lived by the banks of the Kali Gandaki River and came up to the hamlets once every six months. He carried a burlap sack, hollered, 'Jay Shiv Shankar, Jay Bholenath!' and begged for rice. Maiju said he became a *sanyasi* after his wife drowned all three of their children in the Kali Gandaki River and then jumped in herself.

She also said they were related to him. He was part of the Bahun branch of Kal's extended family.

'Is it hereditary?' Kanchhi asked.

'What?'

'Being a *sanyasi*.'

'No,' Maiju said but added that she would break Kanchhi's bones if she dropped out of school and became a *sanyasi*. A *sanyasi* was a weak, tortured man, Maiju said.

'That's not true,' Kanchhi said.

'What's not true?'

'That a *sanyasi* is weak.'

'He is.'

'Can you leave everything behind and live by a river?'

'Yes. Anyone can give up. Living is hard.'

'Right,' Kanchhi said.

Bantering aside, the forecast had done its work. It had distracted Kanchhi from the rejection, leading her to wonder instead if being a *sanyasi* was really in her future. Would she be able to give it all up one day and become an ascetic? Wear a yellow robe, carry an orange bag, go village to village begging for alms? Maiju might think little of them, but Govinda sir held *sanyasis* in high regard. A Bahun man himself, he believed that only a *sanyasi* understood the true nature of everything, which was nothing. Gautam Buddha, Guru Vivekananda, Sai Baba, they were all *sanyasis*, he said, and warned Kanchhi to not be too attached to anything, including dreams. Desires and ambitions, he said, were the root causes of depression, especially in poor people like them all.

'But my *ama* says living is harder,' Kanchhi said.

'It is, especially for a woman, but if you can, you should be a *sanyasi*. If not, you should live like one.'

'How?'

'*Sada jiwan, uchha bichar*,' Govinda sir said.

'Meaning?'

He gave her a book. *Santa Jiwan*, the title read. A Saint's Life. An extremely thin pocketbook of poetry with just twenty pages. The front cover was missing, and in its place was the first page with a five-line introductory poem based on the five precepts of Buddhism, *panchasheel*. At the end of that page was the name of the poet: Govinda Prasad Tiwari. It was his own book.

Kanchhi did not read it, but she thought about what Govinda sir had said.

Simple living, high thinking. Tailor-made for poor people. What else could Kanchhi afford but simple living? Ninety-five per cent of what she owned were objects found in nature, grown in the fields or in the wild. Of the remaining 5 per cent, half were items donated or handed down, almost all once used by Dhan *didi* or Laxmi or by children who lived in cities and visited the hamlet once a year. The rest of the 5 per cent was bought on Maiju's meagre salary as a sweeper in the primary school. High thinking then came naturally. It seemed like an obvious choice, blunted the shame of wearing second-hand clothes and living on credit. It restored dignity, armed Kanchhi against pitying looks. Most of all, it cost nothing. Maybe the whorls were right. Maybe Kanchhi was destined to become a *sanyasi*.

Kanchhi entered a phase of obsession with *sadhus*, *sanyasis* and *yogis*. She pestered Maiju to let her go to the temple in Setibeni and meet Kalighat *dai*, asked her to get her a yellow robe and a begging bowl. Maiju told Kanchhi to wait until Kalighat *dai* came to the village himself. 'He'll be here soon,' she said. And he was, just before the monsoon, with a sack full of rice he had collected on the way there. *Gudulla*, *jarneli*, *anadi*, *mansuli*, *pokhareli* – a mishmash of breeds. Eight *pathis* in total. He sold it to Maiju. He always did that whenever he was in the village. Neither Maiju nor Kanchhi minded the mix. It was cheaper buying from him than from Waling.

After he was paid, Kanchhi asked Kalighat *dai* where she could find a yellow robe that *sanyasis* wore.

'What for?' Kalighat *dai* asked. He himself wore faded black pants, a white shirt, a waistcoat and a pointed *dhaka* hat.

'To be a *sanyasi*,' Maiju said. 'She's obsessed with it. Do you have an old robe that you can get rid of? She'll wear it for a day and get over it.'

'I don't wear a robe,' Kalighat *dai* said. 'That's for those who're part of an institution. You don't need it to be a *sanyasi*.'

'I want it,' Kanchhi said.

'You have to be initiated into a sect then. You can't just wear them.'

Kanchhi went quiet. Kalighat *dai* continued, 'Why do you want it? You have to shave your head, renounce your family, live in a monastery and follow this or that silly rule for the rest of your life. And once you wear it, you can never take it off. Is that what you want? A *sanyasi* is supposed to be free, not chained further.'

Kanchhi thought for a second. It was the hair that changed her mind. The clothes, she did not mind wearing the same for life. She often wore the same skirt and T-shirt for weeks at a time. But the hair – it was finally mid-back long. She was not getting it cut again, let alone shaved. As for freedom and family, she was only ten.

'Live first and then become a *sanyasi*,' Kalighat *dai* said. 'You won't last long otherwise. How old are you?'

'Will complete eleven this monsoon,' Maiju said.

'*Dhat*! Go run and play then,' Kalighat *dai* said, pretending to look for a pebble to shoo Kanchhi away.

By the end of the monsoon, Kanchhi had moved on to another obsession – *Mutra Chikitsa*. Urine Therapy, a pale green book, with a silhouette of a meditating *yogi* on the cover, which Kanchhi had found in Govinda sir's library and borrowed. The book purported that if used correctly, urine could disinfect wounds, cleanse the stomach, cure gallstones and restore youth and vitality. Kanchhi could also use it to get rid of freckles, add a glow to her skin and shine to her hair, and, if she could drink it, to increase her height. She would have to pee in a bottle first and store it away for a few days. The older the urine, the better it was.

Kanchhi decided to test the claim.

She peed in two small, round bottles that used to hold cough medicine and hid them in the room to the left of the kitchen. That room was not her room yet but a storeroom, occasionally a chicken coop, sometimes a goat pen. After three days, Kanchhi took one of the bottles out and poured some pee in its cap. It smelled like what days-old urine would smell like – ridiculously pungent, as if the whole hamlet had peed into that bottle. Kanchhi could not drink it, no matter how hard she tried, could not even rub it in her gums (for healthy teeth), but she tolerated the smell long enough to apply it on her face. The urine was cold and sticky, and the skin quickly absorbed it. Minutes later, Kanchhi washed it off with water.

Kanchhi repeated this process every morning for about a week. Then, she added hair to the routine – 'oiled' it with the urine first and then rinsed it with water, no soap. Amazingly, the hair, when dry, looked very shiny and silky, as if it were radiating and not merely reflecting light. Every girl in the hamlet was impressed and decided to try it out themselves. The face, however, did not seem to register any change, although, in the beginning, Kanchhi did think it glowed. The freckles too remained.

'What are you doing?' Maiju asked her at the end of two weeks when the smell became unbearable. 'Throw those bottles away right now,' she yelled.

Kanchhi had added one more bottle, a bottle that used to hold alcohol.

'I can't even walk by that door,' Maiju said.

'It's not that bad,' Kanchhi said.

'Not that bad? It's like your grandparents are back in that room,' Maiju yelled.

Kanchhi shrugged, but she did empty the bottles and put an end to the experiment. By then, she too had begun to doubt whether the therapy really worked. It was not just the freckles the old urine had failed to remove. The second time she washed her hair, it had ended up sticky and matted, and it stank like an infant's diaper. Ramesh had even asked her if she had a urine problem – of it leaking out of her.

11

'KUMBHAKARNA, *OYE*, KUMBHAKARNA,' MAIJU CALLED from the kitchen. 'Kumbhakarna, get up.'

Kanchhi squirmed in her bed and turned towards the wall. The wall, like the room, was cold and dark.

'What are you doing sleeping this late?' Maiju walked in, sprinkling *akshyata* in the air. 'Get up. Up, up. Up before it's too late.'

'I'm up,' Kanchhi said, burying her head deep in the quilt.

Maiju walked over to her bed and pulled the cover off her anyway.

'I said I'm up,' Kanchhi yelled.

'How will you go anywhere in life if you sleep so much?' Maiju said and began folding the quilt.

Kanchhi curled up her legs for warmth for a bit and then sat up, her legs dangling off the bed.

'Go before other people show up,' Maiju said. She meant at the spring. It was *Dashain* that day, the tenth day, and the ceremony began at 7:25 a.m.

'I need to shit first,' Kanchhi said.

'You can do that later.'

'Can't I sleep a little longer?'

'How is this world going to go on if everyone sleeps all the time?' Maiju said and walked out.

Kanchhi looked at the door for a bit and then followed her.

Outside, the dawn was dim, peppered with darkness that still clung to the air. On the porch, Maiju had gathered a *doko*, an empty water pot and a washbasin with a towel and a petticoat in it.

'Get your clothes and the soaps and go,' Maiju said. She was now flinging *akshyata* in the other room, at the far end.

Yawning and fighting sleep, Kanchhi walked to a rope hanging from the porch wall and pulled down a T-shirt and a skirt. The washing and bathing soaps were tucked on a beam under the porch roof. She grabbed them as well.

'Come right back afterwards, understand?' Maiju said, walking out of the room. 'Don't dawdle. I'll need help with *selroti* here.'

Kanchhi nodded and left. The *doko* perched on her back and the basin on top.

At the spring, there was no one but a woman and her two little daughters, finishing up. The woman was wringing the last of the water out of the last of the clothes she was washing, and the daughters were towelling themselves dry. Kanchhi did not recognize them. Neither did they her.

As they prepared to leave, the woman asked Kanchhi whose daughter she was.

'Syani's,' Kanchhi answered.

'Whose?'

'The woman beyond the bend.'

The woman looked up at the Chiuridanda bend and then at Kanchhi. She could not place Kanchhi or Maiju in her memory. 'Which Syani is it?' she asked, more to herself, and hoisted a *doko* on her back. The little girls were already past the spring and on their way. The woman began to follow them.

'Oh, Kal Bahadur.' The woman remembered and swung around. She peeked at Kanchhi from under the tumpline. 'You're his daughter! I didn't know he had a grown-up daughter. How old are you?'

'Eleven,' Kanchhi said.

'Does he come back at all? Have you ever seen him?'

'No.' Kanchhi shook her head.

'No?' The woman too shook her head. From the distance, the girls screamed, '*Ama. Ama*, look, a millepede.'

The woman looked at her daughters and then back at Kanchhi. 'Well, tell your mother I asked after her. I'll come over later if I find time.'

Kanchhi nodded.

After the woman and the children left, Kanchhi got ready for a bath. She emptied the washbasin and moved it under the water. Then, she slipped into the petticoat that she had brought with her, tied it above her breasts and took off her clothes one by one: a T-shirt, an undershirt, a school skirt that she often wore outside of school, and her panties. It was as she was about to hurl the panties into the washbasin that she noticed something odd in them. The crotch of the panties, usually black and silky, was stiff and dry like a day-old millet bread.

Kanchhi looked around. When she saw no one, she sniffed the panties and then swiped their crotch with a finger. The last time something similar had happened was about a year ago when her underwear was cloaked in white and she had assumed she had accidentally dropped some wheat flour on it. This time, the colour was black or appeared black.

Confused, Kanchhi looked at the ground and checked her thighs. The ground showed nothing, but her thighs, the inner parts of them, were streaked red halfway down to her knees. Kanchhi touched one of the streaks and then checked in between her toes. There was nothing there. Then, she walked over to the basin and picked up the skirt she had just taken off to check its pleats. Nothing there as well. Kanchhi next surveyed the stones – the stones on the stone bench – and then the slopes around her. Nothing there either. Kanchhi was looking for leeches. The spring and the woods around were not known to harbour any. Kanchhi looked at the underwear again and examined it closely. That was when it dawned on her like a slow *ghanse* song wafting through the mountains. This was a period. Her first one.

Kanchhi sat down on the stone bench and stayed there for a long while.

Back home, she did not tell Maiju about her period. She did not know how to without having to observe the rituals afterwards. And the period rituals were ridiculous. She would have to forego celebrating *Dashain*, stay away from everyone for five days, touch no fire or the gods and sleep in a corner of the house with nothing but a mat and an old blanket for warmth, grateful that at least at their place it was a corner within the house. At Saili *didi*'s and at most families with men, it was the buffalo shed.

'What's wrong?' Maiju asked when Kanchhi returned from the spring. Kanchhi had not carried the water pot into the kitchen but left it inside the *doko* leaning against the porch.

'Nothing,' Kanchhi said.

'Come get your tea. It's still warm.'

'No, bring it outside,' Kanchhi said.

'Come and get it. I'm cooking here.' Maiju pulled the water pot out and took it inside.

Kanchhi stayed in the yard, drying her clothes on a bamboo fence around the kitchen garden.

A little later, Maiju walked out with a glass of tea.

'Leave it on the porch,' Kanchhi said.

Maiju brought it up to her.

'I told you to leave it there,' Kanchhi shouted. 'Now, put it on the ground.'

'What's wrong with you?' Maiju asked, a little alarmed. 'Did someone say something to you at the spring?'

'No. I'm trying to dry my clothes here.'

'And who's stopping you?' Maiju stared at her for a bit and then went back into the kitchen. Kanchhi sat down by the edge of the yard and tousled her hair to help it dry.

Once, she had asked Maiju what would happen if she touched someone on their period. Maiju had said it would be a sin.

'Who would be the sinner?' Kanchhi had asked. 'The one touching or the one touched.'

'Both,' Maiju had said.

'Who said so?'

'I don't know. I don't make the rules,' Maiju had said.

'Who does then?'

'I don't know. Ask your grandfathers and their forefathers.'

Around 7:30 a.m., the ceremony began. Kanchhi changed into her *Dashain* clothes for that year – a warm checkered plaid skirt with a cream-white top that was puffy around the shoulders and a checkered waistcoat. Maiju wore a green blouse, a green *lungi* and a green *patuka* that wrapped around her waist like a python. Then, she spread a mat in the middle of the porch and brought out a bowl of *akshyata* and a plate of *jamara*.

'May you be blessed and live long. May Goddess Durga protect you,' Maiju said as she applied a dollop of *akshyata* on Kanchhi's forehead. 'May everything you wish come true. May you never suffer.'

Kanchhi watched the grains fall in her cupped hands. The *akshyata* was red, the *jamara* yellow. Maiju picked up a pinch of the saplings and tucked it in Kanchhi's hair. The push made her head sway. Kanchhi sniffled.

'What's wrong?' Maiju asked again, giving her ten rupees.

'Nothing,' Kanchhi said.

'Was the water cold?'

'A little.'

'I told you to go earlier when it was warmer. Now, you've caught a cold.'

Maiju bowed at Kanchhi's feet.

'Want me to make you some turmeric water?' she asked.

'No,' Kanchhi said.

'Drink some hot water then.'

'No, I'm fine. I'll just have to spend some time in the sun. I'll be okay.'

Maiju picked up the bowl and the plate. 'Come help me in the kitchen then,' she said. 'It'll be faster if we're both at it.'

'No, I want to stay in the sun for a bit,' Kanchhi said.

'Just come in. Stay by the fire for now. You can stay in the sun later.'

Maiju walked inside.

Kanchhi dusted the grains off her lap and followed Maiju a second later.

Inside, a big wok half-filled with oil was heating up. In front of it was a pot, just as large, full of rice batter. The mutton was done. The *selroti* had not even been started. Kanchhi pulled a *pirka* as far away from the hearth as possible and sat on it.

Maiju poured a fistful of batter into the wok. Kanchhi picked up a thin bamboo stick and waited. When the *selroti* was halfway done, she turned it over.

'Do you have a headache too?' Maiju asked when Kanchhi was quiet through two *selrotis*.

'No,' Kanchhi said.

'Take the kettle and fill it up. I'll make you some turmeric water.'

'No, I'm all right,' Kanchhi said.

'Are you hungry then?'

'No.'

'Offer a *selroti* to the gods and start eating.'

'I'm not hungry, I told you. I can wait.'

'Are you tired then? Why don't you get into the habit of waking up early?'

'I said I'm fine.'

Maiju poured another handful of batter into the oil.

'Were there other people at the spring?' she asked.

'No,' Kanchhi said.

'No one?'

'No one.'

'That's surprising. There were very few people when I was there as well.'

'Maybe they all bathed at midnight.'

'Maybe,' Maiju said.

'How long will this take?' Kanchhi asked, no longer trying to hide her irritation. Maiju seemed to have batter for over a hundred *selrotis*, and they were only done with three.

'What's wrong with you?' Maiju asked again. 'If you don't want to help, get back outside. I'll do this myself.' Maiju took the stick from Kanchhi.

Kanchhi did not wait. She got up and walked outside.

The rest of the month was equally tense. Kanchhi had touched everything considered sacred: the food cooked for *Dashain*, the water, the fire, Maiju, Saili *didi*, Bir Bahadur *dai*, their whole family, their kitchen, the tangerine trees, the mango tree, the books, the broom, the vegetables – everything. The logical consequence, according to beliefs, then, was the end of the hamlet. It would either disappear like a mist or crumble like a piece of limestone.

'*Ama*, who came again with the rule that you can't touch a woman on her period?' Kanchhi asked again one day.

'I don't know. Ask your ancestors,' Maiju repeated.

'How?'

'I don't know.'

'Useless mother. Do we really have to follow the customs?'

'Yes. Why do you ask? Have you started to bleed?'

'No,' Kanchhi said.

Fortunately, nothing happened. No one fell sick or died that month. The worst thing that happened to them was someone stealing their firesticks, and the firesticks were not even axed logs or solid branches, just a bunch of twigs Kanchhi had collected in a corner. The second worst thing was Saili *didi* not showing up to help with the millet harvest as she had promised. Maiju was miffed for a bit, but the two patched up by the end of that afternoon. Kanchhi knew she would have to tell Maiju someday, though, and so when she bled again during *Tihar*, another big festival, she told Maiju about her period but only after the festival was over.

'*Ama*, I think my periods have begun,' she said.

They were at the outdoor sink. Maiju was rinsing the plates. Kanchhi was pouring water from a small jug.

'What do you mean?' Maiju didn't believe her.

'I said my periods have begun,' Kanchhi repeated.

'Do you even know what that is?'

'Yes,' Kanchhi said.

'Tell me what happens then?'

'Blood comes out of it.'

Maiju laughed. 'Out of where?'

'Out of *it*.'

Maiju stopped washing the ladle that she was washing and looked at Kanchhi.

'Are you bleeding right now?' she asked.

'Yes.'

'How many days?'

'One,' Kanchhi lied.

'When did it begin?'

'This morning.'

'What? And you're telling me now?'

'I thought I was hurt.'

'Go sit on the porch,' Maiju said. 'And don't touch anything.'

Kanchhi got up and walked to the porch.

'You already touched this water,' Maiju said. '*Chhi*. Why didn't you tell me right away? You know the rules. Does anyone else know about it?'

'No,' Kanchhi said, sitting on the porch.

Maiju went back to washing the dishes. Only a wok remained to be cleaned. Once it was done, Maiju left it with the other dishes in the cauldron and left the cauldron where it was. Since Kanchhi had touched the water that the dishes were cleaned with, the dishes would now have to be left out in the sun to dry.

'I'm going to get Saili *didi*,' Maiju said, rubbing her hands dry on her *lungi*. 'If she asks, tell her you just found out that you were bleeding. You went to pee behind the house and saw blood in your underwear, understand?'

'Understood.'

'Do you need a rag right now?'

'Yes.'

Maiju picked up a lamp that was by the cauldron and walked past Kanchhi to their room. A trunk containing clothes that they did not wear frequently was under her bed on top of sticks. Maiju rolled it out and opened it.

'Come here,' she said, taking out an old cotton sari. Parts of it were already torn and used as rags. She tore two pieces, each about a foot wide.

Kanchhi stood outside by the door. Maiju folded the pieces into pads small enough to fit inside an underwear.

'Do you have safety pins?' she asked.

Kanchhi nodded.

'Use them to fasten it. One on top, one at the bottom.'

'But I thought I couldn't go inside the room,' Kanchhi said.

'Change in here for now. Be quick and don't touch anything but your bed.'

Kanchhi nodded again. She took the pads from Maiju and went inside the room.

'I'll be back in a bit,' Maiju said and left to go get Saili *didi*.

The rags were green with tiny red flowers. They felt old and soft. Kanchhi pinned one to a clean set of underwear and took off the panties she was wearing. It was soaked in blood. This time, the period was heavy. If she had not told Maiju, Maiju would have found out herself.

A little later, Maiju walked back up with Saili *didi*.

'What are you doing?' she asked.

Kanchhi was outside, washing the dirty underwear a little away from the outdoor sink.

'Washing my underwear,' she said.

'Not there. Go behind the house. Don't you have a sense of what's hygienic and what's not?'

'I'm almost done.' Kanchhi poured water over the underwear and wrung it tightly.

'*Alachhini*,' Maiju said.

'Kanchhi,' Saili *didi* called. She was sitting on the porch, holding a blanket in her arms. 'You've grown up, haven't you? Kids these days. They grow up so fast. I hadn't even had my first period when I got married.'

'Really?' Kanchhi asked. 'When did you get married?'

'I was thirteen, I think.'

'Thirteen when you got married?'

'Yes,' Saili *didi* said. 'Had my period a year or two later.'

'I was fourteen when I had my first period,' Maiju said. She was on the porch now, looking for a mat rolled up and tucked on a wooden shelf just below the roof. 'I cried all day,' she added.

'Why?' Kanchhi asked.

'I don't know. Everyone cries their first time.'

'No, they don't,' Kanchhi said. 'What's that, Saili *didi*? Looks like a blanket.'

'It is. It's your period blanket,' Saili *didi* said and showed it to Kanchhi. It was a thin, green, old army blanket that once belonged to Bir Bahadur *dai*. 'You'll be sleeping with it every month from now on,' Saili *didi* added.

Just then, Maiju pulled a mat from the shelf. It was old too; in fact, the oldest of them all, limp and frayed. Next, she got Kanchhi a *lungi*, just as old, with a tear at the hem.

'Start wearing a *lungi* from now on,' Maiju said, flinging it at Kanchhi. 'Go inside and pack.'

'Pack? Where am I going?'

'To Saru *didi*'s house,' Maiju said.

'What? Why?'

'It's your first time, that's why,' Maiju said.

'But I can stay in that room.' Kanchhi pointed to the room to the left of the kitchen, the room where she had hidden the bottles of pee.

'No, you can't,' Maiju said.

'Why not?'

'Don't ask too many questions. Pack.' Maiju began to walk away.

'Where are you going?'

'To the shed.'

'For what?'

'To get some straws.'

'They're going to be your mattress, Kanchhi,' Saili *didi* said.

'No—'

Kanchhi had forgotten that when a Chhetri girl bled for the first time, she was not just stowed away in a corner of the house for five days but hidden from view from everyone and the sun for eleven days. And because Magars did not observe these rituals as strictly as Chhetris did, Chhetri girls were often kept in a Magar house. In this case, Saru *didi*'s house. Saru *didi* was a sixty-year-old Magar woman who lived by herself around the bend from Maiju's.

'Why do we have to go there? We have no men in our house,' Kanchhi argued on the way to Saru *didi*'s.

'Every Chhetri man in the hamlet is a man you can't see,' Maiju said.

'Men could come to Saru *didi*'s too.'

'They won't be our relatives.'

'Why don't you just tell Chhetri men not to come to our house?'

'Kanchhi, just be quiet,' Maiju said.

'It's actually fun, Kanchhi,' Saili *didi* said. 'You get to do nothing for eleven days.'

'I don't like it,' Kanchhi said.

'Just eat and sleep and relax. We'll come see you. Laxmi will come see you too. You'll be fine.'

'No, I don't like it. This is stupid.'

'*Didi*,' Maiju called when they reached Saru *didi*'s house. Saru *didi* was already lying down on her porch, ready to sleep. The lamp was out.

'Who is it?' she asked.

'It's us,' Maiju said. 'Here to trouble you. Were you already asleep?

'What happened?' Saru *didi* asked, a little alarmed.

'Nothing to worry about,' Saili *didi* said. 'Our daughter here has just grown up.'

'Oh. Why else would you come see a poor woman like me?' Saru *didi* said and struck a matchstick.

'Eh, babai,' Maiju said, sitting down on the porch. 'You know how the days pass. You do nothing, and yet, the sun sets in the blink of an eye.'

'That is true,' Saru *didi* said, giving Maiju the lamp. 'That is true. Now, I don't have any other room but that one. You know it. Open it and make the bed. It's unlocked.'

Maiju took the lamp and walked to the room on her left, the room by a cobbled path that they had just crossed.

'Stay out,' Maiju said when Kanchhi followed her into the room. Kanchhi disobeyed.

The room was small like theirs but mostly empty, except for some scraps piled at the far end of the corner: an unused *silauto*, a pair of quern-stones, slippers with broken straps and iron woks rusted to the point of being strainers. There was no bed there.

'Am I going to sleep on the floor?' Kanchhi asked.

'Where else will you sleep? Do you see a bed here?' Maiju asked. 'Go stay outside with Saru *didi*. We'll call you when it's ready.'

Kanchhi walked out and sat on the porch with Saru *didi*.

'Did you have to do this too, *Didi*?' Kanchhi asked Saru *didi*.

'Do what?' Saru *didi* asked. She was leaning against the wall and stuffing tobacco into her pipe.

'Hide during your first time?'

'No,' Saru *didi* said. 'We did everything as usual, except visiting the temples. That we didn't do. I don't know what women these days do.'

'I wish I were a Magar too,' Kanchhi said.

Saru *didi*, who had just taken a puff, coughed. 'It's not that difficult,' she said. 'Marry a Magar man and you will be a Magar too.'

'Is there no other way?'

'No.'

'Then, I can't be a Magar in this life. I'm not getting married.'

'No? Why not?'

'I'm not.'

'What will you do then? Become a spinster?'

'Yes.'

'You say that now, and tomorrow, you'll be the first one to run away.'

'No, I won't.'

'You will. Everyone at your age says they won't, and they do.'

'Kanchhi,' Maiju called.

'What?'

'Come here,' Maiju said.

Kanchhi got up and walked to the room. Maiju had spread the old mat on the floor, the straws on the mat and the blanket on the straws.

'Get me your bag,' Maiju said.

'Why?' Kanchhi asked.

'To be used as a pillow. We forgot to bring it. I'll get you a real one tomorrow.'

'*Hya*,' Kanchhi said, on the verge of tears. 'I'll die of cold here.'

'No, you won't. We didn't even get a blanket in our time,' Maiju said.

'Does everything have to be like it was in your time?'

'Yes. That's how traditions work.'

Kanchhi almost cried then.

'Tomorrow, sweep the floor first thing in the morning, understand?' Maiju said.

'You didn't sweep it just now?'

'No. Who sweeps at night?'

'All these stupid rules.'

'Yes, you're the only one smart here,' Maiju said.

A few minutes after Maiju and Saili *didi* left, Kanchhi got into her bed and tried to fall asleep. It was difficult. Both the straws and the blanket were too thin to keep her warm. Cold seeped in from every direction. To make matters worse, Saru *didi* snored – long and loud snores, punctuated by frantic gasps for breath.

In the morning, Maiju brought her a pillow and a grey *chadar*, and after Kanchhi complained about the cold, more straws. She also brought her lunch and, later, dinner. Morning and afternoon teas were on Saru *didi*. Snoring aside, Saru *didi* was great company and a fantastic storyteller. She made the evenings fun. She told Kanchhi that she'd once had a daughter like her, but she died of pneumonia at just six months of age. Soon afterwards, her first husband too died. She did not know of what. He used to live and work in India. One day, she just received a letter that simply said he had passed away.

It was the afternoons that were tough to live through, the afternoons after the first few days when sleep began to elude Kanchhi and boredom began to set in. Kanchhi read *Gitilahar* at first, a thin book of lyrics that she had picked up from Govinda sir's library. It had about thirty songs from the Nepali movies that had come out between 1984 and 1990. Kanchhi read them all and copied them into her own notebook. Then, she curated a list of female solo tracks from within those songs – from '*Yi Woth Timra Muskan Timrai*' (*Kanchhi*) to '*Adharma Aja Unkai Chha Geet*' (*Anyaya*) to '*Kina Badhdaichha Dhukdhuki Mutuko*' (*Mayalu*). Kanchhi hoped that someday she would be able to tape these songs and dance to them all. There were about eleven of these songs.

When there were no more songs to read and copy, Kanchhi tried writing her own. A *salaijo* tune at first that talked about the month of Mangshir, about millets glinting in the sun and about fire-flame bushes igniting passion and illuminating memories:

Mangshirai lagyo tyo kodo bala salaijo jhalala sun jasto
Hahaa maya jhalala sun jasto
Banama dhayari manama maya salaijo samjhanama goreto
Hahaa maya samjhanama goreto

Tei tala ho ni ghar hamro Kanchhi
angani gheraima saprakka sayapatri

(The month of Mangshir is here. The millet fingers glint like gold in the sun.
My love, like gold in the sun.
The woods have fire-flame bushes, my heart has love, and the memory has dirt trails.
My love, the memory has dirt trails.

Our house is right down there, Kanchhi,
The one with the marigolds flanking the yard.)

Then, a *jhyaure* song about her life that seemed to pass by in just getting grass and firewood:

Yo jindagani ghansai ra daura bokdai jani
Timi aye ramauni natra adhyaro huni
Maya mero, mutu mero, anjuli bhari atauni

(This life that passes by in getting grass and firewood
Is happy when you are near, sad when far
My love, my heart, you fit in the palm of my hands.)

She also attempted to write a short story – about a woman who raises a daughter all by herself after her husband leaves her – but she gave up after a page of trying.

Towards the end of the week, Kanchhi began reading and rereading her own textbooks. She did exercises not yet assigned, studied chapters not yet discussed and even read the pages outside the chapters, including the copyright page, the foreword, the messages from the two kings (the late King Mahendra and his son then-King Birendra) and the patriotic song on the back cover: '*Yo Mero Desh Nepal Hera Kati Chha Ramailo.*' This, My Country Nepal, Look How Fun It Is.

The last three days were a little better. Laxmi too had got her period for the first time, and she came up and stayed with Kanchhi, dragging her own mat and a bundle of straws. The two would then play with pebbles and talk all day, falling asleep when there was nothing else to do.

On the eleventh day, Maiju came to collect Kanchhi before sunrise, with a bottle of mustard oil and a new *lungi*. Together, they walked to a spring first, the one on the left of the hamlet, used by Saru *didi* and Saili *didi*. There, Maiju burned the straws Kanchhi had slept on for the last ten nights, and Kanchhi washed herself. Once done, Maiju rubbed some mustard oil on Kanchhi's hair and proclaimed that Kanchhi was now a woman. 'A pure and free woman.' Pat. Pat.

On the way back, Maiju stopped by a field and stole some string beans. The sun that Kanchhi had not seen for nine days glinted off every surface, shiny or dull. As Kanchhi squinted and watched Maiju pluck the beans and hide them in a fold of her *patuka*, a thought came to her, a thought that said it was okay to lie and hide the truth sometimes. What mattered was the circumstances and the intention. In the grand scheme of things, her lying about her period was as inconsequential as Maiju stealing a few beans from a neighbour's field. Besides, it was much better than feeling powerless in the face of tradition.

Amale diyeka jor bejor tala
Amale diyeka jor bejor tala
Chhudainma rattigo sangi
Chhudainma rattigo

(The rags that the mother gave
Turned red as soon as I touched them, my friend
They turned red as soon as I touched them)

A dragonfly hovered over a millet plant. A breeze swept past Kanchhi's new *lungi*. And her own version of a *sangini* song kept playing in her head.

Never again, Kanchhi vowed to herself, never again would she ever tell anyone about her period. If she got away with it once, she would get away with it again.

Two months later, Maiju asked Kanchhi what had happened to her period.

Kanchhi shrugged. 'It went on a pilgrimage,' she said.

'Are you sure you weren't bitten by a leech then?'

'No.'

'Tatteri ki,' Maiju said. 'You'll have a hard time being a mother now.'

'Who cares?' Kanchhi said.

12

November 13, 2005

THE TEMPLE IS SMALL, ABOUT AS TALL AS MAIJU. A concrete structure with a sloping zinc roof, it is where the woman was said to have washed the petticoat. Under the shade of a big *pipal* tree. The woman is also said to have founded the temple. In penance. Not the concrete structure but the practice of worshipping an idol. There are two idols – one in the laps of the *pipal* tree, nestled among the coils of its roots, a small, shapeless rock smeared in red and yellow powder; the other is inside the concrete temple, a human-like statue of goddess Durga. At some point in the course of history, the god became a goddess.

'*Jay Devi. Jay Mata*,' Maiju whispers as she squats in front of the first idol. She marks it with a paste of yellow and red powder and bows. This god has been abandoned. Leaves pile high around the rock, nearly burying it. Maiju sweeps them away with her bare hands and drops a marigold in their stead.

The concrete temple is better maintained. Haricháur *buwa* cleans it every morning. He sweeps the steps leading to it, the plinth that it stands on and the floor, also made of concrete, inside. The gate too is clean, although it is beginning to rust where the paint has chipped off. Maiju unlocks the gate and pushes it open. Inside, the goddess sits on a lion on a pedestal. The lion can be seen, but the goddess herself is draped in a red, sequined veil. Her skirt is also red and sequined. Ironically, she is wearing a petticoat underneath. Red, as well, and clearly visible under the mesh of the skirt.

Maiju repeats the process with her. Marks her feet and forehead with the yellow and red paste and bows. Leaves a flower at the base and bows again. Here, a bell is installed on a short pole. Maiju rings it, and as she does so, the image of the young boy who returned home after years of being away flits before her eyes. What are the chances, she thinks as she walks out of the temple to the gate. What are the chances that Kanchhi might come home too? What are the chances that she too was only lost on her way home? Could that have really happened? Could she really surprise Maiju after all these years?

'Hey, *Devi*.' Maiju turns around and clasps her hands together one more time.

'Hey, *Devi*,' she repeats.

No other words come out.

13

A FEW WEEKS AFTER SHE CAME OUT OF CONFINEMENT, Kanchhi went to Govinda sir's library to return *Gitilahar*. Govinda sir's library was a bookshelf in his living room, a two-shelf bookcase on top of a table under the stairs that led to the second floor.

'May I come in, sir?' Kanchhi asked from the door.

Govinda sir, who was sitting at another table surrounded by three boys from Kanchhi's class, leaned back on his chair and exclaimed, 'Deepa! Come in, come in. Here, join us.'

The three boys – Shiva Shirish, Tara Prasad Gautam and Ranjan Kunwar – moved towards the wall and made room for her.

'Have you heard of a psychologist?' Govinda sir asked.

Kanchhi shook her head.

'Isn't he someone who understands how the mind works, sir?' Tara Prasad asked. He was known as the smartest of the three.

'Yes, the mind, not the brain,' Govinda sir said. 'There's a difference. You might be interested in it, Deepa.'

Kanchhi shook her head again, unsure of what to say.

'A child psychologist,' Govinda sir continued. 'You will be good at it. Think about it. And you boys.' Govinda sir turned towards them. 'Have you heard of a campus in Chitwan?'

'The one that researches agriculture, sir?' Tara Prasad asked again.

'Yes, that one,' Govinda sir said.

'We've heard of it.'

'You should all consider it. We need a revolution in agriculture as well.' Nepal had just ushered in a multiparty democracy and, with it, its new constitution.

'My father told me about it,' Ranjan said. He was the tallest of the three.

'What does he do again?'

'He's in the Indian army.'

'Ah. Indian army. That's a good job too, but not for you boys. Not for you. You should stay in the country and do something here.'

'What about civil service, sir?' Shiva Shirish asked.

'That's good too, very good, but we need more women there. Kanchhi, have you thought of applying to civil service jobs?'

Kanchhi shook her head.

'You can be the first section officer from this area – not just the first woman section officer but the first section officer in general. Wouldn't that be brilliant?'

The boys looked at her. Kanchhi again said nothing.

'Sir,' Tara Prasad spoke, 'what exactly is a constitution?'

'It is, what you call it, the law of the land,' Govinda sir said. 'It governs everything.'

'Does it govern our school too, sir?'

'Yes and no. For instance.' Govinda sir shifted forward and wrote 'Constitution' at the top of an exercise book. At the bottom, he wrote, 'Janasewa Secondary High School.' 'Now,' drawing a dotted line between the two, he asked, 'what connects them?'

No one said anything. Kanchhi moved towards the bookshelf by the boys.

'The Constitution,' Govinda sir continued, 'guarantees your right to education, and the schools—?'

'They provide education,' Ranjan answered.

'Correct. Now, how can you provide education if you are not allowed to?'

'But, sir, our school was formed a long time ago.'

'We had another Constitution then.'

'If we did, why did we need a new one?'

Kanchhi pulled down a thick book and turned the pages. The first two lines read:

Chimli lochan dirghakal tapama kholera basantika
Nachdi sundar talale pawanma dekhi phuleki lata

(Like a flowering vine dancing beautifully in the wind,
with eyes closed in deep meditation and youth unfurled)

'What's *lochan*, sir?' Kanchhi asked.

'What?' Govinda sir said.

The three boys parted like grass and looked at Kanchhi.

'*Lochan*. What is it?' Kanchhi asked.

'Eyes,' Govinda sir said and tried reading the title of the book she was holding.

'*Shakuntal*,' he said. 'Not for you, not yet, which reminds me.' He looked under the exercise books strewn all over his table. 'Where is it, boys? Where is it?'

'What, sir?' the boys asked.

'The magazine. It was right here. Where did it go? Oh, found it. Here.' Govinda sir threw a magazine to Kanchhi. *Madhuparka*. A literary monthly. On the cover was a picture of a temple Kanchhi did not recognize. Govinda sir did not know it either. Kanchhi leafed through the pages. Except for the front cover, everything was in black and white.

Kanchhi put *Shakuntal* back on the shelf and the magazine inside her bag. Then, as Govinda sir went back to talking to the boys, she resumed her browsing. Next to *Shakuntal* was an abridged version of Mark Twain's *Prince and the Pauper*, and it looked like a picture book of one boy in both rich and poor costumes. Kanchhi briefly wondered if she should take it but decided she was not ready for English literature yet. She fingered through the rest of the collection instead. Two other English books were newly added to the shelf – an abridged version of *David Copperfield* and a *Wuthering Heights* pocketbook. Next to them were the old staples of Nepali literature – *Shirishko Phool*, *Naso*, *Basanti*, *Muna Madan* – a few, random issues of *Madhuparka*, *Ruprekha* and *Sharada*, and books on general knowledge – *Samanya Gyan*, *Gyangunka Kura*, *Bigyan ra Abishkar*. The lower shelf held Govinda sir's own collections of poetry – about ten copies of *Santa Jiwan* and a whole stack of his most recent work, *Phulaka Thunga*, written for children. The latter was still bound in a rope. Kanchhi tugged at the rope as if to test it and moved forward. At the end was a tattered book that caught her eye. Kanchhi pulled it out.

It was a magazine, much smaller than *Madhuparka* but bigger than the *Prince and the Pauper*. On the cover was a picture of a young Nepali woman, probably in her twenties, wearing a sleeveless top and very pink lipstick. In her mouth was a quill, also pink, but so faint it almost disappeared among the scruff marks dotting the whole page. Below, on the right of the woman, was another picture. An inset, with a mugshot of a schoolgirl as old or only a few years older than Kanchhi. The caption underneath read: 'When Lust Blinds You.' Next to it were two other headlines: 'A Tale of a Tattooed Beauty' and 'A Feat of the Impotent.' At the very bottom was the fourth one, stretched as long as the width of the magazine: 'Notorious Women and Their Sex Lives.'

Kanchhi looked at the name of the magazine again. *Tatyakatha*, it said. Real Stories.

Kanchhi slipped the magazine inside her bag.

Kanchhi was sure Govinda sir did not own the magazine; if he did, he didn't mean to put it on the shelf where a student could pick it up. The magazine was lewd and pulpy – so raunchy and so explicit words like *yoni*, *linga*, *birya*, *bhrun* and *karani* were thrown about like spices in almost every story. Almost every story also had death in it (usually a murder), and the black and white pictures of the dead were always displayed in their crudest form – arms and legs splayed about, clothes pushed up against their bodies, their necks in awkward, uncomfortable angles and their helplessness blatant and undignified. Kanchhi read her first *Tatyakatha* story that evening: 'When Lust Blinds You.' It was about two sixth graders who had sex in a field and got pregnant.

The story opened with the girl in jail. Fifteen years old, Chhetri and from a hill in the district of Nawalparasi. The mugshot from the front was reproduced on the first page, alongside a mugshot of a boy as old as the girl. The boy was from the girl hamlet too – same age, same caste and also arrested the same day but the first one to confess to the 'sin' they had committed.

A year earlier, the story went, they were merely innocent children who did not even know they fancied each other. Then, one day during recess, the girl asked the boy if she could borrow his pen. The boy said sure but decided to taunt the girl a bit in the process. He extended his arm as if to give her the pen, but when the girl reached for it, he retracted it. He did this for a while. Extend, retract. Extend, retract. On the fourth extend and retract, he accidentally poked her breast. This, the writer wrote, sent shivers down their bodies, awakening lust. A few weeks later, they attempted sex in a field. He came before he could even go in. They tried again after a few days. This time in another field. Used toothpaste as a contraceptive. It did not work. The girl missed her period and then another. Abortion was illegal in the country. So, alarmed, the girl tried what she had heard would work. She ate ash gourd and bottle gourd, chewed spoonfuls of 'hot' spices like nutmeg, cinnamon and flax seeds, swallowed *sindoor* powder, jumped down from one field to another and even placed a quern-stone on her belly in an attempt to crush it – did everything short of inserting a stick up her vagina. Nothing worked. Eight months later, the girl gave birth to a baby girl and, seconds later, strangled her. She got caught while trying to bury the baby in a heap of manure. A neighbour noticed her.

A year earlier, when Kanchhi had just started fourth grade at Janasewa, a girl in sixth grade had been escorted out of school for 'tongue-kissing' a boy from her own grade. 'What's a tongue kiss?' Kanchhi had to ask Jharana, who told her that it was a kind of kissing where tongues touched each other.

'Touch each other?' Kanchhi was surprised anyone would want to do that. Even more surprising was that the girl had to leave school as a result. Kanchhi still remembered her, short bangs and perky boobs, walking across the school as if guilty of murder. A thin shawl covered her face, and two adult women, one on each side, led her by the arms.

As Kanchhi now lay on her bed, with *Tatyakatha* by her side and a lamp glowing by the window, she wondered if there was more to the story. Was the girl doing it too? Was it even possible for a sixth grader to do it and then get pregnant?

'Don't burn the oil all night,' Maiju said and put an end to her wondering.

Kanchhi never returned *Tatyakatha* to Govinda sir's library (of course), never saw another one on the bookshelf either, nor did she stop finding them. Wherever she went, whoever's house she stepped into, all she had to do was locate the room that a young man (sometimes woman) occupied and begin the search. Sooner or later, she would find them, either buried deep in a stack of books in an alcove or on top of a wall with other book-length erotica written in Hindi. Sometimes, they were in plain sight, usually by a pillow or on a windowsill. One, two or three random issues of *Tatyakatha*. Almost always, she stole them.

One day, Thapa Maila *dai* saw her reading the magazine and shook his head. 'Are you old enough to be reading it?' he asked.

Kanchhi did not understand the question. She could read it just fine, she thought. The legal jargon threw her off sometimes, but it did not hinder the flow.

'Yes,' she said. 'The crimes here are of another world.'

Maiju, who could neither read nor write, only stared at Kanchhi.

Strangely, when fifth grade ended and Kanchhi reclaimed her first position, the school awarded her a book in English as a prize. *The World's Twenty Most Notorious Women*, it said, and included the same women that Kanchhi had read about in her first *Tatyakatha*: Catherine the Great, Countess Elizabeth Bathory, Eva Braun and so on. Their notoriety was based on their sex lives, who they were fucking and how deviant the act was. The school had confused 'notorious' with 'famous' and had not bothered to skim through the pages to make sure the book was appropriate to be an award.

14

THERE WAS ANOTHER REWARD FOR COMING FIRST that year: Kanchhi's own room. The room to the left of the kitchen. Kanchhi had been wanting to move in there for a while now, but Maiju had been against it. She considered the room impure and the act unsafe. Kanchhi's grandparents had died in that room, and the spirits, Maiju said, wandered around.

'Let them,' Kanchhi said one morning. 'There's enough room for all three of us.' Then, she went to fetch Laxmi, and, together, they emptied the room. There was not a lot to carry out, just an unhinged trunk full of muggy clothes, a few old *dokos* used to coop chickens, and some farming tools – a mattock, a hoe, an axe, a share of a plough and the stakes and fulcrum of the grain huller that once used to be in that room. The bed, Kanchhi kept. It was made of *sal*, and despite being decades since her grandfather had built it, it was still strong and free of wood beetles and termites. Kanchhi spread the newest mat she could find on the bed and, underneath it, tucked the rice grains that the Bayarghari shaman had given her.

'Laxmi,' Kanchhi said, unrolling the mattress on top of the mat. 'What do you think of our maths teacher?'

'You mean your maths teacher? The one who failed the tenth grade?'

'Yeah.'

'I don't know what I think of him, but I know he has a thing for the science teacher.'

'He does?'

'Yeah. Haven't you heard?'

'No.'

'Well, they're always with each other. If they aren't together, they should be. They look good together.'

'Hmm,' Kanchhi said and spread a bed sheet on top of the mattress. She held one end of it, Laxmi the other. What Laxmi said made sense to her. Both teachers were tenth graders preparing for their second attempt at the School Leaving Certificate (SLC) exams, and both, while preparing, were teaching at Janasewa. They had a lot in common to not fall for each other, but that was not why Kanchhi had asked Laxmi about her maths teacher. He could play the flute very well, and Kanchhi liked that.

'You know who you would look good with?' Laxmi asked.

'Who?' Kanchhi asked.

'Yog Bikram?'

'Who?'

Laxmi laughed. 'Yog Bikram or Lata Thakuri. They're both very tall. You'll look funny with them.'

Kanchhi shook her head. Yog Bikram was a boy in her class. Definitely tall but someone she had never paid any attention to precisely because he was so tall. Thirman Thakuri, on the other hand, was hard to overlook. He was both deaf and mute (hence the nickname Lata Thakuri), and he was Saru *didi*'s second husband's third son from his third wife. He lived in the Thakuri hamlet.

'What about yourself?' Kanchhi asked.

'What about me?'

'Who do you like?'

'Nobody,' Laxmi said. 'I'm too well-behaved to be involved in all this.'

'As if.'

'For real,' Laxmi said. 'I'm going wherever *Ama* sends me.'

'We'll see about that.'

'See it then.'

A few weeks later, sixth grade began in the middle of January. When it did, there was a surprise. Over the winter break, the police station had been moved up to Bagar from Hatiya because one of its walls had collapsed one night, almost killing a recruit. The recruit was a seventeen-year-old constable named Sukh Bahadur Subedi. He and his three other policemen colleagues could be seen from Kanchhi's classroom window, sitting on a stool and polishing their boots, greeting people and chatting with them, or just milling about under the shadow of a gigantic, west-facing mountain.

'Want to go see that constable?' Laxmi asked that first day when she came over during the lunch break.

'Why? I can see him from right here,' Kanchhi said.

'Want to go see the wall then?' Laxmi asked.

'The wall?'

'Yes.'

'No.'

The wall in Hatiya was a half-hour walk away. By the time they would get back, the lunch break would be over.

'So what?' Laxmi said. 'I'm skipping school after this.'

'Why?'

'Because it's only the first day. I won't miss anything. Everyone skips school on their first day.'

'No, they don't.'

'Yes, they do.'

'How will you pass exams if—'

'The same way as usual. Luck. Besides, don't you know how they grade our papers?'

'How?'

'They throw them up in the air and see which ones land on the table. The ones that do, passed. The ones that don't, failed. The marks don't matter.'

'That's not true,' Kanchhi said.

'It *is*. Wait two years, and you'll find it out yourself.'

Kanchhi shook her head in disbelief.

'Anyway,' Laxmi said. 'Your boy, look.'

'Who?' Kanchhi turned right to look through the door. On the ground in front was Yog Bikram Thapa, flying paper planes with his friends. Kanchhi shook her head. It was not happening.

'What's wrong with him?' Laxmi asked.

'Nothing,' Kanchhi said.

'We should make a list of odd pairs,' Laxmi said.

Soon, the fifth bell rang, and the lunch break was over. Laxmi was right. Half of Kanchhi's class had skipped school. The total number of students was already less than twenty, and now it seemed as though they were all sitting for exams – two students fanned out on every bench, most of them without a book in front, sending a clear message to the teacher that they wanted him to tell them a story and call it a day. But the maths teacher, Nirajan sir, did not care. He went straight to the blackboard and wrote 'Sets.'

'No, sir, not today,' someone from the other side of the aisle shouted.

Nirajan sir turned around and smiled. He had a beautiful smile, like that of Madhav sir's from primary school. A wide smile that flashed his well-set teeth. Kanchhi could not believe that he had failed the tenth grade.

'Introduction to Set,' he read from the textbook. 'Tara Prasad, read the first few lines until I say stop,' he said.

Tara Prasad got up. He usually sat on the second bench on the other side, with Shiva Shirish, Ranjan Kunwar and Ramesh from Kanchhi's hamlet. That period, he had moved to the front, along with Shiva Shirish.

'Introduction to Set,' Tara Prasad read out loud in Nepali. 'This is a potato. This is a tomato. This is a turnip. This is a cabbage. These all are vegetables. This is a set of vegetables in a basket.'

'Good. Stop,' Nirajan sir said. 'Sit down.'

Tara Prasad sat down. Nirajan sir then turned to the rest of the class and asked if they understood. Kanchhi nodded.

'There are vegetables in a basket, and this is a set of vegetables in that basket,' the teacher summarized. 'Deepa, read the next section.'

Kanchhi got up and read the next few lines. This one was a set of four prime numbers less than ten. At the end, the teacher asked again if everyone understood. Kanchhi nodded again. Up next was a set of nations in SAARC. Ranjan was to read that out loud. He had just begun and was saying 'Bhutan' when Kanchhi looked out of the door and saw a group of villagers walking across the bridge over the Setikhola River. They were coming towards the school, and as they reached the teashop that faced the two school buildings, Kanchhi noticed that one of the villagers was carrying a sick person in a *doko*.

'Who is it?' Everyone on the other side of the aisle stood up and looked out of their windows. Nirajan sir walked to the door and looked out as well. The other students, those on Kanchhi's side of the aisle, did the same. Soon, Thirman Thakuri crossed the school yard and joined the villagers carrying the sick person.

'It's Thakuri *baje*,' Ramesh said.

'Who?' the teacher asked.

'Lata Thakuri's father, sir,' Ramesh said. 'They live below our hamlet.'

'Looks like they're taking him to a hospital,' Nirajan sir said and turned around. Everyone else continued to stare out.

'All right.' Nirajan sir clapped his hands. 'Back to the lesson. Ranjan—'

Ranjan turned around. The other students took their time.

Thakuri *baje* was a jolly drunk. That was how Kanchhi remembered him. Another retired Indian army man, but someone who had risen to the rank of a sergeant. He drank in the afternoons and danced with a flower tucked behind his ear. Any flower that was in bloom: rubber plant, *simal*, marigold, malabar nut. Sometimes, a sprig of a wild plant. *Chhamchham nachideu niurera* ... One thing he disliked was being called a *baje* (an old man). 'Call me *mama* instead,' he would say. An uncle. 'I'm around your mother's age.' And he was. Only fifty years old then. Maiju was just over forty.

Turned out Thakuri *baje* had developed throat cancer.

End stage. A week later, the men who had carried him to a hospital in Palpa carried him back to Torikhola. The doctors had advised them to let him die in peace among his family in the village. A few days afterwards, Kanchhi and Maiju went to see him with a bunch of mustard greens as a gift. Thakuri *baje* was sitting on a mattress on the porch, wrapped up in a checkered blanket, drinking a cup of hot water. He looked healthy to Kanchhi. A little gaunt perhaps and a little uncomfortable maybe, but still fit and strong. He joked as soon as he saw them.

'Maybe it's all the greens that's killing me,' he said. 'Should have brought a big, fat goat, Syani.'

'Should have, *Dai*, should have, but this is all that grows in a poor woman's garden,' Maiju said and handed the greens over to his fourth wife. The fourth wife was much younger than Maiju and had a toddler in her arms. All three wives, except Saru *didi*, who was the second, lived in that house with Thakuri *baje*.

'Do you want a biscuit, *Nani*?' the fourth wife asked Kanchhi.

Yes, Kanchhi nodded.

The fourth wife went inside the kitchen. She and the other wives ran a small shop out of a trunk in the attic and sold items that did not cost too much, like biscuits, candies, cigarettes, tobacco, tea, *bindis*, matchsticks, and such – items that could be carried in a *doko* from Waling.

The biscuits Kanchhi received were half a packet of Nebico Glucose. Kanchhi held on to them.

'And,' Maiju asked Thakuri *baje*, 'what did the doctors say?'

'What else could they say? Said I'll die of this,' Thakuri *baje* replied.

'Really?' Maiju asked.

'Yes. The cancer's spread everywhere, they said. No cure.'

Maiju tsked. 'What exactly is this cancer?'

'Death,' Thakuri *baje* said, slurping on his hot water. 'Death's come to collect me. That's what it is.'

'Is there no option left? Any shamans, priests, lamas?'

'We did all that and more,' the third wife said, coming out of the kitchen with more hot water for Thakuri *baje*. She looked just like Thirman Thakuri – a long, oval face with close-set eyes and high cheekbones.

'Lunkhu, Bayarghari, Waling, Pokhara,' the third wife continued. 'Took him to shamans here, there and everywhere. Nothing worked. I told him to go to the hospital a long time ago, but he wouldn't listen to me. Don't they say an army man has no brain? Well, that's true. He has no brain.'

'Shut up. Why are you talking too much?' Thakuri *baje* said. 'This army man's pension is what's keeping you alive. It's also what's going to keep you alive after I'm gone.'

'As if.' The third wife rolled her eyes. 'How much do you think we get after it's divided among four wives? Nothing.'

Thakuri *baje* made a hacking motion at his wife. She returned it and then asked Maiju if she wanted some tea.

A month later, Thakuri *baje* died. A conch shell announced his death. A long, uninterrupted note that echoed through the mountains.

'Ram-Ram, Ram-Ram,' Maiju chanted and walked past the tangerine trees to the end of the terrace field. Kanchhi followed her. The Thakuri hamlet was on a flatter ridge far below Saili *didi*'s house, and Thakuri *baje*'s house, right in the middle of it all, had a small crowd gathered in the yard – splotches of red and green in a field of grey.

'Looks like he died a while ago,' Maiju said.

'Are we going down too?' Kanchhi asked.

'In a bit. Let them finish their work first.'

'Can *I* go now?'

'No, not now.'

'I want to see what they do.'

'It's not a wedding,' Maiju snapped.

Kanchhi went quiet and watched the crowd for a while. More people walked up from below Thakuri *baje*'s house. At Saili *didi*'s yard too, Laxmi and Dhan *didi* appeared at its edge and looked down.

'No. I'm going now,' Kanchhi said and ran to her room to get a shawl. When she walked out, Maiju told her to at least wash her face first. Kanchhi walked to the outdoor sink, splashed some water on her face and then left, stopping by at Saili *didi*'s to get Laxmi.

When the two girls reached Thakuri *baje*'s house, he was already laid out on a bed of bamboo by a mound of holy basil. An ewer that must have been used to pour him water during his last breaths was by his head. His face could not be seen. The whole body, including the face, was wrapped in a white shroud, and his two younger brothers, both clad in white dhotis, were in the midst of spreading a yellow one on top.

'Where's Lata?' one of them shouted when it was time to carry Thakuri *baje* to Setibeni, the point where the Setikhola River met the Kali Gandaki.

'I told him not to go anywhere,' the other uncle said.

'He was right here,' Thirman's mother said. She was on the porch with Saru *didi* and Thakuri *baje*'s two other wives.

'He's going to make us all late. It's already nine in the morning,' the first uncle said. It took six hours to get to Setibeni.

'Let me go find him.' Thirman's mother got up and went to look for him inside the house. In the meantime, three of Thirman's cousins positioned themselves to carry Thakuri *baje*. When Thirman could not be found anywhere, a young man from the crowd stepped in to be the fourth carrier. Up ahead in the corner, a flag bearer got up, and an old man next to him blew the conch again. The same long, sad note.

'Ram nam satya ho. Ram nam satya ho.' The chants began.

The four young men bent down and lifted Thakuri *baje* onto their shoulders.

Kanchhi and Laxmi followed the procession as far as the primary school. That was the furthest most girls and women went. They could have gone further, but right below the primary school, the woods sloped downwards, and since women were not allowed to witness the funeral and since they would have to turn back sooner or later, it was wiser to turn around then. Maiju and Saili *didi* had already left for their homes, going up, instead of right, from Thakuri *baje*'s house.

'Know the story of Lalu and Kal?' Kanchhi asked Laxmi, stepping off the *chautara* they were on. The procession was now out of sight.

'I do,' Laxmi said, getting off the *chautara* as well. 'Lalu and Kal' was a story included in the ninth-grade Nepali textbook. It was about a man named Lalu who kidnaps Kal, the lord of death, and no one dies for decades.

'Wouldn't it be nice if we could lock Death up too and never die?' Kanchhi asked.

'Why? I don't want to live forever,' Laxmi said.

'Why not?'

Laxmi shrugged. 'My grandmother did not die well. She struggled a lot.'

'That's because she was dying. If she didn't have to die, she wouldn't have suffered.'

'Doesn't Lalu regret locking Death up too?'

'He does.'

'See. Even he didn't want to live forever.'

That was true. Lalu does get tired of being old and frail and lets Death out in the end. Once out, Death asks the god to make him invisible, and the god obliges. People, as a result, according to the story, never get to see their death coming.

'My *ba*'s name is also Kal,' Kanchhi said.

'Oh, yes, isn't it? Funny name. You should lock him up and see what happens.' Laxmi laughed.

Kanchhi laughed too, and the two walked by the school building, looking in through the windows for no reason. At the end was the third-grade classroom tucked in a corner.

'Oh, look, Lata Thakuri,' Laxmi said.

'Where?'

'There.' Laxmi pointed at a shape across the room, a shape facing away from them.

'And they're looking for him everywhere,' Laxmi continued. 'How did he get inside? Lata, *oye*, Lata,' Laxmi called, despite knowing that he could not hear her.

They walked back to the door and saw that it was closed but not locked. The small AA88 padlock hung open in the loop. Kanchhi pushed the door open. Something about it startled Thirman and he looked back. He was smoking a cigarette.

'When did you begin smoking?' Laxmi asked in gestures.

Thirman Thakuri smiled in response and held out his hand holding the cigarettte, asking if the girls wanted to try it too.

The girls shook their heads and walked across the aisle to where he was sitting on a table, with his legs pushed up against the windowsill. Once there, Laxmi brought her fists up on her shoulders and said, 'They've left already. You should go.'

Thirman pointed at himself, his eyes and in the direction of the woods and mimed that he had seen the men leave. 'Don't worry,' he moved his hands in front of him. 'I'll run down.'

'No, no, go now. They'll be mad at you otherwise,' Laxmi said, pulling on his arm.

Thirman brought his legs down and smiled at Kanchhi. In the far distance, the conch sounded again. Thirman took one long last puff of the cigarette and threw the rest out of the window. The butt landed on a bamboo sheath right next to a dead wasp.

The next day, Kanchhi saw him on the ground in front of the school building, kicking a *chungi* in his white mourning attire.

'Why did you come to school?' She gestured from afar.

Thirman did not understand her and resumed kicking the *chungi* up in the air.

Later, she saw him at the Setikhola River, fishing for crabs.

'Not going home?' Kanchhi gestured from the bridge above.

Thirman shook his head and went back to shaking a big rock.

Kanchhi did not bother him after that. Govinda sir had asked her to participate in a nationwide essay contest for the ninetieth anniversary of the newspaper *Gorkhapatra*, and she began preparing for it. The topic was on democracy and how Nepalis could strengthen it as they moved into a new era of governance. A difficult topic to write on. Kanchhi had never paid any attention to any of those concepts.

But then, a few days later, Thirman Thakuri appeared right outside her classroom window, glanced in and passed by. He did that again the next day and the day after that, trying to make it seem as though he was doing just that – passing through – but the girls noticed it. 'Who is he looking at?' they tried to guess. Kanchhi's ears went red.

The following Saturday, he showed up at her house, with a cousin in tow. The cousin, one of the four whom Kanchhi had seen carrying Thakuri *baje*, asked her if she wanted to join them. They were headed up to Tauka Kanchha *dai*'s house, he said, to speak to his nephew, who was their classmate. Tauka Kanchha *dai*'s house was right next to Ramesh's. Kanchhi said no. Maiju, who was in the yard with Kanchhi, asked them if they could return an aluminium glass to Tauka Kanchha *dai* for her.

A few days later, they were in Kanchhi's yard again. This time, the cousin said they were headed towards the volleyball court past Saru *didi*'s house. Again, Kanchhi said no.

'What happened?' Thirman asked her one day in the woods below the primary school. Kanchhi smiled in response. He was not amused.

15

THREE THINGS HAPPENED DURING THAT MONSOON of 1991. One, Kanchhi turned twelve, unmarked and unnoticed. Two weeks later, *Kanyadan* came out in cinema halls in some parts of the country, and the people got its first super-hit Teej song, '*Teejako Rahara*.'

The song and the movie were such massive hits that when monsoon vacation ended and classes resumed, Kanchhi sat among a group of students and listened to a scene-by-scene narration from Jharana, who herself had heard the story from someone else. The movie was about child marriage and remarriage. A little girl gets married to a little boy but then becomes a widow when he dies young. Unable to remarry, the girl grows up in her in-laws' house, where she is treated as their servant. Years later, a young man walks into the hamlet, and the girl, now a young woman, falls in love with him, but her mother-in-law, instead of letting her go, continues to harass her, tying her to a pillar in a buffalo shed in the climax and setting it alight. That scene, even when narrated, traumatized Kanchhi to such an extent that she asked Maiju if she had any plans of getting married again and if she had, not to tell anyone. 'Are you on *bhang*?' was Maiju's answer.

Three weeks later was that year's Teej, and on that year's Teej, on the day of Rishi Panchami to be exact, Maiju found out that Kanchhi had been lying about her period for a whole year. Rishi Panchami was the day when women, married and unmarried, huddled in groups around springs and bit into 365 sticks of chaff flower 365 times, hoping to cleanse their bodies of the sins they had committed during their periods. Of all the days.

'Kanchhi, *eh*, Kanchhi.' Maiju banged on the door that morning at four. Kanchhi, as usual, squirmed and tried to sleep a little longer, except that this time she was on her period – the third day – and she sat up instantly when she realized that the rag she was wearing could be completely soaked in blood.

'Get up. Up,' Maiju shouted again. Kanchhi could hear her darting around outside.

Kanchhi got off the bed and lit a lamp. Indeed, the rag she was wearing was completely soaked, and some of the blood had leaked out on the bed. The other rag, which Kanchhi had washed the night before, was hanging from a rope on the wall behind her. Kanchhi reached for it. It was damp, too damp to wear after the ritual. Kanchhi looked around, searching for a piece of clothing that she could rip and turn into a rag. She could not find any. None were as soft and absorbent as

Maiju's old cotton sari. Kanchhi would have to wait and tear herself one later then.

'Kanchhi, please,' Maiju pleaded from outside. 'Saili *didi* and her girls will be here soon. The sun will be out too if you don't hurry.'

Kanchhi took down the bar shutting the door and walked out.

On the porch, Maiju had assembled almost everything needed for the ritual that morning: chaff flower twigs in seventeen bundles of twenty-one, one bundle of seven and one of one; two long leaves from the sugarcane plant (one for Maiju, one for Kanchhi); two sprigs from a *kush* plant (again, one for Maiju and one for Kanchhi); and five different kinds of mud, each on a *badahar* leaf – one came from a termite's mound, another from the holy basil's, the third from the tip of a plough, the fourth from a slope with some generic red mud, and the fifth came from a spot supposedly trodden by an elephant. A man in Hatiya sold that elephant mud, and women bought it. The only items missing were some fresh cow dung and cow piss. Maiju came out of the kitchen with a plastic bottle and ordered Kanchhi to go get the piss and the dung from Ramesh's. Ramesh's house was the only Bahun house in the hamlet, and therefore the only house with a cow.

'I can't,' Kanchhi said. 'I have to go use the latrine.'

'Always the latrine,' Maiju said, looking immediately

for her slippers. 'Hurry up then. Don't take half an hour. Also, see if I left the big tumpline in the fields down there. I couldn't find it here.'

'It's too dark to see anything.'

'Just look for it,' Maiju said and started to walk up towards Ramesh's house. 'Use the rest of the water that's already there,' she added.

Kanchhi waited until Maiju was out of sight and chatting with Thapa Nani *didi* by her house. Thapa Nani *didi* too was getting ready for the Panchami rituals. Kanchhi could not understand what they were saying to each other, but the mumblings she heard assured her that Maiju would not be down anytime soon. Kanchhi then checked on Saili *didi*. She walked to the edge of the terrace field and looked down. Neither Saili *didi* nor her women were on their way up. Kanchhi checked her immediate surroundings next, the paths and fields around, just in case. When she was certain no one was nearby, Kanchhi ran to Maiju's room. There, from underneath Maiju's bed, Kanchhi pulled the old trunk out and from the trunk, the old cotton sari. She was about to tear a piece off when Maiju stepped back into the yard.

'What are you doing?' she asked.

'Nothing,' Kanchhi said, standing up so fast she kicked the trunk and its lid closed with a thud.

'What's that?' Maiju asked, walking up to the room.

'I was looking for something to wear after the bath,' Kanchhi said.

Maiju did not believe her. 'Have you started stealing from me?' she asked.

'No,' Kanchhi said, reflexively showing her the sari to prove her innocence.

'What is it?'

Maiju took the sari in her hand, and it hit her. 'Are you on your period?' she asked.

Kanchhi, who had taken a step back towards her old bed, nodded. Maiju did not see her nod and asked again, 'Are you?'

'Yes.'

'What day?'

'First.'

'First? First in a year?' Maiju asked.

'Yes.'

'Where are the rags I made you a year ago?'

'I don't know. I lost them.'

'Lost them? How could you? Get back outside and don't touch anything.'

Kanchhi walked past her and out of the room into the yard – as far away as possible from Maiju. Maiju tore two rags out of the sari and then put the sari back in the trunk. As she pushed the trunk back under the bed, the second fact hit her.

'You're lying,' she said.

'No, I'm not,' Kanchhi said.

'This isn't the first day, is it?' Maiju asked, walking out of the room with the rags.

'No,' Kanchhi said.

'This isn't the second time either, is it?'

'No.'

'I knew it,' Maiju said. 'I knew it.'

'Nothing happens,' Kanchhi said.

'Nothing happens?' Maiju stepped into the yard, angry at being lied to. 'How do you know nothing happens?'

'Nothing happened for a year.'

Maiju threw the rags at Kanchhi. Kanchhi ducked and then caught them.

'Don't touch anything,' Maiju shouted and then saw the items on the porch. '*Dankini*, *papini*, why did you have to touch everything?'

'Just sprinkle some gold water on them. You'll be fine,' Kanchhi said.

'Sprinkle some gold water?' Maiju looked around for something to throw at Kanchhi.

Kanchhi ran away.

'Where are you going? Come back, you *papini*. Come back,' Maiju shouted.

It turned out that Maiju had walked back from Thapa Nani *didi*'s house to get a banana for the cow. Thapa Nani *didi* had mentioned it in passing, and Maiju realized that she had to go back and get one too. A banana in return for some piss.

'What if I hadn't turned around then?' Maiju kept murmuring for minutes afterwards. 'What if I hadn't?

When were you going to tell me? How long were you planning on hiding it?'

'Forever,' Kanchhi said.

'Aren't you ashamed?' Maiju asked.

'Ashamed of what?'

'People are going to remember you for this.'

Kanchhi shrugged.

'Did you go to temples too while on your period?'

'No,' Kanchhi lied.

'Good.' Maiju took a deep breath. 'Okay, what's done is done. Now, you'll fast for a month come January, understand?'

Kanchhi nodded.

'You'll fast and go take a dip at the Kali Gandaki at the end.'

Kanchhi nodded again and then asked, 'What about today?'

'What about today? You're not coming with us,' Maiju said.

'Why not?'

'What do you mean why not?'

'But I thought this was the day to wash off the sins committed during my period.'

'It is, but you are on your period.'

'Stupid customs,' Kanchhi said.

'Don't be too smart. You know nothing about the sins of your periods.'

'Looks like you know nothing either.'

In a way, it was a relief. Maiju now knew about Kanchhi's periods and knew that periods were not to blame for anything unfortunate. A girl in her period was going around touching everything, even gods and ancestral shrines, and nothing devastating had happened. The harvests were fine, no one in the family had fallen sick, and no one had died unexpectedly. All the other unfortunate events, such as Thakuri *baje*'s death, a few chicks being snatched by eagles and the buffalo's miscarriage, were all chugged as facts of life, and there was no reason to reinterpret them. Still, for a while afterwards, Maiju went around the house sprinkling every corner with gold-touched water. And for months, she would suddenly think about what Kanchhi had done and get angry. 'You've lost my trust,' she would say. 'You've lost all of my trust.'

16

November 13, 2005

AT AROUND SEVEN, THE SUN FINALLY SHINES through. It rises above the mountains in the east, and the fog lowers itself closer to the Setikhola River. At a fire pit outside, by the black pipes, Maiju stirs a large cauldron of gruel for her buffalo – a mixture of rice husks and ground corn, leftover millet *dhedo* and potato curry, and rocks of salt. From there, she can see that Thapa Nani *didi*'s house, three fields above to the right, is already coming alive for the party that evening. Her two sons are on two trees in front, tying a string of colourful pennants around the branches. The party is to welcome the youngest son's wife into the hamlet, but Maiju cannot tell who is whom on those trees, not even from their voices. What they are saying to each other is muffled by the sound of their radio playing at first a slow *kauda* song and then the Gayatri mantra on repeat.

Om bhu: bhuwa: shwah:
Tat sabitu: barenyam
Bharga devasya dhimahi
Dhiyo yo: na: prachodayat

(Let the lord of the earth
The heaven and the self
The source of divine light
Illuminate and enlighten)

Maiju hums along. So does Saili *didi*, who is on Maiju's porch, sweeping the area around the quern-stones. The festive atmosphere in Thapa Nani *didi*'s house is contagious, the Gayatri mantra calming.

'Let's dance till dawn tonight,' Saili *didi* says. She is happy. Bir Bahadur *dai* will stay in Pokhara for at least two days – today and tomorrow. The earliest he can return is the day after, on Tuesday, that too if everything goes as smoothly as planned. The plan is to sell a plot of land he owns in Pokhara and help Bhime *dai*, their oldest son, buy a used bus. Bhime *dai* wants to run a route from Pokhara to Waling. The irony is that after years of being nagged, Bhime *dai* was finally out of the hamlet, but he did not leave of his own free will. The Maoists kicked him out during the last ceasefire in 2003. Him and Thapa Maila *dai*.

'I can't dance,' Maiju says. 'My wrist hasn't healed properly.'

'You and your wrist.' Saili *didi* throws the broom to the side and pulls herself in position to start grinding corn. 'The devils will never let it heal, will they?'

'*A-han*,' Maiju says and examines her wrist. She broke it more than a month ago when she fell from the *badahar* tree right off the front yard.

'Will it ever be straight?' Maiju asks. The wrist *is* healing but is bent slightly outwards, as if she is in the midst of opening a lid.

Saili *didi* looks at her and says no.

'It's going to be like your husband then,' Maiju says. 'He does not know how to give straight answers, does he? What was wrong with him this morning?'

Saili *didi* chuckles and says, 'The same old.'

'What do you mean?'

'What else could I mean?'

Maiju understands. The alcohol, she means. It has always been that ever since it morphed into an addiction. Saili *didi* cannot function without it, won't even come help Maiju in the fields unless promised a bottle in payment. It is also the reason she always fights with Bir Bahadur *dai* and fought again that morning. This time, Saili *didi* says, he caught her shuffling through his trunk looking for some money. Bir Bahadur *dai* was supposed to be in the latrine but came right back to get water. When he saw her hunched over the trunk, Saili *didi* says, he grabbed her by her hair and slapped her hard.

'Did it leave any mark?' Maiju asks. 'Let me see.'

'No.' Saili *didi* turns to Maiju and shows her her left cheek, but Maiju is too far away to see anything.

'Well, what can I say? You guys are a match,' Maiju says.

Saili *didi* laughs and then changes the topic, 'Remember the daughter-in-law who disappeared a few months ago?'

Maiju remembers her. She was a young Chhetri woman who had married into the only Chhetri family that lived up in Balakot. Maiju has heard that they are related but does not know how.

'Yes, what about her?' she asks.

'The one from Balakot.'

'I remember. What about her?'

'They found her yesterday.'

'They did? She came back?'

'No, they found her body.'

'Her body? Where?' Maiju looks up in the direction of Balakot.

'No, not there. There.' Saili *didi* points past the gorge behind Maiju, in the direction opposite to the Gurung hamlet, towards Bayarghari. 'Nothing but bones,' Saili *didi* adds.

Maiju puts a hand above her eyes and squints hard to see if she can detect any movement that far away. The Bayarghari bazaar is obviously out of view, but the mountains in between are also very distant. The Setikhola gorge is just massive. All Maiju sees is a curtain of green and yellow, with lines of red winding across. Signs of newly cut roads.

'The dozer unearthed her,' Saili *didi* says.

'How do you know all this?' Maiju asks, more curious than doubtful of the story.

'Thapa Nani's youngest son told me. He was up in Balakot inviting his friends to the party, and someone there told him.'

'How do they know it's her body?' Maiju looks up in the direction of Balakot again. 'It could be the Maoist woman's. Remember her?'

Saili *didi* does but is sure it is not her. The body, she says, was found close to the Bayarghari bazaar, more than eight hours away on foot. The Maoist woman, on the other hand, was raped and dumped in the jungle right across the Setikhola River. Less than an hour away.

'Besides,' Saili *didi* stops grinding and lowers her voice, 'just add two and two.'

'Wait, wait,' Maiju says and extinguishes the fire. She pulls the burning wood out of the pit and shoves it under the ashes. The buffalo's gruel, she cools it by pouring cold water into the cauldron. Then she walks to the porch and sits next to Saili *didi* to hear her more clearly.

'The woman disappeared two months ago,' Saili *didi* continues. 'Her husband has been in Qatar for a year. Now, who goes to Bayarghari?'

'Anyone can go to Bayarghari.'

'From Balakot? No, it makes no sense for her to walk

down all this way and go to Bayarghari. Even we don't go to Bayarghari.'

That is true. For people in Balakot and around, including Torikhola, Waling in the southeast has always been the closest and the most preferred city, even when they had to walk for eight hours to get there in the past. These days, all one needs to do is walk down to Hatiya and get on a jeep. They can walk down to Bagar and travel on a jeep to Bayarghari as well, like Bir Bahadur *dai* did that morning, but Bayarghari is not, and was never, as big or convenient of a hub as Waling is. Only people like Bir Bahadur *dai*, who want to avoid those they know in Waling or along the way there, prefer to travel to or via Bayarghari.

'So…?' Maiju asks.

'So, the rumour is she was pregnant when she disappeared.'

'Who was the lover?' Maiju lowers her voice.

'I don't know. But she must have been on her way to abort the kid.'

'In Bayarghari? Do they do that there?'

'If not there, then in Pokhara. Why else would she go that way?'

'Are we sure it's her?'

'They are.'

'How did she end up there?'

'I don't know. Maybe she died on her way back. Maybe her mother-in-law killed her. I would have done the same,' Saili *didi* says and resumes grinding corn.

Maiju does not say anything for a while. Then asks, 'How are we related again?'

'I don't remember,' Saili *didi* says. 'I think her husband's great-grandfather and Kal's great-grandfather were the same. Or is it great-great-grandfather? One of the two. I forgot which one it was.'

'*Eh. Eh*,' Maiju nods and gets up to walk back to the fire pit. 'We should go there sometime,' she says.

'We should. I need to get some wandering nettles from there.'

'Wandering nettles? For what?'

'For Bhime's father's eyes. They were very red this morning.'

'From being mad at you, perhaps.'

Saili *didi* laughs. Maiju walks to the fire pit and lifts the cauldron. It is heavy.

17

AS EXPECTED, LAXMI FAILED THE EIGHTH GRADE. She did not even go collect the report card. Kanchhi did it for her after picking up her own. Laxmi had failed in maths, science and English. In science, her marks were only four. Four out of a hundred. She had not even tried.

'What was four for? For writing your name?' Kanchhi asked.

'I guess my paper landed on the floor,' Laxmi said.

'What now?' Kanchhi asked.

'What now?' Laxmi shrugged and then looked around at the ground dotted with shredded pieces of notebooks. Up ahead was the teashop, swarming with students ready to celebrate the end of another academic year.

'Well, we go get tea now,' Laxmi said, and the two headed towards the shop.

A few days later, Laxmi went missing. Bir Bahadur *dai* came up to Kanchhi and asked if she had known anything about Laxmi and the constable Sukh Bahadur Subedi. Laxmi had run away with him.

'What?' Kanchhi was as stunned as Bir Bahadur *dai*.

'Did you know?' he asked, handing her the note Laxmi had left under her pillow.

'I didn't know anything about this,' Kanchhi said.

'How could you not know?' Bir Bahadur *dai* asked.

'I really didn't know, *Buwa*. *Satya*,' Kanchhi said. 'She never told me anything about him.'

Maiju did not believe her either and said that Kanchhi was to blame if anything happened to Laxmi.

'Like what?' Kanchhi asked.

'Like abandoned, sold, killed.'

Kanchhi laughed.

'This is *not* a laughing matter.'

'He *is* a cop,' Kanchhi said.

'And cops are gods? One just stole our daughter.'

Kanchhi laughed again. Maiju slapped her head hard.

It took Bir Bahadur *dai* that whole winter to locate Laxmi. She turned out to be in Chitwan at the house of one of Sukh Bahadur's uncles. Sukh Bahadur had apparently quit his job and taken her there after going to Pokhara first, where the two had gotten married at the Bindabasini Temple and spent a week at another constable's house, the other constable at the Bagar station. Sukh Bahadur was fortunate that the assistant sub-inspector, in charge of the Bagar station, never reported him as missing or a deserter. So, when he returned to Bagar, Sukh Bahadur got his job back easily. Even better, he was soon posted to Pokhara.

Laxmi and Sukh Bahadur were married the 'proper' way in a grand ceremony that cost Bir Bahadur *dai* more than a lakh and fifty thousand rupees. A retired Indian army man, he could afford it. He gave Seiko watches to the men in Sukh Bahadur's family and fabric for *gunyo cholo* to the women. Torikhola itself got an all-night party. Kanchhi's job was to peel garlic and ginger in the afternoon and, in the evening, guard the gifts the groom's team had brought with them: yards of cloth, fruits, yogurt, flowers, nuts. She also had to watch over the gifts/dowry they would take with them: a cauldron, water pots, plates, cooking pots. Kanchhi fell asleep while guarding the items in a small room once shared by Dhan *didi* and Laxmi.

At five the next morning, Maiju woke her up.

'Go say bye to Laxmi,' she said.

'Where is she?' Kanchhi asked.

'Outside.'

Kanchhi stepped out into the yard. There, Laxmi was surrounded by a group of women, all of whom were crying, with their faces buried in their *chadar*s. Kanchhi walked back inside.

'What's wrong?' Maiju asked.

'Too much crying. I don't want to cry.'

'Just go say bye. It might be years before you see her again.'

'It won't be,' Kanchhi said. 'I'll see her soon. I know.'

She went back to sleep.

When seventh grade began, Kanchhi realized that Laxmi was not the only one who had left their hamlets that winter. Thirman too was gone. He had been admitted to a deaf and mute school in Pokhara and would now be back only on school vacations. Saru *didi* confirmed the news one evening and shared that his mother had always wanted him enrolled in such a school but his father had been against it.

Kanchhi did not ask why. The boughs in front were red from the setting sun, and she only stared at them.

In July, Dhan *didi* too left, after becoming the first woman in the hamlet to pass the SLC exams. She had passed it in third division, missing the cut-off by a mark.

'*Ama*, do we have anyone in Pokhara?' Kanchhi asked Maiju late one day. They were both on the porch – Kanchhi lying on a mat, chewing on a stick of sugarcane; Maiju combing through wild mushrooms and patting them gently so that the insects fell off the gills.

'You have an aunt there,' Maiju said. 'One of your father's sisters.'

'Which one?'

'I don't know. The third one, I think.'

'Where in Pokhara is she?'

'I don't know. Ask Bir Bahadur *dai*.'

Kanchhi spat the cane out.

'Chhi,' Maiju said. 'Don't lie there and eat like that. You'll become a snake.'

Kanchhi got up and faced Maiju. '*Ama*, I want to study in Pokhara too.'

'And stay at your aunt's?'

'Yes.'

'And they'll let you too?'

'Why won't they?'

'They haven't been back here, not even once, since your grandparents died.'

'So? Maybe they're busy. You haven't been back to your village either.'

'That's different. I have no one there to go back to. They have me, you, Bir Bahadur *dai*, Saili *didi*, all this land. Saili *didi* and I might not be blood, but you are.'

'And that's why they'll let me stay with them. I won't be asking for a lot. I just need some food in the morning, some food in the evening and some space to lie down at night. In return, I can cook, do the dishes and look after their children too.'

'And you think it's that easy, huh?'

'Have you never really met them since that day?'

'No.'

'Wait, I'll arrange the next meet then.'

'Right.'

'Really. You just wait. I'll go to Assam and bring *Ba* here too. I'll pull him by his ears and drag him to the village.'

Later, while doing her Nepali homework, Kanchhi drafted a letter to her aunt in Pokhara. The actual assignment was to imagine that she was in a city for school but had fallen sick and needed some money. 'Write a letter to your father,' the assignment said, 'asking him to send a few hundred rupees over with someone who comes your way.' Kanchhi decided to write two.

Date: Asadh 27, 2049

My dear, respected phupu,
Namaste and lots of love.

Phupu, my name is Deepa Chhetri, also known as Kanchhi, daughter of Kal Bahadur Chhetri, granddaughter of Sher Bahadur Chhetri, your niece. I and Ama are both fine here and hope that you, your husband and children are all well and healthy too.

Phupu, let me not meander and get straight to the point. I am writing this letter to you because I am currently in seventh grade. SLC is only three years away. Recently, Saili didi's oldest daughter, Dhan didi, passed it in third division and went to Pokhara to study further. You must have met her by now. She is enrolled in Prithvi Narayan Shah campus and is studying arts. I too want to join the campus after my SLC exams and study there. I am a very good student, Phupu, and I know it will happen. I believe in education. So does Ama. I am writing to you because I have no one else in the city. I hope you will help me succeed in my objective. I will repay your debt. I can cook and do the dishes and the

laundry, and one day, when I am able to stand on my own two feet, I can take care of you too.

Please convey my love and namaste to your family.

Your obedient niece,
Deepa, aka Kanchhi

Govinda sir told her she need not worry about education beyond SLC. If she passed the exams, it would be his responsibility to make sure that she studied further. 'If you need help, don't hesitate to ask, understand?' he said, giving her the notebook back. 'Anything. Money, books, advice, anything.'

Kanchhi nodded.

18

SHIVA SHIRISH WAS A TORTURED SOUL. THAT MUCH was clear. What was torturing him was unknown. The third wheel in the gang of three – him, Tara Prasad and Ranjan Kunwar – and a poet, his alias 'Shishir' meant winter, and it suited him well. He was gloomy. Not cold but gloomy. Kanchhi got to know him better that year after Govinda sir showed him a love poem she had written in memory of Thirman Thakuri. Twenty lines, nineteen syllables each, inspired by the syllabic poems included in her textbook.

Maya dui aksharko tara wogateko thulo sansar
Tyo muskan, tyo herai, lochan sara batika bahar
Tyasaima mero naun, mero gaun, mero swapana lukeko
Tyasaima mero hriday, mero samarthya, prachin adeko

(Love, made up of only two syllables, envelops this vast world
That smile, that look, those eyes – all blossoms in a garden

Hidden in that word are my name, my village and my dreams
Leaning against that word are my heart, my strength and my history)

Govinda sir sent the poem to *Gorkhapatra*.

A few days later, Kanchhi found a letter tucked in her textbook. It was from Shiva and was written in pencil. He had beautiful handwriting – big and round, smooth letters. He said he liked the poem and asked her who her favourite poet was. His was Bhupi Sherchan. Kanchhi noticed that his Nepali was much stronger than hers.

She replied a few days later. She had never heard of Bhupi, she wrote. The poem she drafted was just for fun. 'Time pass,' she wrote. She preferred prose and asked him if he had read *Basanti*. While the political intrigue went over her head, the romance had left her shaken. Not the separation of the lovers – no, she wrote. Nor was it Gagan's doubts over Basanti's love for him or what those doubts made him do. It was the fact that they were cousins. 'Cousins. How can cousins marry each other?' she wrote. 'He was her uncle's son!'

Magars do it all the time, he wrote back. Maybe he was a Magar. She should read some poetry, he said and sent her a transcription of one of Bhupi's poems. '*Chiso Ashtray.*' His favourite, he underlined.

Chiso Ashtray

Yeha jo aunchhan
Mutubhari ago, wothbhari jwala bokera aunchhan!
Yeha jo baschhan
Hatkelabhari kharani ra ankhabhari dhuwa bokera baschhan
Ra yehabata jo janchhan
Poltabhari nibheka biswas ra thuta sapanaharu shohorera janchhan

Yesto chha yo char bhanjyang khalto
Yeuta chiso ashtray jasto chha,
Yo char bhanjyang khalto!!

(**A Cold Ashtray**

Those who come here
come with hearts in flame and lips ablaze!
Those who live here
live with ashes in hands and smoke in eyes.
Those who leave from this place
leave with a bundle of dead beliefs, with butt-ends of snuffed dreams.

This is the valley of four passes
It's a cold ashtray,
This valley of four passes!!)

Kanchhi glued the poem up on her wall. She did not ask Shiva what an ashtray was or what 'this valley of four passes' referred to.

By the third letter, it got more personal. Kanchhi learned that Shiva was from a hamlet on the other side of the Setikhola River, towards the north, where she had never ventured. He was the only son, he wrote, the only child, and loved his mother a lot. All that he desired in the world was to keep her happy. His father had died when he was a toddler. Was found dead with his head submerged in a bucketful of water. A few men were charged with murder, but none convicted, he wrote. 'A bucketful of water?' Maiju asked. 'Maybe he was an alcoholic.'

Kanchhi's letters were simpler in contrast, rather chirpy, as if it was her duty to show him the bright side of life. 'Have you been to Paiyunkot?' she wrote in one letter after walking to the palace one Saturday. 'They hold a big fair during *Dashain* there. You should go. You can also see the full expanse of the Hatiya bazaar from the top.' In the same letter, she sent him a leaf fallen from her jackfruit tree. 'I like how glossy they are,' she wrote. 'My great-grandfather planted it.'

He sent her an entry from a journal in response. In it, he lamented how confident his friends were but not him. On the margins were some calculations he had made on how much he needed to pay for schoolbooks and *Dashain* clothes.

'*Ama*, how much do you make as a sweeper?' Kanchhi asked Maiju one day.

'Why? Is that your homework?'

'No. I'm just curious.'

'Hundred rupees a month.'

'Hundred rupees a month? Is that a lot?'

'No, but it's enough to buy you books and clothes.'

'Books? I thought I always got them from Laxmi.'

'What about notebooks?'

'Oh, yes.'

'And the pens and pencils and the rice you love so much. Expenses, Kanchhi, they never go away.'

'Wait until I get a job. They'll go away.'

'Wonder when that will happen if that will ever happen.'

'It will happen.'

'I'll probably be dead by then.'

'No, you won't.'

'The lines of fate, Kanchhi. Who's seen them? Go get some earth from the field. No, wait, you haven't even washed your face. *Phohori*.'

It was the day of Ghatasthapana, the first day of *Dashain*, and Maiju, freshly showered and half-naked, with a *chadar* wrapped around her breasts, was planting *jamara* on a *tapari*. Kanchhi, sitting on the porch next to her, looked on. She was forbidden to touch Maiju or the *tapari* because she had just woken up and did not want to take a bath.

'*Ama*,' Kanchhi said, 'what's Shirish?'

'Shirish? As in the last name?'

'Yes.'

'They're Magars. Like Saru *didi*.'

'Is that what *Shirishko Phool* means then? A Magar flower?'

'That I don't know. What's that flower?'

'It's a book.'

'Maybe it's a city flower.'

'Maybe.'

'Why are you asking these questions?'

'No reason.'

Maiju dropped the last of the barley seeds on the *tapari*.

'*Eh, babai*,' she sighed, stretching her legs in front. 'You can't trust a man, Kanchhi. If they get you pregnant and leave, it's over.'

'Who's talking about a man?'

'It's the woman who has to be careful. Always.'

Kanchhi said nothing, just let out a sigh louder than Maiju's.

Later that afternoon, just as Kanchhi dropped a bundle of paddy sheaves in the yard, she got a surprise. Thirman was back in the village for *Dashain* holidays and stood in her yard with the same old cousin in tow.

'Where to, boys?' Maiju asked them. She was right behind Kanchhi, with her own sheaves of rice on her back.

'To Saru *kaki*'s,' the cousin answered.

'When did you come back from Pokhara? I heard that's where you are these days,' Maiju asked Thirman.

'This morning,' the cousin replied for him. 'I went to get him.'

'To Waling?'

'No, just down there to Bagar. Waling's too far.'

'Of course. And Lata, what did you get us from Pokhara then?' Maiju asked.

Thirman gestured 'a shawl,' opening his arms wide and closing them.

'Really?' Maiju asked.

'Yes,' the cousin said. 'We can go back down and get it for you. We didn't think we would see you here.'

'No, no.' Maiju laughed. 'I was just playing with you. I don't want it. Why are you headed to Saru *didi*'s?'

'Just to see her. It's been a while. Don't want her thinking we don't care,' the cousin said. 'And, Kanchhi, how are you?'

'All right,' Kanchhi said.

'Do you want to go to Saru *kaki*'s too? Let's go there once you're done here. She's always asking after you.'

'No,' Kanchhi said, untying the sheaves.

'There's so much work here,' Maiju said, spreading her own bundle in a corner of the yard. 'There's never ever any time to go anywhere. Actually, if you young boys are free, can you hack off those branches for me?' Maiju pointed at the mango tree behind her. It was huge, and its branches intertwined with those of the jackfruit. Together, the canopy they formed blocked the afternoon sun.

'Look at it,' Maiju said. 'It feels like evening when it's only afternoon.'

The cousin looked at the trees and asked, 'Right now, *Kaki*? You want us to hack them off right now?'

'Yes, if you're free. You can come back tomorrow or the day after if you're freer then. Take some mangoes with you in return. Take a jackfruit too if you want.'

The cousin looked at them and said, 'I doubt they're edible.'

'Why won't they be?' Maiju asked. 'These just flowered a little late. If they're not any good, then it's still dharma helping out an old woman.'

Thirman tapped on the cousin's shoulder and asked what they were talking about. The cousin explained it to him. And then, after a short exchange, the cousin said, 'All right, we'll do it now,' and picked up a sickle Maiju had left on the porch.

'Let me get you a bigger one,' Maiju said and went inside her room to look under the beds.

'Why don't you look in your room too, Kanchhi?' the cousin asked.

'Why? I know it's not there,' Kanchhi said.

'Check and see first. Maybe it's under your bed or on top of your pillow?'

Kanchhi looked at Thirman. He was studying the mango tree, as if sizing it up before climbing it.

'Just go inside and take a look first and then tell us if it's there or not. Just go,' the cousin insisted.

Kanchhi became suspicious. She peered at the cousin first and then at Thirman. Thirman was now looking at the millet fields below.

Kanchhi walked up to her room. The door was bolted shut just as she had left it – with the hasp firmly over the hoop. Kanchhi unbolted the door and opened it. It took her a while to adjust to the darkness inside, but when she did, she saw a white envelope on her pillow. Kanchhi immediately looked behind her. The cousin had followed her and was peeking from under the porch roof with a huge grin plastered on his face. Thirman Thakuri was more cautious and stayed where he was.

Kanchhi closed the door and opened the envelope. Inside was a greeting card, hand-drawn, with a picture of a flower flanked by candles on each side. On top, in an arch, were the words, 'Happy Bijaya Dashami and Shuva Deepawali 2049.'

Kanchhi opened the card. 'Meet me at the abandoned house after dark?' a note read.

'Kanchhi,' Maiju shouted from the yard outside. She had found a small *khukuri* under Kanchhi's old bed. 'Go make tea for the brothers,' she said.

The abandoned house was around the bend from Saru *didi*'s house. Her brother-in-law used to own it, the brother of her first husband, whose family moved to Waling in the early seventies once the Sunauli–Pokhara Siddhartha highway came into operation. For a while afterwards, another brother-in-law of Saru *didi* and his family moved into the house, but then they too migrated, these ones to the plains, to Butwal. Now, the house just squatted there like an old grandmother, locked, with its porch coming apart and its roof about to cave in.

Kanchhi walked to the house a little after dark. There, Thirman and the cousin were already on the porch, drinking from a bottle of a popular brand of alcohol (Shree) and smoking cigarettes, the glow of which startled Kanchhi. She had forgotten that Thirman smoked.

'Should I say Kanchhi or my sister-in-law?' the cousin asked.

Kanchhi stood closer to Thirman and said nothing.

'Sit here, *bhauju*. Sit here.' The cousin got up. He was a short man, only a few inches taller than Kanchhi.

'No,' Kanchhi said.

'Why not?'

'I can't stay for too long. *Ama* doesn't know I'm here.'

'So? Don't be scared of your mother. We'll take care of her.'

'How?'

'We know how,' the cousin said.

Kanchhi didn't budge. The cousin pulled her by her arm and then paused in the midst of it. 'I can touch you, can't I?'

Kanchhi nodded, and he sat her on the porch like a little child.

'Don't be afraid,' he said again. 'I'll be right there looking out for your mother. If I hear anything, I'll sing. And if I sing, hide.'

'Hide where?'

'Anywhere.'

'What song will you sing?'

'Does it matter?'

'No.' Kanchhi shook her head.

'Then? Don't be so scared of your own mother. We'll take care of her, I told you.'

Kanchhi shrugged. The cousin turned to Thirman, and they talked to each other in gestures for a while, after which the cousin asked Kanchhi if she wanted to drink as well. She said no.

The cousin took the bottle and left. As he disappeared around the field, Thirman took a small notebook out of his pants pocket and scribbled on it.

It said: *The tea was not tasty.*

'Why did you drink it then?' Kanchhi asked.

Thirman laughed and then gestured. His gestures had become advanced, more nuanced. She did not understand most of it.

'Where did you learn to sign so well?' she asked.

He wrote again: *The tea was good. How was the card? Did you like it?*

Kanchhi smiled. 'Yes.'

Then, they were quiet. Thirman had had a haircut. A high and tight army haircut. Kanchhi watched him light a cigarette and take a puff. The puff was so long it burnt the first half of the cigarette in a second.

'Pokhara must be nice,' Kanchhi said. 'Do they grow millet there too?'

He didn't reply.

Kanchhi tugged at his sleeve. Thirman looked at her, trying not to blow smoke on her face.

'Pokhara must be nice,' she said again. 'How was it?'

He scribbled: *Pokhara?*

'Yes.'

'Nice,' he gestured, and they were quiet again. This time, Kanchhi focused on the path in front and on the wild bushes of ferns, *banmara* and nettles that had reclaimed the spaces around them, including the edges of the front yard. Everything here felt abandoned but also beautiful and warm, as if the silhouettes of the wild were about to crawl up and dance with the fireflies flitting about.

'I have to go,' Kanchhi said and got up suddenly. Thirman looked at her a little shocked but stood up as well. He did not ask her why she had to go. He walked up to the path ahead and looked for his cousin. Kanchhi followed him.

The cousin was sitting by a path. When he saw them, he walked over and said, 'That was fast.'

'I have to go,' Kanchhi said.

'Are you a parrot? You've been repeating the same line

since we got here,' the cousin said. 'You were here for less than five minutes.'

He had a hint of irritation in his voice. Kanchhi looked at him, taken a little aback by it. Then, she turned around and began to walk home.

'*Oye*, *oye*, sorry,' the cousin shouted. 'I was just kidding. Wait, wait. Kanchhi—'

Kanchhi slowed down. The cousin muttered his shock at her reaction and walked past her. Thirman took his time. He stared at the bushes in front and then at a millet plant by his side. Then, he took another long drag from the cigarette. Just then, someone far above called for another Kanchhi – Ramesh's sister. Kanchhi and the cousin both looked up. They could not tell who it was. Nothing could be seen, except the silhouette of the abandoned shed that once belonged to the family of the abandoned house and the dark sketches of fields and trees buzzing all around them. The cousin answered the call anyway. '*Hoi, hoi,*' he said and then laughed. Kanchhi turned to look at Thirman. He was inches away from her.

'*Abui*,' she said, a little startled and then embarrassed at being startled.

Thirman walked past her, his arm almost brushing against her *chadar*. A few steps later, he slowed down, and that was when she saw it – his hand, his right hand, stretched slightly behind him, slightly upturned, slightly curved like a scoop, clearly asking for her hand. Kanchhi smiled, and as if led by a magical force, with a swiftness that surprised her as well, she did as asked – she put her hand in his. His grip was big and rough, warm and tender like the autumn sun. Kanchhi walked hand-in-hand with Thirman for a while. Him leading her. Her following him. In front, the cousin hummed a slow *jhyaure* tune, a song about two lovers seeing each other after a long time:

> *Mayalulai bhetinna sandhain bhet hunchha kahile kahi*
> *bheta hunda bolaunu maila mayale maile jhain*
> *maya nirmohi muskaideu mitheri lagaideu pirati*

> (You don't always get to see your lover
> When you do, call him like I do
> My cruel love, smile a sweet one and make love to me)

Thirman let go when they reached Saru *didi*'s house. Saru *didi* was on the porch, sifting chickpeas by lamplight.

At home, Maiju was milking the buffalo. The sound of milk pattering against an urn could be heard from a distance. Maiju milked the buffalo twice every day. Only she was allowed to touch it.

'Kanchhi?' Maiju shouted when she heard her in the yard. 'Is that you?'

'Yes, it's me,' Kanchhi shouted back.

'Where were you? Go take a look at the curry inside. Take it off the fire if it's boiling.'

'La,' Kanchhi said and picked up the tumpline she had left on the paddy spread.

Inside, the kitchen was dark, except for the fire that burned on the ground. On it was a wok with potatoes and wild fiddleheads submerged in boiling water. Kanchhi stirred the curry once and then, with the help of a ladle inserted through an ear of the wok, lifted it off the fire. The rice was already done. The pot sat on top of the ashes close to the fire. When Maiju came in a little later, carrying the milk urn and a lamp, Kanchhi fetched the milk wok from the windowsill in front.

Without a word, Maiju emptied the urn into the wok. She then poured some water into the urn, gave it a little shake and poured the mixture into the wok as well.

'Move,' she said.

Kanchhi realized Maiju was upset. She shifted onto a tiny square mat to her right and watched Maiju take her spot on the *pirka*. Maiju looked into the curry just as Kanchhi had and then proceeded to insert more wood into the fire. A pile of wood always lay beside her on the left. Kanchhi reached for a blowpipe and blew air through it. When the wood caught fire and everything around glowed in warm yellow, Maiju stirred the milk with a ladle.

'What happened now?' Kanchhi asked.

Maiju did not answer.

'Why are you upset?'

No answer again. Instead, Maiju broke a twig with

a loud snap and threw it into the fire. Then, she lifted a kettle and shook it hard to check if it had any water inside. Very little. Maiju got up and walked to the water pot kept in a corner behind Kanchhi. Her bangles clanged, the water sloshed, and Maiju's breathing rasped. It was going to be a long night of unbearable silence, Kanchhi understood. She got up and left for her room. Maiju still did not say anything.

In her room, the air was cold. Kanchhi tightened the *chadar* around her and got under the quilt without lighting the lamp first. The quilt, made of rags and old clothes, was colder, and it took a moment for her body to warm up. When it did, she stretched her legs straight and turned on her back. A flash of red passed by the window, and for a moment, her heart leapt at the thought of Thirman up to see her again. But it was only a firefly, darting about inside the room lost. Kanchhi followed its movement for a while, and when it disappeared in between the wall and the roof, she looked back out of the window. The darkness outside matched the darkness inside, and nothing but the trills of crickets and cicadas punctured it. Kanchhi thought back on the evening and how surreal it had been – the card, the abandoned house, the hand, the touch. At Saru *didi*'s, Thirman had stood only a few feet away from her, with his legs splayed and hands in his pockets, his face turned straight at Saru *didi* but his eyes on her. Even now, she could feel them piercing through the night like the hoot of an owl.

'Oye, Kulankini,' Maiju shouted from the kitchen.

Kulankini. The tainted one. Maiju knew where she had been.

'Come eat, *Kulankini*,' Maiju shouted again.

Kanchhi got up and walked out.

In the kitchen, Maiju sat like a blown-up monsoon frog, with a plate of rice and curry in front of her. The milk was done, and she was scooping some into a bowl. Out on the porch, a regular stray cat, attracted by the milk, meowed. Kanchhi got its bowl from behind the door and placed it in front of Maiju. Without a word, Maiju poured milk in it, and Kanchhi carried it to the cat. The cat began to lap it up. Kanchhi walked back into the kitchen and sat on the mat. Maiju pushed the plate of food towards her. The potatoes in the curry were not peeled as Kanchhi would have liked and some of the fiddleheads were too mature to chew and swallow, but Kanchhi sat on the mat and ate without a complaint. The joy of eating had long evaporated, and the food tasted like grass, but she was never one to go hungry when angry. It was Maiju who was forced to break her own silence.

'You think you've grown up, haven't you? Walking around with a *natho* after dark?'

The word *natho* clanged like a plate dropped on the floor.

'Who told you that?' Kanchhi asked.

'You think no one knows? Going around the hamlet

with that boy like his little bitch. You think he's going to marry you and take you to Pokhara?'

Kanchhi squirmed.

'Did you find no one better?' Maiju continued. 'Tell me if you're done studying and want to get married. I'll find you a man myself. A man with two arms, two legs and a good government job.'

Kanchhi pushed her plate away and said, 'I'm done.'

'Of course, you are. *Randi*,' Maiju said.

The next day, Thirman came up again. Again, with the same cousin. But this time, Maiju, without bothering to make any small talk, launched directly into a diatribe: '*Eh*, *Babu*, please tell me without hiding anything or lying about anything. Is there something going on between Lata and Kanchhi or between you and Kanchhi? If that is the case, tell me who among you wants to marry her, and I'll gather everyone in the hamlet and start the process right away. If there's nothing, then stop coming up. This house has no men. If word gets around that boys have been visiting this house, that too Thakuri boys, we'll be done for. Let Kanchhi be. Let us be. If you are only friends, behave like one, come over during the daytime and have some tea. I'll make you a cup myself, but don't ask her to come see you after dark. Please don't.'

'No, *Kaki*.' Shocked, the cousin fumbled for words. 'What are you talking about? We're only here to see how the tree was shaping up and then move on to the

Magar hamlet. You know Lata here does not live around anymore. So, he has to go and see his friends himself. Don't worry about us. He has a girlfriend in Pokhara, and I have my own in Balakot.'

'I'm only saying because,' Maiju said, a little calm now, 'you know how the hamlet works. This isn't Pokhara. This is not Kathmandu. If you come to the house, they'll say you've touched her. If you see her after dark, they'll say you've slept with her. And once they start talking, there's no stopping it. You know how the gossips work. *Padyo bhane bagyo, bagyo bhane chheryo, ani chheryo bhane maryo.* Where will we go then? Where can we go?'

'Don't worry, *Kaki.* Don't worry at all,' the cousin said.

'Your mother's a little off,' the cousin later said when they met again at the abandoned house.

Kanchhi laughed.

'She was threatening to marry you off to either one of us. Didn't even care which one it was. What a woman. Completely ruined my morning.' The cousin grabbed his head in his hands and shook it.

Kanchhi kept laughing.

'It's not funny,' he said. 'What if she really gets the villagers together? We'll have a Thakuri versus Chhetri war.'

'No, we won't.'

'How do you know?'

'I know.'

The cousin got up and began to dust his pants. 'Lata here will be safe in Pokhara, but I'll be the one who gets all the beating. I don't want to die over nothing.'

'What are you saying?' Kanchhi asked.

'I'm leaving. I can't be your bodyguard every day. Start meeting at Saru *didi*'s house from now on. They won't kill her.'

'Are you serious?' Kanchhi asked.

'Yes.'

'No—'

'No, I'm going,' the cousin said and then turned to Thirman, who, with a tilt of his chin, asked what was wrong. 'I don't want to die,' the cousin both said and gestured.

'No one's going to die,' Kanchhi said.

Thirman looked at the cousin and then at Kanchhi. The cousin would not listen to anyone. He began to walk away. Thirman motioned Kanchhi to wait and ran after him. On the path ahead, they argued, but the cousin would not relent. Thirman looked at Kanchhi once again, motioned her to keep on waiting and then ran after the cousin one more time.

Neither of them came back.

19

MAIJU KNEW ABOUT KANCHHI'S RENDEZVOUS WITH Thirman Thakuri just as she had long suspected Kanchhi had lied about her periods. It was a mother's instinct, a result of being born and raised a woman in the same mountains. Such acts are not abnormal. There have always been women who hated period customs and did everything they could to subvert them. Back in Baglung, for instance, Maiju knew a woman who used to hide bloody rags under her porch roof and irk her family. They called her crazy. The woman also met a lover after sundown. That – everyone had done it, almost everyone.

Knowing about the rebels, however, is not the same as knowing what to do with them. The latter requires heart, a courage to go beneath the surface and confront the real issue: the absurdity of some norms and rules. Like most people, however, Maiju hated confrontations. It was much easier to pretend instead, pretend that no rebellion exists, and when it becomes difficult to keep pretending, seethe in anger instead, punish the rebels with disapproval, talk before they do, rather loudly and over them, and silence them. A regret that haunts Maiju.

November 13, 2005

In the kitchen, the tea comes to a boil. Maiju pours it into a steel glass and walks out to the porch with both the kettle and the glass. Tea is all Maiju is ingesting today. Tea and water and fruits. Another integral part of the anniversary ritual. Fasting. At one point, Maiju had fasted a day a week for years, beginning with Mondays because Kanchhi had left on a Monday. She prayed to god Shiva then. A year later, she switched to Tuesdays for goddess Kali. Then to Saturdays for goddess Sankata. She was a month in on Thursdays for Satya Sai when she lost faith. But by then, fasting, like prayers, had begun to provide a sense of peace. Maiju now skips lunch regularly or eats either leftovers or just berries and fruits, sometimes just buttermilk, sometimes whatever Saili *didi* brings, and sometimes all she drinks is water until her flanks ache and she has to eat something. Hunger works because it distracts. The right intensity keeps the arms moving but not the brain. Pull, grab, snip. Pull, grab, snip.

The tea is bland. No sugar, just a pinch of loose tea powder. Maiju finishes it in three large gulps. A mynah hops in the yard, eyeing the millet and rice beans. Both are on the porch. The millet, unthreshed and still in fingers, is under a straw mat by Kanchhi's room.

Maiju throws the last bit of tea at the bird. It streaks the yard in between, but the mynah remains unnerved.

'I know what you're here for,' Maiju says.

The bird jerks its head from side to side.

'You're not getting it,' Maiju adds, and as if to show the bird she means it, Maiju walks to the chicken coop right outside her room and pulls the twig keeping the hasp locked. A mother hen and her five chicks as big as Maiju's fist walk out. The mynah flies to the *simal* tree, currently in red bloom. The sixth chick stays inside.

'What happened?' Maiju gets on her haunches and peers at it. It is sick. She pulls the chick out of the coop and puts it on the ground. The chick refuses to peck around and stands with its head drooping low into its chest instead. Maiju picks it up and walks back to the porch. She has paracetamol tablets tucked under the roof there. Maiju tears one out of its package, crushes a tiny bit with her fingers and pushes the powder down the chick's throat. The chick resists a little but swallows the powder. Maiju then takes the chick to the pipes and lets it drink water from her hand. When it remains lethargic, she puts it back inside the coop and closes the door.

The other chickens chirp and flap and scuttle after their mother to the field below.

A few minutes later, Maiju follows them, with a sickle and a *thunse*. The *thunse* has inside it a bottle of water and a few tangerines. Maiju's goal that morning is to collect the millet fingers from that field and from the field above the house before the school bell rings.

In the background, Thapa Nani *didi*'s radio gets turned off, and for a moment, there is no other sound, except the clucking of the chickens and the rustlings from Maiju moving among the millet plants. Then, the radio comes back on. The tail end of a song, followed by three beeps and an announcement that it is eight in the morning. Normally, that means it is time for news. Not today. King Gyanendra has barred FM stations from airing news highlights, and so it is time for another entertainment programme. A female host says namaste and welcomes her listeners. Someone at Thapa Nani *didi*'s fiddles with the modulation nodule. Radio Nepal. It is broadcasting news but in English. The female host comes back on. She is now listing songs that her listeners can request on air. The list is a medley of Nepali folk, pop and movie numbers. The host takes a call.

'Hello. Namaste. Who is speaking from where?' the host asks.

The man is a shopkeeper from Butwal. One Nawaraj Khatiwada.

'Is it getting cold there too, Nawaraj *ji*?' the host asks.

'Yes, Swikriti *ji*,' the man says, 'but not as cold as last year.'

'Really? I thought the plains never got cold.'

'No, they do. It gets colder here than on the hills sometimes.'

'Does it? In that case, Nawaraj *ji*, what do people in Butwal do to protect themselves in winter?'

'The same as everywhere, Swikriti *ji*. Staying out in the sun, drinking tea, wearing warm clothes, burning firewood and, if you can, getting an electric heater. I'm more concerned about this war and when we might get some peace.'

'Ah, yes. Aren't we all, Nawaraj *ji*?'

'I hope this time we get everlasting peace. The king needs to talk with the Maoists. That is the only way to end this. People need peace.'

'I understand, Nawaraj *ji*. We need peace. Peace is important. Peace is when we all flourish, don't we? One moment, Nawaraj *ji*.' The woman goes off the air. There is silence for a bit. And then, she comes back on. 'Excuse me, Nawaraj *ji*. There was some technical difficulty at the studio. Nawaraj *ji*, are you still there?'

'Yes,' the man says.

'Well, I would have loved to keep on chatting and finding out more about Butwal, but my technician friend here tells me that it's time for a song. Would you like to choose one and dedicate it to someone?'

'Yes,' the man says. 'The song from the movie *Bhagya Rekha*.'

'"*Dhakamakka Phula Phulyo*"?'

'Yes, that one.'

'It's a nice old song, isn't it?'

'It is. It's from the first movie I ever watched. I want

to dedicate that song to my wife, my children and to all the citizens of this country. For the peace and prosperity of this country.'

'Thank you, Nawaraj *ji*. Bye-bye. Take care.'

The song comes on air. It is about a young man who encourages a young woman to embrace her youth and laugh and play with him. The woman responds, sure, but what if the villagers dispprove. What then?

20

ONE OF THE STORIES IN *TATYAKATHA* WAS ABOUT A mother who, while chopping vegetables for dinner, ends up chopping her three children with a sickle. Kanchhi asked Maiju if that was at all possible – for a mother to kill her own children.

'Why not?' Maiju said. 'If I can give life, I can take it too.'

'Why do you have to answer it like that?'

'Like what?'

'Like a hero,' Kanchhi said.

'She's not being a hero, Kanchhi. She's being a writer,' Bipana *bhauju* said and laughed. Bipana *bhauju* was Saili *didi*'s daughter-in-law, married to her second son, Surya *dai*. She had a hearty laugh, one that seemed to come from deep within her throat, and a few of the passers-by glanced at her, intrigued by its hoarseness. They were all at the Dumre Pass – Maiju, Kanchhi, Saili *didi* and Bipana *bhauju* – halfway to Waling, sitting on a *chautara*, watching a line of mules walk up from below. This was an annual custom – walking eight hours to Waling every winter to buy essentials in bulk and stopping by at Dumre on both ways to dry off the sweat.

'Wonder why we didn't settle here,' Kanchhi said. 'Why do we have to live so far away from everything?'

'Don't ask me,' Maiju said. 'Ask those who decided to settle in Torikhola.'

'Can't we move closer to Waling?'

'And eat what?'

'The same thing we eat at home.'

'If only it were that easy.'

'Why isn't it?'

'Ask Saili *didi*.'

'What do you mean?'

'She means,' Bipana *bhauju* stepped in, 'if Saili *didi*, married to a rich and retired Indian army man, is still in the village, who are we to think of leaving?'

Kanchhi looked down at a group of children playing tag-and-run on the cobbled path and thought how unfair it all was.

'What are you going to buy in Waling?' Bipana *bhauju* asked her.

'Nothing.' Kanchhi shrugged.

'You're just a porter too then,' Bipana *bhauju* said. They all had a *doko* each, empty then except for a few sacks and a gallon jug or a jerry can, themselves empty.

'Didn't you make any money during *Dashain* or *Tihar*?' Bipana *bhauju* asked.

Kanchhi shook her head.

'Nothing?'

'Nothing.'

'Well, let's go around the bazaar anyway once we get there, okay? Be my friend and come with me.'

'Okay,' Kanchhi said.

They reached Waling at 2 p.m. The suspension bridge over the Andhikhola River came first and then a long line of shops on either side of a narrow street. The air here was thick and dusty, but Kanchhi loved it. It reminded her of a lost season. A fresh poultry house, a fancy shop, a Bhusal general store, a Palpali kitchen, a Dhaulagiri restaurant, a pharmacy, a national bank – Waling seemed to have it all, and every year, it was only growing, stretching in every which direction between the Andhikhola River and the highway like a *roti*.

'This shop wasn't here the last time, was it?' Bipana *bhauju* asked, pausing at a sari shop and feeling the fabric of one of the garments hanging from a hanger. The sari was bright yellow with tiny red flowers all over it.

'I don't remember,' Kanchhi said.

'Do you like it?' Bipana *bhauju* asked.

'It's nice,' Kanchhi said.

'It is, but where are we to go in a sari?' Bipana *bhauju* said and moved on.

Up ahead, Maiju and Saili *didi* had already reached their destination: Torikhola Magar General Store, owned and run by one of their own – Saru *didi*'s brother-in-law, who at that moment sat on a *moda* in the middle of a regular 12'x12' room and sold almost everything that Torikhole women could ever want – from grains and lentils to slippers and shoes to *lungi*s and T-shirts. He also gave them discounts and credits, and once they were done shopping, looked after their baskets and sacks so that they could roam around the streets unencumbered.

'Isn't it wonderful to have a familiar face in an unfamiliar bazaar?' Bipana *bhauju* asked, sitting in front of an open sack of rice and running her fingers through the grains.

'What else can we do but be here for our own?' Saru *didi*'s brother-in-law said.

'You're the only reason we come to Waling,' Maiju said. 'What's the going rate for rice these days?'

'Five per kilo,' Saru *didi*'s brother-in-law replied.

'And the salt?'

'Five per *pathi*.'

'Kerosene?'

'Five per litre.'

'Everything is five here,' Kanchhi said.

'I know,' Bipana *bhauju* said. 'Can't you lower the price a little?'

'It's already been lowered for you all,' Saru *didi*'s brother-in-law said.

'He'll lower it some more a little later,' Saili *didi* said. Saru *didi*'s brother-in-law chuckled.

'Kanchhi, let's leave the old women here to handle

this, and you and I go see the bazaar,' Bipana *bhauju* said.

'*Ama*, can I go?' Kanchhi turned to Maiju.

'Where are you going?' Maiju asked.

'Where are we going?' Kanchhi asked Bipana *bhauju*.

'To the highway and back,' Bipana *bhauju* said.

'Okay,' Maiju said. 'But don't go too far, and come back right away.'

Two shops ahead, Bipana *bhauju* stopped at a cosmetic store and bought a small bottle of nail polish. She tested the colour on Kanchhi first. Dark red. Next, they passed by a stationery store, where Kanchhi paused briefly, eyeing the magazines clipped to a rope like clothes, looking for *Tatyakatha*. It was not there. The shopkeeper, who could have helped her find it, was not interested in doing so. He did not even glance at her, immersed as he was in reading a pocketbook on Libra.

'I'm going to shift to the bazaar someday,' Bipana *bhauju* said as they continued up the street.

'Why?' Kanchhi asked.

'*Why*? Look around.'

'I mean, I understand, but apart from the shops and stores, what's here that—'

'Listen, Kanchhi. If you aren't careful, your whole life will go by in making these occasional trips to Waling and back. Is that what you want?'

'No.'

'Then?'

'I meant—'

'I know what you meant.' Bipana *bhauju* bent over and picked up a hair scrunchie someone had dropped on the ground. She dusted it off and wrapped it around her wrist. 'What I'm saying is for you to be careful. If you aren't, this's what you'll get. This's what all of us get. Listen, as a woman older than you, let me tell you this: when the time comes, choose wisely. Don't marry the first one that comes asking for your hand. Don't make the same mistake I made. Find a boy who lives in a bazaar and marry him.'

Kanchhi laughed.

'I'm serious. You'll regret otherwise.'

'I'm not getting married.'

Bipana *bhauju* did not care. She repeated her message as they reached the highway and walked up the steps of a shuttered store to sit down. Kanchhi repeated her answer too, but this time Bipana *bhauju* fell silent. Kanchhi did too. In front was a bus parked by the side of the highway, and they watched it get ready to leave. On its windshield was the itinerary board: Waling, Pokhara, Damauli, Khairenitar, Kathmandu.

'Does that bus really go to Pokhara?' Kanchhi asked.

'Ask him,' Bipana *bhauju* said. She was referring to the driver's assistant, a young boy of Kanchhi's age, who was crouching on the roof of the bus securing the passengers' luggage. Every now and then, he would shout to anyone who looked a little dressed up or had any baggage with them if they wanted to go to Pokhara or Kathmandu.

'Want some peanuts?' Bipana *bhauju* asked.

'No,' Kanchhi said.

'I want some. You stay here.' Bipana *bhauju* walked to a vendor, who had a basket full of roasted peanuts, and came back with a cone of them.

'Are you sure?' Bipana *bhauju* asked, shoving the peanuts towards Kanchhi, tempting her to take one.

'Yes.' Kanchhi nodded. 'I don't like them.'

Just then, the young boy got off the bus and walked towards Kanchhi and Bipana *bhauju*. When he got close, Kanchhi asked him if the bus really went to Pokhara.

'Yes, want to go?' he asked.

'No, was just asking,' Kanchhi said.

'Yes, yes, we want to go,' Bipana *bhauju* said. 'But we have no money. Can you still take us there?'

The boy looked at Bipana *bhauju* and shook his head as if he were sixty. 'The kind of people you meet,' he said.

Bipana *bhauju* laughed. 'This little boy is funny,' she said.

Soon, another bus came from the south and stopped right in front of the first bus. Everyone could hear it honk before it appeared around the bend. The banner at the front read: Butwal, Galyang, Waling, Pokhara, Kathmandu.

'Where's Galyang?' Kanchhi asked.

'I don't know,' Bipana *bhauju* said as the helper of the

second bus got out and climbed to the rooftop as well, this time to drop off luggage. He was older than the first one, a little older than Thirman perhaps, and had long hair with light-brown highlights. Bipana *bhauju* commented that long hair did not suit boys. 'It makes them look like monkeys,' she said.

'No, it doesn't,' Kanchhi said.

'Why? You like him?'

'No.'

Bipana *bhauju* laughed again.

'What a sweet laugh,' a policeman said. He had just gotten off the bus and was walking past them.

'*Murdar* police,' Bipana *bhauju* whispered. 'I don't like their kind at all.'

The policeman grinned and winked.

Kanchhi wondered where Laxmi was.

The second bus left right away. After the first one too departed, Kanchhi and Bipana *bhauju* walked back. Maiju and Saili *didi* were done talking to Saru *didi*'s brother-in-law and were now across the shop at a roadside eatery, eating *selroti*. The eatery did not have a name, just two tables on the porch and a counter behind it with food on display: chickpeas, eggs, potato curry, beaten rice, soybeans.

'You shouldn't be eating these,' Bipana *bhauju* said, taking a piece of *selroti* from Saili *didi*'s plate and biting into it. 'They are made in Dalda ghee. It's unhealthy.'

Saili *didi* examined the piece in her hand, doubting that anyone would use ghee to make *selrotis* in a bazaar.

'It's a different kind of ghee,' Bipana *bhauju* said and, when Saili *didi* seemed unconvinced, added. 'Ask the woman there if you don't believe me.'

The woman she was referring to was behind the counter.

'*Aaa*,' Maiju said. 'We're not eating this every day. A bite won't kill us.'

'That *is* true,' Bipana *bhauju* said and ordered a plate each for her and Kanchhi. Kanchhi, who was starving, cleaned up her plate in minutes.

'Slow down,' Maiju said. 'You'll choke otherwise.'

'*Hantakali*,' Bipana *bhauju* said.

At 4 p.m., they began walking back, with *doko*s heavy on their backs pulling on their necks. Kanchhi's *doko* was comparatively lighter. It contained only a 20-litre jug of kerosene and a new pair of flip-flops. Maiju carried all the sacks of food and spices. Their destination that evening was a house in Bayakhola, an hour past the Andhikhola River, where another Magar man from around their village had moved to – this time, a Magar man from a hamlet below Harichaur. Just like Saru *didi*'s brother-in-law, he was a man the Torikhole women trusted and thus stayed at his house whenever they went to Waling and needed shelter on their way back.

The man's house was on a field below a dirt trail and

looked like any other house in the mountains around – a thatched hut with a front yard and an animal shed. When the women stood on the trail above it, Magar *dai* seemed to have just got back from the fields. He had a hoe in his hands.

'Where are you headed, sisters?' he asked. 'Need shelter for the night?'

'Did you not recognize us, *Dai*?' Saili *didi* said. 'We're headed to *your* house.'

'Huh?' Magar *dai* said. 'I can't see very well these days. Who is it?'

The women descended to the yard.

'Oh, Torikhole *nani*.' He really had not recognized them. 'Come in, come in.'

'You have a room, don't you, *Dai*?' Saili *didi* asked.

'We always do.' Magar *dai* said.

'Who is it?' his wife asked. She was in a corner on the porch, tending to a fire.

'Sisters from Torikhola,' Magar *dai* said.

'*Eh. Eh.* Walking back from Waling?' she asked.

'Yes,' Saili *didi* replied.

'Where's the key, *Budhi*?' Magar *dai* asked.

'It's not locked,' his wife answered.

Magar *dai* turned to the women and asked if they wanted to leave the *doko*s down on the first floor or take them up with them. 'You can leave them here,' he said. 'No one will touch them. It's just me and her.'

Saili *didi* said it might be better to carry them upstairs.

'Your decision,' Magar *dai* said and walked up a ladder. The women followed him to their usual room at the end of the second floor, where there were two single beds across from each other and a window in the middle – a room like any other in a rural hamlet. The women dropped their *doko*s out by the door and stepped in.

'Do you want to rest a little or come right down?' Magar *dai* asked, lighting a lamp in an alcove by the door.

'Rest a little,' Maiju said.

'Any tea or hot water in the meantime?'

'A glass of hot water,' Maiju ordered.

Saili *didi* wanted millet liquor. 'You have some, don't you?' she asked.

'No,' Magar *dai* said. 'But I'll check with the house next door.'

'God bless you,' Saili *didi* said.

'Get me a glass too, *Dai*.' Bipana *bhauju* spoke.

'For me too?' Kanchhi said.

'No,' Maiju shouted. Everyone laughed.

Magar *dai* waited by the door for a bit, as if for Maiju to change her mind, and then left. The women kept the door open and lay down – Maiju and Kanchhi on one bed, Saili *didi* and Bipana *bhauju* on the other. They were all exhausted.

'One glass might not be enough,' Saili *didi* wondered aloud.

'One more, and you might not get up tomorrow,' Maiju said. 'Who's going to carry your *doko* home?'

'It's nothing but water in there,' Saili *didi* explained. 'They put three-quarters water and one-quarter liquor. Even a rat doesn't get drunk on it.'

'Why can't I try some too?' Kanchhi asked.

'This isn't *kheer* for you to try,' Maiju said and pulled a quilt over herself while yawning loudly. 'Looks like I might fall asleep,' she added.

Kanchhi too yawned loudly but sat up and looked around. Saili *didi* and Bipana *bhauju* were already under their quilts. Kanchhi got off the bed and walked to the alcove by the door.

'What are you up to now?' Maiju asked, lifting her head a little.

'Nothing,' Kanchhi said and walked back with the lamp. There was a shelf above their bed, a wooden board mounted on two wooden stakes, and on it was a pile of papers. Kanchhi wanted to see if there was anything worth reading in it. Most of the items turned out to be old eighth-grade textbooks and notebooks. A few of them were government forms. Some were SLC exam papers and SLC exam guidebooks, and some were pictures – a passport photograph of a young man who was possibly once the owner of the room, a 4'x5' picture of the same man but in a garden outside somewhere, a few postcards with pictures of women Kanchhi did not recognize, and then, an image of a young woman in a frilly top revealing ample cleavage, a cover picture of a magazine Kanchhi instantly recognized. *Tatyakatha*. Beneath it were three more issues. Kanchhi took one and sat down with it.

'You read that?' Bipana *bhauju* asked.

'Yes,' Kanchhi said.

'I heard only useless people read it.'

'I'm useless then,' Kanchhi said.

About a month after the Waling trip, Bipana *bhauju* came up to Kanchhi's. Spring was in the air by then. Everything smelled sweet, and the sun was just the right temperature, lolling everyone everywhere into a deep nap. Kanchhi too was sleeping on a mat in the yard.

'Get up, Kanchhi,' Bipana *bhauju* said. 'Come with me to the shop.'

'The shop? Why?'

'Need to get a few things. Just come along. I need a friend.'

Kanchhi sat up and stared at the ground like a sick chicken.

'Quick, quick,' Bipana *bhauju* urged.

'What's the rush?' Kanchhi asked.

'We've got to catch them while they're taking a nap too.'

Kanchhi walked to the outdoor sink and washed her face. 'Where's Punti?' she asked. Punti was Bipana *bhauju*'s seven-year-old daughter.

'Taking a nap too.'

'Everyone seems to be taking a nap.'

'That's why we go up now. We'll catch them in the shop that way.'

The shop she was referring to was a one-shelf shop that Tauka Kanchha *dai* had recently installed in the front half of a small room in his house, the house at the top of the hamlet next to Ramesh's. The shop was often closed because no one but Tauka Kanchha *dai* could run it, and he, like any other farmer, was mostly in the fields. Fortunately, that afternoon, Tauka Kanchha *dai* was in the house. The door to the shop was closed from inside. Bipana *bhauju* walked up to it and knocked.

It took a minute, but Tauka Kanchha *dai* came out, slipping into an inner vest and looking groggy. Bipana *bhauju* had woken him up from a nap as well.

'What do you want?' Tauka Kanchha *dai* asked.

'Tea,' Bipana *bhauju* said.

'Just tea or sugar too?'

'No, just tea.'

Tauka Kanchha *dai* yawned.

'*Chhi*, close your mouth while yawning. It stinks,' Bipana *bhauju* said.

'You shouldn't have woken me up from a nap then. What do you expect? Kanchhi, do you want anything?'

'No.'

'Don't sit on the *doko*, please. It will break,' Tauka Kanchha *dai* said.

Kanchhi was on an upside-down *doko* in the yard. She got off.

Tauka Kanchha *dai* then stepped back inside the shop and took down a set of wooden planks boarding up the shop from inside. 'How much tea do you want?' he asked Bipana *bhauju*.

'A *pau*,' Bipana *bhauju* said.

'A *pau*? You woke me up for a *pau* of tea?'

'Yes,' Bipana *bhauju* said. Tauka Kanchha *dai* shook his head.

'Have you brought anything new lately?' Bipana *bhauju* asked.

'I got some *bindis* and hairbands.'

'Can I see them?

'Sure.'

'Kanchhi, want to come in with us?' Bipana *bhauju* asked.

'No,' Kanchhi said and looked at a tiny ancestral temple at the edge of a field past Ramesh's house. It was a favourite hangout for local boys, and Kanchhi wanted to see if any of them were there.

'I'm going to go there for a bit,' Kanchhi said and began walking towards the temple.

There was no one there, just a grand view of rows and rows of freshly ploughed fields and the mountains that supported them. Kanchhi sat by the temple's short metal gate and looked out. Spring, while soothing to the skin, was painful to the eye. Nothing but haze and dust was in the air, and everything only looked grey, brown and dull.

'Kanchhi,' Bipana *bhauju* yelled.

Kanchhi got up, walked around the temple and yelled back, 'Done? So soon?'

'Yes, done,' Bipana *bhauju* yelled again and headed towards Kanchhi. She had bought nothing but tea.

'Want to go to the fair on Saturday?' Bipana *bhauju* asked on the way down.

'The new year fair?' Kanchhi asked back.

'Yes, the one in Setibeni.'

'I don't know. It's too far. *Ama* won't allow it.'

'Ask her anyway. Tell her I'll be there with you.'

'I'll try,' Kanchhi said.

Maiju did not allow Kanchhi to go to the fair. Six hours to Setibeni and back with just Bipana *bhauju*, she said, was too unsafe. Kanchhi told her some of her female schoolmates would be there as well. Maiju still said no. Without Kanchhi, Bipana *bhauju* didn't go either, and as usual, all they did on that New Year's was nothing.

'2050, 2051, what difference does it make?' Maiju said.

'It's 2050. It's the end of a decade.'

'It will be the end of a decade in a decade again. Go then,' Maiju said.

'*Hya*,' Kanchhi said.

'What *hya*? Get your *doko* and the sickle and go welcome the new decade,' Maiju said.

Towards the evening that day, Bipana *bhauju* came up again, this time to let Kanchhi know that there was someone waiting for her at the *chautara* below the primary school.

'Who is it?' Kanchhi asked.

'I don't know. Punti came up with the message. Two young boys,' Bipana *bhauju* said.

'Two young boys?'

At first, Kanchhi wondered if it was Thirman and his cousin again, but she doubted it. After Maiju's outburst, they had not dared contact her again. Besides, she knew Thirman would not be back from Pokhara for the new year. The next obvious answer then was Shiva Shirish. But again, why would he be up here? She had not written to him after the same outburst and neither had he. Their relationship had just fizzled out.

'Where's Punti?' Kanchhi asked.

'Somewhere around,' Bipana *bhauju* said.

'I don't believe you.'

'What do you mean?'

'Why isn't Punti here giving me the message? Why are you here?'

'I don't know why she's not here. She's a little kid.'

Kanchhi still didn't believe her. She sat where she was, doing her homework, without the slightest intention of walking down.

'Aren't you going down?' Bipana *bhauju* asked.

'No.'

'Aren't you curious to see who it is?'

'I don't care. I don't think there's anyone there. I think you're pulling my leg.'

'*La*, why would I do that?' Bipana *bhauju* began to laugh. 'Don't keep your boy waiting. Go.'

'No,' Kanchhi said.

Bipana *bhauju* continued to laugh. Maiju, who was on the slope below the yard digging for ginger, asked what was so funny.

'Our little Kanchhi here has an admirer,' Bipana *bhauju* said.

'An admirer?' Maiju asked.

'Yes, an admirer.'

'No, I don't,' Kanchhi said.

'Little Kanchhi's not little anymore,' Bipana *bhauju* said and laughed again.

Later, after she left, Maiju told Kanchhi to stay away from Bipana *bhauju*.

'Why?' Kanchhi asked.

'She's got a horn in her butt, that's why,' Maiju said.

'What?'

'Nothing. Stay away from her.'

Turned out there were rumours flying around about Bipana *bhauju* and Tauka Kanchha *dai*. Kanchhi did not believe them. The rumours were bound to fly, she thought. Bipana *bhauju* was a young daughter-in-law whose husband was never in the hamlet. Her husband, Surya *dai*, was a serial migrant labourer. He was in Macau then, tending to horses at a horse stable. Before that he was in Delhi, working at a restaurant until he got into a fight with the local men and they beat him up unconscious. Before that, he was in Butwal. He had, in fact, never been in the hamlet since he was twelve. Kanchhi sometimes forgot that Saili *didi* had three sons. Tauka Kanchha *dai*, on the other hand, was always around. He had never left the hamlet, was as young as Bipana *bhauju* (both twenty-three years old) and was married too but childless. His own fault, people said, the doctor said. Who better than him to have an affair with?

'Why do you believe what other people say about them?' Kanchhi asked Maiju.

'Because they know. They've seen them together,' Maiju said.

'No, they haven't. People will say anything.'

'Why would they say things they don't know?'

'Have you seen them together?'

'No.'

'Then, why are you saying things you haven't seen for yourself?'

'Because they have.'

'How do you know they have?'

'Shut up. Just stay away from her. There's no difference between you and her.'

Some of the rumours were ridiculous. Kanchhi heard a woman tell Maiju that someone had seen Bipana *bhauju* and Tauka Kanchha *dai* naked in a *khar* field high above the hamlet. The *khar* field, where thatch grass grew, was too rocky and too steep to be naked in. 'How is that even possible?' Kanchhi asked.

'She meant the woods below,' Maiju said.

Another rumour alleged that they were found in the abandoned house, not exactly them but a gold chain, which people believed belonged to Bipana *bhauju*. 'It could have been anybody else's,' Kanchhi said.

'It's hers,' Maiju said.

'Didn't you say they said things about you as well?'

'They did.'

'Then, why are you taking their side?'

'Because I know me, and I know her.'

'What do you know?'

'I know everything.'

Kanchhi shook her head, but when she saw Bipana *bhauju* next, she did not tell her any of this. Bipana *bhauju* had come up to her to walk up to the shop again. This time, the shop was closed from outside.

'Kanchhi, you stay here and wait for him. I'll go around and check the fields,' Bipana *bhauju* said.

'Okay,' Kanchhi said and sat on Tauka Kanchha *dai*'s porch. There was no one around but Ramesh's father, taking a nap on his own porch. Both Tauka Kanchha *dai*'s and Ramesh's porch were unusually high and wound around the sides of their houses as well. Kanchhi watched Ramesh's father sleep for a bit and then watched a large beetle buzz by. When the beetle flew out of sight, Kanchhi decided to walk to the temple again. This time, there were three boys there – Ramesh, Tauka Kanchha *dai*'s nephew and Thapa Nani *didi*'s youngest son Thapa Sana – all around Kanchhi's age, all crouching by the metal gate, and each doing their bit to prepare *ganja*.

'*Abui*, *ganja*,' Kanchhi said.

'It's not *ganja*. It's herbal medicine,' Ramesh said and everyone laughed. Ramesh was in charge of crumbling the *ganja* leaves into smokeable bits.

'Wait till I tell your father,' Kanchhi said.

'Wait till I tell your mother,' Ramesh said.

'Tell her what?'

'Everything.'

'Like what?'

'*Like what?*' Ramesh repeated after her, and everyone laughed again.

Kanchhi shook her head. 'Useless boys,' she said.

Tauka Kanchha *dai*'s nephew, who was cleaning a bamboo pipe, blew on it and, when nothing but air came out of it, handed it to Ramesh. Ramesh stuffed it with the *ganja* crumbs.

'Where did you get it from?' Kanchhi asked, meaning *ganja*.

'Lord Shiva,' Ramesh said, with his arms half-stretched towards the sky, and everyone laughed again.

'Are the boys bothering you?' Tauka Kanchha *dai* shouted from far behind Kanchhi.

Kanchhi turned around.

Tauka Kanchha *dai*, in a dirty blue vest and long track

pants, was standing in his yard, pinching snuff to put in his mouth. A few feet behind him was Bipana *bhauju*, twisting a long stem of grass in her hand. When she came close, Bipana *bhauju* walked directly to Kanchhi and said, 'Let's go.'

She had not bought anything. The rumours were true.

Two days later, they were caught. Kanchhi was working in Saili *didi*'s field then, the field right above the primary school, sowing corn, when it happened. It was Punti who started the process when she came over crying and would not be consoled. Punti had been feverish that day, and Bipana *bhauju* was supposed to look after her.

'Where's your *ama*?' Saili *didi* asked. 'Do you still have a fever? Did you eat anything? Did you sleep? Where's your *ama*?'

Punti continued to cry, forcing Saili *didi* to lift her in her arms and walk up. She told Maiju she would be back in a bit. No one else was home that afternoon. Bir Bahadur *dai* was below the school, grazing goats, and Bhime *dai* was in Hatiya, getting fertilizer from the government. Saili *didi*'s third son, who was as rare a sight as Surya *dai*, was in India, in its army.

While Saili *didi* was gone, Kanchhi and Maiju continued to sow corn, Kanchhi hoeing in front and Maiju dropping seeds behind her. A little later, Saili *didi* came running back.

'What happened?' Maiju asked.

'Kanchhi, go get your uncle,' Saili *didi* said.

'What happened?' Maiju asked again.

'They're in there,' Saili *didi* said.

'Who? Where?'

'Bipana and her lover. In her room. I locked them from outside.'

Maiju looked up at Saili *didi*'s house and then at Kanchhi. 'Go, didn't you hear? Go get Bir Bahadur *dai*.'

Kanchhi dropped the hoe and walked down.

'Run,' Maiju said.

Kanchhi ran and once at the *chautara* past the school, she shouted, '*Buwa, Thulobuwa.*' No one replied. It took her a while to find Bir Bahadur *dai*. He had fallen asleep under the shade of a chestnut tree.

'What happened?' he too asked.

'*Ama* and Saili *didi* want you up.'

'Why?'

'I don't know. Something about Bipana *bhauju*.'

Bir Bahadur *dai* put on his hat and picked up his old radio and a stick. Then, he told Kanchhi to stay behind and look after the goats.

'No,' Kanchhi said and followed him up. Maiju and Saili *didi* were well on their way.

In the house, the first room past the buffalo shed was Bipana *bhauju*'s. Saili *didi* had bolted it shut from the outside. There was absolutely no sound coming out. Bir Bahadur *dai* squinted at the door for a while and then asked Saili *didi* to go get his brothers. His brothers, two in total, lived right next door. Only one of them, his older brother, was home.

'Bipana,' Bir Bahadur *dai* said, opening the door hasp and trying to sound as calm as he could. The door was locked from inside. 'Bipana, open the door,' Bir Bahadur *dai* said and waited.

When nothing happened, he tried again. The door did not open.

'Bipana *buhari*,' Bir Bahadur *dai* called again.

The door stayed locked.

'How long have they been in there?' Bir Bahadur *dai* stepped down to the yard and asked.

'It was locked from inside when I got here,' Saili *didi* said.

'Are you sure it's them in there?' Maiju asked.

Saili *didi* said she was sure. She had heard them talk and laugh.

'Where's Punti?' Bir Bahadur *dai* asked.

Saili *didi* pointed to the other room, the room that had once belonged to Laxmi and Dhan *didi*. Saili *didi* had locked Punti in as well. Bir Bahadur *dai* looked at it and then at the people starting to gather in the yard. Apart from his older brother, both his sisters-in-law and their families were now in the yard.

'Go get Thapa Maila *dai*.' Bir Bahadur dai turned to a little boy in the crowd. 'Get Tauka Kanchha's wife and his mother too.'

The little boy, one of Bir Bahadur *dai*'s older brother's grandchildren, ran up the hill to get them all.

In the meantime, Bir Bahadur *dai* tried again to get the door to open. 'Bipana. *Buhari.* Come outside. We'll just talk,' he pleaded.

There was no response, except the sound of some movement from inside.

'You can't stay in there forever, you know,' Bir Bahadur *dai* said. 'We'll break the door if we have to, but we need to talk and figure out what to do next.'

'They will never come out if you talk that sweetly to them,' Saili *didi* said. 'You have to scream. *Eh*, Bipana,' Saili *didi* screamed.

'Shh,' Bir Bahadur *dai* said. 'Let me handle it.'

'Yes, better to remain quiet,' one of his sisters-in-law said. 'She's not our daughter. If something happens to her, we'll be in trouble.'

'What's going on?' Thapa Maila dai asked. His two sons had followed him down as well.

'What happened?' he repeated.

'*Dai*, thank god, you're here,' Bir Bahadur *dai* said to Thapa Maila *dai*, suddenly sounding anxious. 'We've allowed this to go on for too long. Now, look what they've done. They are in there in my house in the middle of the day.'

Thapa Maila *dai* looked at the door as Bir Bahadur *dai* had and walked over to it.

'Kanchha, *eh*, Kanchha,' he called Tauka Kanchha *dai*.

'Open the door, Kanchha, and come outside. We're not going anywhere until you do, you know that.'

The door still did not open. Thapa Maila *dai* turned to the crowd and said, 'Let's not get riled up and do something we might regret later.'

'We haven't done anything,' Bir Bahadur *dai*'s older brother said.

'I know. I'm saying let's not do anything.'

'What are we to do? They did everything,' the brother spoke again.

Everyone laughed. Just then, Tauka Kanchha *dai*'s mother and Ramesh's father arrived in the yard. Neither of them said anything, but as if sensing their presence, Tauka Kanchha *dai* opened the door and walked out, bolting the door shut behind him. His vest was turned inside out.

'Let's go up to my house and talk about this in a small group,' Thapa Maila *dai* said. 'You, you, you, us, let's go up.' He pointed at Bir Bahadur *dai*, Bir Bahadur *dai*'s older brother, Tauka Kanchha *dai*, Tauka Kanchha *dai*'s mother and Ramesh's father. 'Others, please stay here or return to your houses, and *bhauju*—' Thapa Maila *dai* turned to Saili *didi*. 'Let Bipana out if she wants to. Don't raise your hand against her. We'll talk and decide what should be done next. Punti? Where's Punti?'

Saili *didi* pointed to the other room.

'Take care of her too. We'll be down soon,' he said.

The men did not come down for two hours. The women and children waited in Saili *didi*'s yard for a while and then left. When Bir Bahadur *dai* and his older brother finally walked down, they were both drunk. The men had come to an agreement that Tauka Kanchha *dai* would pay four thousand rupees in compensation and stay away from Bipana *bhauju* forever. In return, Bir Bahadur *dai* would not lodge any kind of police complaint against him – that of rape or polygamy or character assassination. As for Bipana *bhauju*, she would be allowed to stay in the hamlet for as long as Surya *dai* willed. She was his concern, they said.

For a while afterwards, it was all quiet. No one from Tauka Kanchha *dai*'s came down to Bipana *bhauju*'s, and no one from Bipana *bhauju*'s went up. Kanchhi too stopped visiting Tauka Kanchha *dai*, shopping at Thakuri *baje*'s instead when needed. A silent war had begun. The only whispers were about Bipana *bhauju*. People said this was inevitable. A young woman without a husband was a tragedy waiting to happen.

Then, about a month later, Bipana *bhauju* disappeared. So did Tauka Kanchha *dai*. Two weeks later, he came back. Alone. 'She didn't want to,' he said. Bir Bahadur *dai* slapped him hard this time. Tauka Kanchha *dai* fell on his knees and promised to pay more. Two more thousand, he cried.

'He sold her,' Saili *didi* said.

'Maybe she went back to her mother's,' Maiju said.

Once again, Thapa Maila *dai* played the mediator. Once again, they talked (at an open field this time) and came to another agreement. Three more thousand was paid in compensation. No one went to the police station. No one went to Butwal either, where Tauka Kanchha *dai* said Bipana *bhauju* was. Tauka Kanchha *dai*'s wife – a Magar woman – too was left out of the conversation. She had married him when they were both sixteen. Love marriage, they said. No one asked her how she felt. Punti cried for weeks. So did Saili *didi*. Then, right before Teej, Bipana *bhauju*'s mother came down from Bhoksingh, a village far above and west of Balakot, and took Punti with her. Saili *didi* let her go.

'*Ama*,' Kanchhi asked Maiju the evening Punti left. 'Do you think Bipana *bhauju* will ever come back someday?'

'No,' Maiju said.

'Why not?'

'If you leave like that, you can't come back.'

'Why not?'

'You can't.'

'I'm coming back. If I ever leave like that, I'm coming back.'

'You're not leaving like that.'

'If he can, so can I. This is my hamlet too.'

21

BIPANA *BHAUJU*'S DISAPPEARANCE SHOOK KANCHHI. That Tauka Kanchha *dai* could just come back, pay for his right to stay in the hamlet, but not Bipana *bhauju* deeply unsettled her, and Kanchhi kept thinking about how unjust the whole process was, especially for Punti. They did not even think about her, and she was the one who lost everything that day. Punti never had a father to speak of, and now, her mother too was gone. Not even eight, and she had become an orphan.

'No, she hasn't.' Maiju tried to believe otherwise. 'Bipana is in Bhoksingh. Why else would her mother come and get Punti?'

'I doubt she's back in Bhoksingh,' Saili *didi* said.

'Where else would she go?'

Kanchhi did not believe it either. She thought something much more sinister had befallen Bipana *bhauju*. *Tatyakatha* was full of stories like that – stories of men who took their lovers to faraway places, killed them there and went back to their hamlets as if nothing had happened.

'I don't think he killed her,' Maiju said. 'He must have come to his senses and left her in the bazaar.'

'What senses?' Kanchhi asked.

'What else is he going to do with her? He can't marry her and bring her here. Neither can he stay in the bazaar forever. What is he going to do there? How is he going to feed himself? Here at least, he's got a house, the fields, a mother, a wife, a shop. He can't give everything up for her.'

'He killed her.'

'No, he didn't.'

Use the following phrases in a sentence:

Farar hunu: Bhaujulai Butwalko junglema marera nij abhiyukta farar bhaye.

(To run off: The accused ran off after killing *bhauju* in the jungles of Butwal.)

Kan samaunu: Aparadhilai kan samauna lagayera matrai hundaina jail ni halna parchha.

(To hold one's ears: The criminal should be jailed, not just ordered to hold their ears and say sorry.)

Lampasar parnu: Bhaujuko bepatta bare sara gaunle kehi garna nasakera lampasar pare.

(To lie prostrate: When it came to solving *bhauju*'s disappearance, the villagers lay prostrate, unable to do anything.)

Govinda sir noticed the thread.

'Are you trying to write a story, Deepa?' he asked, handing Kanchhi her notebook back.

'No,' Kanchhi said.

'Expand on it and write one. We'll send it to *Gorkhapatra* again.'

Kanchhi hesitated. The poem she had sent a year earlier had not been published yet.

'Publication takes time,' Govinda sir said. 'Shiva's writing a poem about child labour, and Tara Prasad is compiling a list of the ten most interesting facts about this area. You can't be the only one who doesn't submit.'

Kanchhi did not write anything. A few weeks later, Govinda sir wrote a story himself, about a boy who bumps into a blind old man but does not realize he is blind, and submitted it under her name. That too never got published.

It was Laxmi's visit that finally shook Kanchhi's mind off Bipana *bhauju*. She came home that monsoon for two months and brought along her year-old son, Basanta – a chubby little toddler who lifted spirits just by existing. The first time she saw the child, Kanchhi dropped a coin at Laxmi's feet and bowed deeply.

'Kanchhi,' Laxmi said. 'I thought I would never see you again.'

'How is Lamjung?' Kanchhi asked.

'The same as here, just a lot more Gurung hamlets. We're surrounded by them.'

'Too late for you. You chose a Bahun man,' Maiju said, bowing to Laxmi and the child as Kanchhi had.

Laxmi laughed. She seemed different. For one, she was decked in red from head to toe – a line of red *sindoor*, a red *bindi*, red lipstick, a red *pote*, a red blouse, a red sari and a red *chadar* covering both her and her son. The only things not red on her were the big, brown sunspots on her nose and cheeks.

'*Bahuni bajai*,' Maiju said. 'Why do you have to wear red all the time?'

'No red, husband dead,' Laxmi said and laughed. 'Everyone wears red there, *Chhyama*. Only a widow doesn't.'

'*Eh*, *barai*, the things we do because others do it too,' Maiju said. 'Kanchhi, want to hold the child for a bit?'

'Want to?' Laxmi asked.

Kanchhi nodded. Laxmi opened her *chadar* and passed Basanta to her. He had been playing with beads on Laxmi's necklace and did not want to let go.

'Careful,' Maiju said. 'Be gentle.'

'This is the third one I had to get after he broke the other two,' Laxmi said, unfurling Basanta's fingers and taking the necklace back.

'It's just begun,' Maiju said. 'Wait until he starts walking around. You won't have time to even breathe then.'

'He's already a handful.'

Kanchhi nestled Basanta in her arms and cooed at

him. He seemed tired but cooed back at her, bursting a bubble in his mouth in the process.

'It's going to rain now,' Maiju said.

'It's monsoon. He can fart and it will rain,' Laxmi said and everyone laughed.

Towards the end of Laxmi's stay, Dhan *didi* too came back for a visit. She had changed a lot as well but in the other direction. Done with her first-year IA exams, she was awaiting the results and had just begun working at the front desk of the Nepal Telecommunications office in Pokhara. With her first pay, she had got a very short haircut, one that fell right above her ears, and a set of sky-blue *kurta surwal*, which she wore to the hamlet. Kanchhi had never seen anyone in such a piece of clothing before.

'Where did you get this, *Didi*?' she asked.

'Everyone wears this in Pokhara, Kanchhi,' Dhan *didi* said. 'Do you like it? Want me to get you one next time?'

Kanchhi did not say anything, only stared at the dark blue flowers on the *kurta*. The trousers were plain blue, but both the top and the bottom were silky to the touch.

'Let me know before I go, and I'll get you one next time,' Dhan *didi* said.

'Did you ask about psychology on campus?' Kanchhi asked. Dhan *didi* had promised her that she would find out about it.

'I did,' Dhan *didi* said. 'Not a popular major, but they do teach it there. What are you going to do with it?'

'I don't know,' Kanchhi said.

'I think you should study political science. It's a very popular major.'

'What does it do?'

'Helps you get into politics.'

'Govinda sir says it's a dirty game.'

'That's what they tell you to keep you away.'

'Why?'

'Because they are smart. It keeps women like us away. If I were a man, I would get in it.'

'If you were a man?'

'Yeah. It's too dirty right now,' Dhan *didi* said and laughed. 'Here, since you love reading—' She reached into her tote and got a book out: an IA first-year English grammar book, written in both English and Nepali.

'I'll need it back if I fail the exams, but until then it's yours,' Dhan *didi* said.

—

A search for Surya *dai*'s second wife began right away. Laxmi promised to look around her husband's hamlet in Lamjung and Dhan *didi* among her own friends and extended network in Pokhara. Even Maiju thought of a few faces, going through a list of people she knew in Baglung, wondering whether any of them had children old enough to get married. It did not work out. None of the suggestions made it past the brainstorming stage.

It was Saili *didi*'s sisters-in-law who brought forth three proposals, all from Tindhara, a hamlet right across the Kali Gandaki River two hours up from Setibeni, a hamlet where the two sisters-in-law had both been born and brought up. Tindhara had a long, strong marital history with Torikhola. Women from Torikhola went to Tindhara. Women from Tindhara came to Torikhola.

Two of the matches did not make it to the viewing ceremony. Surya *dai* wanted a literate wife this time. One of them had never been to school, and the second one, who had studied until the third grade – Bir Bahadur *dai* did not like her aunt. He said he had run into her in Hatiya one day and she talked down about Torikhola. 'As if there are better places and better men for her niece,' Bir Bahadur *dai* said. 'Of course, there are, but why tell me? I don't want to form relationships with people like that.'

The third one, who had also studied until grade three, was already married, but her husband had run away with his girlfriend a day after the wedding. Maiju said he probably wanted to make everyone happy except her. 'Thank god her parents took her back,' Maiju said.

In winter, Saili *didi* and Bir Bahadur *dai* went to see the third woman in Tindhara. Kanchhi joined them. The woman's name was Tara and at 5'9", she was the tallest woman Kanchhi had ever seen. She was also the fifth of thirteen children, and five of them were below ten. It was a constant ruckus in their house. One of them loved to catch daddy-long-legs spiders and race them against each other. One of the others loved to eat them. Even more memorable was the hamlet itself. Kanchhi had never seen such wide terraces up on the mountains before. They were as big as those often found in river valleys like Bagar or Hatiya. The houses too were different. Most of them were wooden, with wide balconies and concrete porches, and almost all of them had beautiful gardens, with roses and gardenias and coffee plants hemming the front yards. If she had thought Torikhola was a hamlet full of Indian army veterans, this one acted like it. Kanchhi had to ask Bir Bahadur *dai* if he really was a retired serviceman. Where was his money? 'In Pokhara,' Saili *didi* said. He had invested all his money on land in Pokhara. They planned to retire there someday.

Saili *didi* and Bir Bahadur *dai* said yes to Tara and left behind a gold chain and a gold ring to seal the deal. On the way back, they stopped by at Hatiya and called Surya *dai* from an old, solar-powered rotary dial phone. They did not reach him right away and left a message asking him to call back as soon as he could. When he called back the next day, he told the shopkeeper he would call in a week.

"If you like her, keep her," Saili *didi* said Surya *dai* told them. 'But he wouldn't be able to be back until *Dashain*.'

Tara *bhauju*'s family promised to wait.

In October, ten whole months later, Surya *dai* came back, jacked with biceps as big as banana trunks. If he was furious that his family had sent his daughter away, he did not show it. He never talked about Bipana *bhauju* either. All he did, as if in a nod to the episode, was beat Tauka Kanchhi *dai* up after Surya *dai*'s younger brother too got home for *Dashain* and the wedding. The three brothers, including Bhime *dai*, assembled three other men and dragged Tauka Kanchha *dai* to the woods above his house. There, they broke his right arm and left leg, leaving his face untouched, and threw a thousand rupees for treatment. Tauka Kanchha *dai* had to be taken to Pokhara the next day.

'You didn't have to hurt him like that,' Maiju said to Surya *dai* later. 'What if he'd died or been permanently disabled. You would have destroyed not only your own life but that of his wife's as well.'

Surya *dai* only smiled and asked Kanchhi instead if she needed help with hanging a swing for *Dashain*. Kanchhi said no. They were not installing one that year. Then, he asked her if she had ever seen a camera before.

Kanchhi had not.

'Come with me then. Your job tomorrow is to take pictures for me.'

The next day was the day of *Astami* celebrations, the eighth day of *Dashain* when villagers from Torikhola and the hamlets around it – the Thakuri hamlet, Haricharur and the two Magar hamlets below and above Harichaur

– slaughtered animals at the village temple, which back then was still a mere rock snug in the laps of a *pipal* tree.

The next afternoon, Kanchhi walked to the front of the temple and sat above a slaughter pit. The camera, a grey Panasonic, swung from a strap around her neck.

The slaughter pit was small and square, about five feet deep, and had a wooden pole at its centre. At one point in the past, the pit used to be a mustard mill, and the pole was used to press oil out of mustard seeds. Now, the pole steadied animals for beheading and the pit received their blood. On each face of the pole was a painting of an ewer, a *khuda*, a sword and a *khukuri*. Kanchhi watched a man walk an adult buffalo to the top of the slaughter pit and pass it to Surya *dai*. Surya *dai* walked the buffalo down a set of steps and to the pole. He was one of the three designated priests for the occasion. The other two were Ramesh and Thirman – Thirman, who had just been back home for *Dashain*. Each of the priests were clad in white dhotis and sacred threads, and each brandished a weapon – Surya *dai* a large *khuda*, Thirman a large *khukuri* and Ramesh a tiny one.

'Ready?' Surya *dai* asked Kanchhi. He wanted her to take a group picture first, with the buffalo in the middle and the priests around it.

'Ready,' Kanchhi said, and when the priests posed, holding on to the buffalo and raising their weapons high in the air, Kanchhi pressed the big button down as Surya *dai* had taught her.

'In one clean sweep. In one clean sweep,' people began to chant. They were all around Kanchhi, sitting and standing around the pit, segregated by gender. Women were mostly directly in front of the temple, and the men on the other three sides of the pit. To Kanchhi's right, by the *sal* trees, was a team of *panche baja* players. As the chants soared, they began to play their instruments.

'Take one as I do it,' Surya *dai* shouted to Kanchhi.

'Okay,' Kanchhi shouted back. Just then, the *narsinga* player blew the trumpet hard. It was so loud and so doleful the sound rose above all the others like a battle cry. People started to clap and cheer.

'Swing it. Swing it,' they chanted.

The three priests took their positions. Thirman grabbed the rope tied around the buffalo's neck and led it closer to the pole. Ramesh grabbed its tail. Surya *dai*, who cleared the leaves from the floor first, walked behind the buffalo and stood by its neck, ready to strike as soon as it stood still.

The buffalo, however, took its time. It looked up first and then around, sniffed the air and the post, and then, as if sensing malice in the air, began circling the pole, dragging both Thirman and Ramesh around as it did so. People began to laugh.

'Looks like the buffalo isn't ready to go,' someone said.

'Hold on to it,' the others said.

'Yeah, yeah. Hold on to it. It'll tire soon,' the rest chimed in.

They were wrong. It was the priests who got worn out first. After a few more rounds around the pole, Surya *dai* lowered his *khuda* and took a step back towards the wall. Thirman too let go of the rope, and Ramesh the tail. For a second then, the buffalo was completely free, and that, more than anything, must have calmed it down because then it stood still and lowered its neck as if to sniff the dry leaves fallen on the ground.

Surya *dai* sensed an opening and raised his *khuda* and brought it down. The buffalo buckled under itself and fell but not on its side. Swiftly, Surya *dai* raised the *khuda* again and struck the buffalo one more time. *Chhyak*, *chhyak* and *chhyak*. That really was the sound of the *khuda* slicing flesh and bones. *Chhyak*. On the tenth swing, Kanchhi took a picture. Ten more swings later, the buffalo was beheaded. By then, everyone had fallen silent. Even the music had stopped.

'*Tait*,' people said when it was over. 'What did you do, Surya? Are those biceps just for show?'

'Frustrating,' they said. 'That wasn't nice at all.'

A man jumped into the pit and asked Surya *dai*, 'You did well. First time?'

Surya *dai* glanced at him and shook his head. 'It's just been a long time,' he said.

'Yeah, I know. Everything needs to remain sharp,' the man said and picked up the buffalo's head. Thirman, Ramesh and two other Thakuri boys lifted the body out of the pit.

'Don't you have anything to offer?' The man holding the head turned towards the women.

'Where's that accent from?' one of the women asked.

'Where do you think it's from?' the man asked back.

'Baglung, Myagdi,' someone said.

'How did you know? You've been there?'

The women laughed.

'It's a Baglunge Magar's accent,' the man said with pride and then winked at no one in particular.

'*Abui*,' the women said and laughed again.

The next slaughter was cleaner. A day-old calf. Surya *dai* beheaded it in one clean sweep. No one had to hold it steady. It was too weak to run around. Surya *dai* also slaughtered the next few: two goats and two more young buffaloes. When it was time for another adult buffalo, Thirman stepped in. It took him two swings. Kanchhi took a picture of him as he finished it. Towards the evening, Saili *didi* brought a baby goat. Ramesh slaughtered it. '*Jaya parameshwori*,' Saili *didi* chanted as she received the lifeless body back. Just the body. The head was left behind for the priests. The blood for the goddess.

22

November 13, 2005

Theki lade jastai mana ladyo samaune hat chhaina
Mare Kali nadilai banchhe ramaune bat chhaina

(The heart fell like a pot, but there's no one to catch it
If I die, I'm for the Kali River. If I live, there's no point in it.)

THE SUN CLIMBS STEADILY. THE FOG DISSIPATES, except far away where clumps of it float above the Setikhola River in the south. Maiju stands in the field, chopping off the millet fingers with a sickle and throwing them in the *thunse* on her back. She is a quiet field worker, does not hum or sing. The rhythm of pull and snip is engaging enough.

Far in the distance, another jeep honks. The last one on its way to Bayarghari. A crow flies to a *badahar* branch in front. Below it are the bottle of water and the few tangerines Maiju brought with her. She looks up at the crow. The jeep honks again. At every turn, it honks – a soothing sound hinting at something somewhere being stirred, being in motion.

Maiju looks up at the sun. It is in a straight line above two trees in the distance, exactly where it should be moments after nine.

'Ka, ka,' the crow caws.

'Subol, subol,' Maiju says.

23

THE MAN WHO HAD PICKED UP THE FIRST BUFFALO'S head came back again the next day. His name was Jhalnath Gharti Magar, a twenty-six-year-old policeman who had recently been promoted to the post of head constable and transferred from Mustang to Bagar. He came up to Torikhola with Laxmi's husband after the latter had stopped by the station on his way up and the two had hit it off. Kanchhi was taking a nap on a bed of rice hays when they walked into her yard.

'Who's this sleeping in the middle of the day?' Sukh Bahadur yelled.

'*Oho*, *Babu*,' Maiju said to him. She was next to Kanchhi, setting up a loom to weave a mat. 'When did you get here?'

'A while ago,' Sukh Bahadur said, going up to her and bowing at her feet. 'Now just walking around, showing our sir here our little village.'

'*Oye*, Kanchhi, get up,' Maiju said.

Kanchhi squirmed. Her ninth-grade history textbook was on top of her face, shielding it from the sun.

'Get up,' Maiju said again, poking at her shins.

Kanchhi peeked from under the book and reluctantly sat up. '*Venaju*, namaste,' she said to Sukh Bahadur and greeted Jhalnath as well.

'I don't think I recognize you,' Maiju said to Jhalnath.

'Our new *hawaldar* sir,' Sukh Bahadur said. 'Got transferred to Bagar only a few days ago. I brought him up so that he can see the hamlet.'

'*Eh, eh*,' Maiju said and ordered Kanchhi to go get mats for the men.

'Not for me.' Jhalnath shook his hand in the air. 'I'm fine standing here. Been sitting down for too long. I'm tired of it.'

Sukh Bahadur, on the other hand, did not object. Kanchhi fetched a mat for him, and he spread it over the edge of the yard to sit.

'Where's Laxmi?' Maiju asked.

'Trying to get the son to sleep,' Sukh Bahadur replied.

'*Bara*, he must be tired. It's a long journey.'

'Isn't it? The trail seemed to never end,' Sukh Bahadur said.

'*Haina*, how far does this Torikhola extend?' Jhalnath asked. He had walked over to the chicken coop and was surveying the trees, the shed and the terraces around.

'The VDC is big. The hamlet isn't. Twenty-five, twenty-seven houses maybe. Isn't that right, *Kaki*?' Sukh Bahadur asked.

'I don't know, *Babu*. Never counted, but that sounds about right,' Maiju said.

'Twenty-seven?' the head constable asked, a little incredulous. 'Where are the other houses?'

'Obscured. There are some on the way to the temple and some beyond that ridge.' Sukh Bahadur pointed at the slope past the Chiuridanda bend.

'*Eh, eh*,' Jhalnath said. 'All Chhetris?' he asked.

'No, four families are Magar and one Bahun,' Maiju said.

'Magar? What kind of Magars?'

'Saru, Thapa, Rana,' Maiju said.

'There's a big Magar hamlet right below the temple and one far up,' Sukh Bahadur said and then pointed in the opposite direction. 'There's another one past the Thakuri hamlet too, and one around the bend this way.'

Jhalnath looked in the direction Sukh Bahadur was now pointing to, towards Saru *didi*'s house.

'A Chhetri hamlet surrounded by Magars,' he said.

'Magar, Gurung, Bahun, Thakuri – all kinds of hamlets,' Sukh Bahadur said.

'What about you, *Babu*? Where are you from?' Maiju asked Jhalnath.

'Baglung,' Kanchhi said.

'How did you know?' Jhalnath turned to her, surprised that she knew.

'You said it yesterday at the temple.'

'I did?' He looked at her, trying to locate her in his memory. 'I don't remember it. What's that book?' he asked.

Kanchhi turned the book around so that he could see the cover page. Jhalnath walked over and read out loud, 'History. Grade 9 and 10. Part 1. *Eh*, *bafre*. *Khoi*, let me see.'

Kanchhi gave him the book.

'Is it compulsory or optional?' he asked.

'Compulsory.'

Jhalnath flipped through the pages slowly. 'Looks like nothing but stories of kings and kingdoms,' he said, giving the book back. 'Do you know who the last king of Parbat was?'

'Nayab Shah,' Kanchhi said.

'Wrong. Fail. You don't even know who your last king was?'

Kanchhi looked at him and then at the book. She was sure he was mistaken. 'It's Nayab Shah,' she said again.

'It's Thir Bam. Read it right.'

'No, sir,' Sukh Bahadur said and then explained that Thir Bam was the ruler of north Parbat. The southern part, then called Paiyunkot, was ruled by Nayab Shah. Torikhola fell under Paiyunkot, and Nayab Shah was their last king.

'Really? Nayab Shah?' Jhalnath asked. 'I've heard of Paiyunkot. Where is it?'

'In that direction.' Sukh Bahadur leaned back in the yard and pointed past the mango and the jackfruit trees. 'You can't see it from here, but one of the palaces still stands. You should go there someday, sir, before you get transferred again. They hold a big fair there every year on *Dashain Astami*. You missed it this year, but you have to go next year. The Kafle people there kill a goat and then hold a game to see which family gets to take it.'

'You say they do that every year?' Jhalnath asked.

'Yeah. They kill a buffalo too but leave that for the leopards.'

'The whole buffalo?'

'Yes.'

Jhalnath stared in the direction of Paiyunkot for a while and then shook his legs, as if he was raring to go right then.

'Do you want some tea or water?' Maiju asked.

'No, we should go,' Jhalnath said.

'Yes, we should,' Sukh Bahadur agreed and got up and stretched his arms over his head.

'Are you sure?' Maiju asked again.

'Yes, *Kaki*. We need to go, but Laxmi will be here soon.' Sukh Bahadur dusted off the back of his pants and rolled up the mat.

'Kanchhi, don't go back to sleep, understand?' he said. 'Naps are for lazy people.'

Kanchhi clutched her book and chewed on a rice straw in response.

'*La, ta*,' the men said and left.

Five days later was Surya *dai*'s wedding. By the time Kanchhi woke up, the groom's party had already left for Tindhara. Only fifteen–twenty people were invited – fifteen to twenty, excluding the palanquin bearers. So, only the men went (a man from each house). The women, on the other hand, stayed behind and prepared Saili *didi*'s house for the *ratyauli* party that would be held later that day. Saili *didi* and Maiju made *selroti*s and mutton, Saru *didi* brewed alcohol (in her own place), and Laxmi and Kanchhi cleaned and beautified the whole house. They sewed garlands, strung together pennants and hung them over doors and trees.

In the afternoon, long before the groom's party arrived with the bride, women, most of them members of the Torikhola Mothers' Association, descended with jugs and glasses, *madal*s and tambourines, and the party began. They sat on mats in the yard and sang:

Kati ramro suntala joda yo
Sasu amai sunenau bolako?

(Look, how sweet these tangerines look
Mother-in-law, didn't you hear me call you?)

Thapa Nani *didi* drummed the *madal*, Ramesh's mother tapped the tambourine, and Harichaur *bajai* (Harichaur *buwa*'s wife) sang the couplets. Kanchhi clapped and joined in the chorus for a while. She did not dance. Saili *didi* did. Dressed in her usual sari and a blouse – the only woman in the hamlet who wore them every day – Saili *didi* was the woman of the hour.

Soon afterwards, Kanchhi went to Saru *didi*'s and carried gallon cans of liquor back to Saili *didi*'s. Some women decided to wait to drink, but most began right away, filling and refilling the glasses they had brought with them.

Sano paila tekinna janinna
Nachna khojda kammar bhachinna

(These small feet don't know how to step
I try to dance but my waist won't bend)

The songs went on.

It was past five when the groom's party made it back to the village. They were seen on the grounds of the primary school first, with the *panche baja* band at the front and the palanquin bearers right behind them. The palanquin was a red cloth tied to a straight piece of wood that Maiju said came from the coconut tree and looked highly uncomfortable. It swung a lot when the bearers moved. Someone in the groom's party shouted, '*Jhyanakuti jhyanakuti jhyain jhyain.*'

'Is that what it means?' Kanchhi asked.

'What?' Maiju asked back.

'*Jhyanakuti*? Is it referring to the way the palanquin swings?'

'Maybe. I don't know.'

'If *jhyain* is the sound of the music, *jhyanakuti* must be that,' Kanchhi said.

'Ask Thapa Nani *didi*. She must know.'

'How would she know?'

'Because she's a teacher.'

Kanchhi looked at Thapa Nani *didi*. She was up ahead, negotiating with the *janti* team. The groom's party had to pay a certain sum, a thousand and one rupees in this case, to the mothers' party before they were allowed in the hamlet.

'No,' Kanchhi said.

'No,' Bir Bahadur *dai* too tried to say to the mothers, but the women would not budge. He had to pay the amount for the procession to continue forward.

The feast began soon afterwards. Saili *didi* came out of the kitchen with a *nanglo* of *selroti* and asked Kanchhi to start distributing them to the crowd. Later, Kanchhi was in charge of passing the jug of alcohol around. She herself took sips only after boys her age came down at around eight. When they did, they were already drunk. They hooted and hollered and danced right away. The girls loved it. *'Bokaharu,'* one of them said.

Kanchhi looked for Thirman among them. He was not there.

As the night progressed, groups began to segregate more visibly along the lines of gender, age, kinship and the level of drunkenness. The men in Saili *didi*'s family sat on the porch, drinking, talking and watching the women in the yard sing and dance. The women in Saili *didi*'s family, including the new bride, stayed inside the kitchen. Most of the young crowd was gathered in the yards of Saili *didi*'s sisters-in-law. Kanchhi, who stayed mostly in Saili *didi*'s yard with other women of the hamlet, walked past them when she went to pee. The surprise was in seeing even more of them beyond the yards and the houses, huddled in twos, some peeing, some chatting and a few feeling each other up under the cover of the full-moon darkness. One young boy, teetering drunk, stopped Kanchhi on the way and asked her if she wanted to kiss him. Kanchhi laughed him off.

On her way back, someone shouted, '*Oye, solti.*'

Kanchhi did not stop.

'*Solti*, stop.'

This time she recognized the voice. Jhalnath's. He was at the edge of the middle yard, sitting in the midst of young boys, all drunk. A group of young girls was standing next to the boys.

'Have you ever had Mustang tea?' Jhalnath asked.

'What?' Kanchhi asked back.

'Tea. Mustang tea.'

'Tea?'

'Yes, tea.'

'No,' Kanchhi said.

'Want some?'

'No.'

'Boys, go get her some Mustang tea.'

The boys laughed. Kanchhi realized she was being held up for exactly that and began to walk away.

'Wait, wait, don't go.' Jhalnath stood up. 'We were just kidding. Here, come sit with us. Boys, go get her a mat. Get these sisters a mat too. Why are you all standing?'

Ramesh got up and fetched a stool for Kanchhi and a mat for the girls. Kanchhi refused to sit. The other girls too continued to stand.

'Don't worry,' Jhalnath said, sitting down again. 'We are two cops here. There's one more in that house. Nothing will happen to you girls.'

The other cop, sitting right by Jhalnath, lifted his head for a bit and then went back to staring at a glass in his hand.

'Sir, what are your boots made of?' Ramesh asked.

'Huh? These boots?' Jhalnath pointed at his feet.

'Yes.'

'Ox leather,' Jhalnath said.

'Ox leather?'

'Yes, ox leather.'

'Are they warm enough for Mustang, sir? I hear it's very cold up there,' Thapa Sana, Thapa Maila *dai*'s youngest son, asked. He was drunk too and slurred his words.

'They are, *Bhai*. They are.' Jhalnath patted his boots. 'But these are windproof. Not waterproof but windproof, and that's what you need there. It's very windy up there. Dry and cold and windy.'

'Sir,' Ramesh spoke again. 'What do we need to get in the force as well?'

'Why? You want to be a cop too?'

'Yes,' Ramesh said. A few other boys also said yes.

'The same as usual, *Bhai*,' Jhalnath said. 'A wide chest, athletic legs, some education and someone you know in the police force. But I say don't be a cop. It's a lot of hard work for nothing. You never know where they'll send you either. I almost died during the 1990 protests.'

'Died? What happened?'

'You know the protests during the revolution?'

'Yes.'

'Well, I was lent to a station in Pokhara then. My first time in the city. We were standing on a street close to the dam. You know the Fewa Lake? Well, there is a big lake in the middle of Pokhara, and I was stationed close to its dam. I don't know what and how it happened, but suddenly a mob came down a street and started pelting stones at us. Soon, I got separated from my group and encircled by the mob. They kicked me until they thought I was dead and threw me in the lake. Luckily, the water woke me up. If it hadn't, I would have died. The lake saved me. That and knowing how to swim.'

The boys could not believe it.

'Really, *Bhai*,' Jhalnath said, taking a swig from his glass. 'Five of us were killed and put on display on a cart in Kathmandu for days, I swear. That's all we get. Stories. A lot of them. You know the salary. It's enough to just get your hand to your mouth. But stories, if they were money, I would be feeding this whole hamlet every single night. Kanchhi, you want to become a cop too?'

'No,' Kanchhi said.

'Why not?'

'Police are brutal,' she said.

'Brutal? Didn't you just hear the story? I told you we're the ones who get it all the time. Brutal.' Jhalnath shook his head and then looked at her. 'You are a little too short, anyway.'

The boys laughed.

'But what's height?' Jhalnath slapped the back of his constable. 'Just a number on a page. If you want to be six feet tall, we'll make you six feet tall.' He chuckled and emptied his glass. '*Ja*, it's done,' Jhalnath said.

'What are you doing here?' Laxmi asked, startling Kanchhi.

'Why? Are they looking for me?' Kanchhi asked back.

'No.'

'Oh. I was just listening to stories here. Was about to head back.'

'Laxmi *buhari*!' Jhalnath exclaimed and raised his left hand as if he was about to sing. 'Laxmi *buhari*. Our sister-in-law. Come, come, come join us.'

'*Am-ma-ma*, drunk men,' Laxmi said. 'Who is this passed out on the ground?'

'Sete,' Thapa Sana said. Sete was from a house in Harichaur.

'Sete? Is he old enough to drink?'

Nobody answered. Someone asked Jhalnath if a cop could choose where they got posted. Jhalnath said yes and no and proceeded to explain what he meant.

'Come with me,' Laxmi said to Kanchhi.

'Where?'

Laxmi had come out to pee as well. Kanchhi followed her back to the pissing field.

'There's a fair set up here,' Laxmi said when she saw the groups of teenagers and young people that had gathered there. 'This whole place is going to stink tomorrow.'

'A lot,' Kanchhi said.

Laxmi waded a little deep into the middle of a millet field and squatted. 'It's a beautiful moon, though,' she said.

It was. The moon was large and bright and hung low just over the mountains.

'Where's Basanta?' Kanchhi asked.

'Sleeping on *Ama*'s lap,' Laxmi said and walked back. 'Was that policeman bothering you?' she asked.

'No,' Kanchhi said.

'He's a smooth talker, isn't he?' Laxmi said. 'Watch out for him.'

On their way back, Jhalnath tried to stop them again, even walked up to them and begged them to stay. 'For a bit. Just for a bit,' he said, but Laxmi refused and Kanchhi, although she loved his stories, no longer had a good excuse to stay behind and listen to him.

'Killjoys,' Jhalnath said.

'Too drunk,' Laxmi said.

In Saili *didi*'s kitchen, Maiju asked them if there were still guests outside.

'Yes,' Kanchhi said.

'Let's go out and dance then,' Maiju said.

'Jaba rati taba budhi tati,' Saili *didi* said and everyone laughed. It's the dead of night and the woman wants it.

Nothing happened for the next five days. Kanchhi came down with a bout of common cold that quickly led to an ear infection, and she kept to herself, skipping school and sleeping all day, until she was forced to walk to the health post in Hatiya. There, she ran into Jhalnath again. He was in full police uniform this time – dark blue pants and a sky-blue shirt with a navy-blue sweater on top. He had heard about her ear infection and asked if it was getting any better. Kanchhi touched her infected ear, embarrassed that he knew. 'It's getting better,' she said.

'Good. Doctor *sa'ab*,' Jhalnath turned to the health assistant at the health post, 'treat her well, *hai*. She's one of our own.'

The doctor nodded and, after Jhalnath left, asked Kanchhi if they were related. Kanchhi said no. She was related to a constable who used to be at the same station, she said.

After this encounter, Kanchhi did not see Jhalnath for a while. First, because *Tihar* began right on the heels of the wedding and then the 1994 general election took place ten days later. *Tihar* that year was as special as *Dashain*. After years of not dancing, Kanchhi danced to two songs: '*Suna Suna Mayalu Jodi Ho*' from the movie

Kasam and '*Tiharai Ayo*' from *Sworga*. Both movies had come out that year, and both songs filled the air non-stop. In the first performance, Kanchhi was the lead female dancer and wore a set of *lehenga choli* for the first time. In the second, she was part of an ensemble. Together, her *Deusi-bhailo* troupe walked to eight hamlets that night, dancing at one or another Indian or British military family's house and raking in more than fifteen thousand rupees in *dakshina*. It was 3 a.m. when they all returned to Torikhola, completely exhausted.

After *Tihar*, there was the election – the second parliamentary election that Kanchhi had not realized was the second. 'When was the first?' she asked Bhime *dai* as they posted posters around the primary school. He told her, 'In 1991, after the 1990 protests.'

'Oh,' Kanchhi said. Somehow, she had not heard of it, even when she had taken part in the essay contest that *Gorkhapatra* had organized soon after the revolution.

'Who did you vote for then?' Kanchhi asked.

'The Nepali Congress,' Bhime *dai* said.

'Why?'

'Wouldn't you rather have a green tree that provides you shade than the red sun that bakes you?' The tree was the logo of the Nepali Congress, the sun that of the Communist Party of Nepal (United Marxist–Leninist).

Govinda sir had told her to always vote for the sun. The sun, he had said, was for the poor.

Jhalnath said she should always vote for the communists too, but mostly because the mob that had beat him up in Pokhara comprised students affiliated with the Nepali Congress. 'They will never get my vote,' he said. 'Even if they promise to raise my salary and pension, I won't vote for them. I'll take the raise and all, but I won't vote for them.'

Kanchhi looked at the teashop behind Jhalnath and at a group of students watching them. Jhalnath had stopped her as she was about to get on the bridge and head home.

'Are you going this way too?' Kanchhi asked.

'No,' he said. 'I actually came to say that I got you something from Kushma.' He had been lent to the city for the duration of the election. 'It was for someone else, but she did not like it. Now, I don't know what to do with it. Then, I thought of you. You can have it if you want.'

Kanchhi stared at him. He had a tic that she had not noticed before. A blinking tic.

'It's inside the police station,' Jhalnath continued. 'I can go and get it right now, or you can come over later and get it yourself. I can order you some tea too if you want. Why don't you come over now? I'll walk you up later.'

'I don't want it,' Kanchhi said and turned around to walk up.

'You don't even know what it is,' Jhalnath said.

'I don't want it.'

'Kanchhi—'

'I don't want it.'

Kanchhi ran across the bridge and up the mountain.

It was a *lungi*, dark brown in colour with long, snake-like patterns, made of polyester and therefore too slippery to be of any use to a village woman. He gave it to her the next day, or rather left it on her desk inside a black plastic bag. Kanchhi gave it to her classmate. 'Heartless woman,' Jhalnath said when he found out about it later.

'What am I going to do with a slippery *lungi* like that?' Kanchhi said. 'It won't stay in place. Don't you know we have to work in a *lungi*?'

'He said the girls these days love it,' Jhalnath said.

'Who said?'

'The man at the shop.'

'Maybe the women in the bazaar do. We don't. Give it to them.'

'Well, you already gave it to someone else.'

'Next time, I meant.'

The next time, he got her a big bar of chocolate. Cadbury Dairy Milk. To celebrate the end of ninth grade, he said. 'Congratulations.'

Kanchhi took the chocolate and kept the wrapper as a keepsake.

'*Ama*, are you scared of policemen?' Kanchhi asked Maiju one day while they were in the fields in Gairabari far above the temple, dumping manure.

'We used to be,' Maiju said.

'Why?'

'I don't know why. Everyone was, and so were we.'

'Maybe I should be a cop too.'

'If you want to. Be whatever you want to be.'

'No, I want to be a psychologist.'

'What's that?'

'Someone who understands minds, not brains. There's a difference.'

'*Eh*, *barai*. What are you going to do by trying to understand minds? You'll go mad yourself.'

'Who's going to go mad?' Jhalnath asked, surprising them both. 'Namaste, *Didi*,' he said to Maiju. Jhalnath was in a tracksuit this time. So was the constable who was at the party with him.

'*Oho*, namaste,' Maiju said.

'Fertilizing the fields, *Didi*?' Jhalnath asked.

'Yes, *Babu*,' Maiju said. 'How else are we to eat otherwise?'

'True, true. Life in the mountains is all about working in the fields, isn't it? It's the same with us too. You work in the fields, we work around them. Look at us patrolling the area.'

Maiju smiled.

'*La*, *la*, we'll let you work. How many more trips left?'

'Maybe two or three. Got to work until the sun sets,' Maiju said.

'True, true,' Jhalnath said and walked away. He did

not talk to Kanchhi at all, only glanced in her direction once or twice.

After the men turned around a corner, Maiju picked up a sickle and wondered why they were there.

A few days later, he showed up again. This time in Waling. Kanchhi was standing at the stationery shop, poring over the contents inside a glass cabinet when he threw a magazine on top of it and blocked her view. 'What a—' she was about to say when she saw him, grinning from ear to ear.

'How much is the magazine, *Dai*?' Jhalnath asked the shopkeeper.

'It's written right here,' Kanchhi said, pointing at a pencil scribbling on the cover. 'Seven rupees.'

Jhalnath smiled and, after paying for it, gave her the magazine. *Yuwamanch*. The cover page had three pictures of a young woman in karate attire. Two of them were identical. In those pictures, the woman wore two medals, one gold, one silver, and held a giant silver cup in front of her.

'I'll be at the highway. Come find me there,' Jhalnath said.

'Where?'

'At the highway.'

'No, I can't. *Ama* won't let me.'

'I don't care. You have to be there,' Jhalnath said and, without letting Kanchhi speak further, left.

At Saru *didi*'s brother-in-law's as usual, Maiju was taking her pouch out to pay the last year's due amount.

'What did you get?' she asked Kanchhi. Kanchhi showed her the magazine.

'Do you need anything here?' Maiju asked.

Kanchhi shook her head. She could not figure out how and when she should ask Maiju about seeing the bazaar by herself. It was just her, Maiju and Saili *didi* then. Tara *bhauju* had not joined them. She was pregnant.

'Are we going to walk around the bazaar later?' she asked.

'I can't,' Saili *didi* said. 'I'm too tired.'

'We don't need to see the bazaar every time we come here. It's the same as always,' Maiju said.

'No, I want to see it,' Kanchhi said. 'I'll go by myself then.'

'No, not by yourself,' Maiju said.

'Just to the highway and back.'

'No,' Maiju repeated, but then something made her change her mind. 'Okay, don't go too far. Only to the highway and back. Be careful of the buses. Also, buy a towel if you find one. A cheap but good one.'

'Okay,' Kanchhi said.

'Don't spend money on anything else.'

'Okay, okay.' Kanchhi said and, after taking the money for the towel, left.

At the highway, Kanchhi stopped at the shuttered store

on whose steps she had sat with Bipana *bhauju* two years earlier. Jhalnath whistled from its second-floor balcony. The shuttered store, no longer shuttered, turned out to be a restaurant with seating spaces on the first and second floors. Kanchhi went through a narrow hallway and climbed up a staircase. At a plastic table on the balcony, Jhalnath was pouring himself a glass of beer.

'Want some?' he asked.

Kanchhi shook her head.

'Want to eat then? They make good chowmein here.'

Kanchhi looked at the menu and nodded. This restaurant looked more upscale than the nameless one she and Maiju frequented. Soon, a little boy came to pick up their order, and Jhalnath ordered chowmein for her.

'Veg or—?' the boy asked.

'Veg,' Kanchhi said.

'Why veg?' Jhalnath asked. 'Order egg or chicken. Do you eat buff?'

'No,' Kanchhi said. 'Veg is good.'

'Veg,' Jhalnath told the boy. 'Nothing for me.'

When the boy left, Jhalnath asked her if she had ever tasted buff.

'No,' Kanchhi said.

'It's good,' he said. 'Very chewy.'

'Aren't you going to eat anything?' Kanchhi asked.

'No, I'd had a big plate of *dal-bhat* before I saw you.'

'How did you know I was going to be here?'

'I know.'

'How?'

'I have spies everywhere, that's how.'

Kanchhi laughed.

'I'm serious,' he said.

'I mean, really. How did you know?'

Jhalnath didn't say, only smiled and lit a cigarette.

'You smoke too?' Kanchhi asked.

'Too?'

'Every man seems to smoke these days.'

'I only smoke sometimes,' Jhalnath said. 'It feels nice, especially after a meal or with a beer.'

'I have to go back early,' Kanchhi said.

'The food isn't even here.'

'I know. I meant later. I'm just saying I can't stay for too long.'

'I know. I'll walk you back.'

'No.'

'Let me walk you back. Your *ama* will be happy that you were with me. Safe with someone she knows.'

'Safe?' Kanchhi said and chuckled.

'Yes,' Jhalnath said. 'Safe with someone more mature and reliable.'

Kanchhi shook her head. Below, a small crowd had gathered by the highway and she shifted from its view.

'Don't worry,' Jhalnath said. 'I know them all. They won't say a word.'

'You know them all?'

'No.' Jhalnath laughed. 'You worry too much.'

A little later, her order arrived. Soy-sauce-brown noodles with sprinklings of chickpeas and strips of carrots and cabbage. Jhalnath told her to use ketchup. Kanchhi squirted some and cleaned up the plate.

'*Hantakali*,' he said and then told her that she had a habit of looking down too much. But he liked it. 'No time for bullshit, huh?' he said.

Afterwards, he walked her out and, from a shop by the main street, bought her the towel that Maiju had asked for. A short but thick blue towel, with white stripes at the ends. 'The best one,' he said. 'Very good at drying off.'

He bought one more. 'For you,' he said. 'Only for you.'

24

ONCE TENTH GRADE BEGAN, KANCHHI STARTED TO see Jhalnath every day. He waited for her at the teashop at first, then at the bridge and then at the wooded slopes above. Each time, she had to pretend that she did not see him and keep on walking. He would catch up a few minutes later and ask her if he could walk along with her. 'Sure,' she would say as to anyone from her hamlet, and he would walk alongside her up until a *chautara* in the middle of the woods. There, they would sit and talk for a bit while his constable friend, who always tagged along, would wander around, giving them space. Jhalnath did most of the talking. He told her that he was from a hamlet in Baglung called Gahate Bari, but unlike Torikhola, his village still grew horse gram and was still famous for it. He also told her that his father was dead. Died when he was only eight. 'Feverish one day and dead the next,' he said. Kanchhi asked him if he was there at the funeral. 'Yes,' he said. 'But it's hard to watch a body burn. Things change in you afterwards.'

As time went on, Jhalnath began to walk Kanchhi

further and further up, eventually going beyond the wooded slopes to a Bahun hamlet nearby. There, he would drop her off by Govinda sir's house. That was usually his limit. He never crossed it, except once when he took her to his friend's house in a Magar settlement past the Bahun one. His friend, a family man with a wife and three kids, was visibly confused at seeing Kanchhi with two adult men, but he brought her a stool to sit on and then a glass of tea his wife had prepared. The tea had both salt and sugar in it. Kanchhi wondered if Magars drank tea that way.

'Do you drink tea that way?' Jhalnath asked.

'No,' Kanchhi said.

'Why would we then, *Kala*? Huh? Why would we?'

Kala was her nickname for that day. Each time they met, he had new names for her – *goriya*, *kali*, *nakkali*, *dalli*, *chuchchi*, *chhuchchhi*, *phuchchi*, *naramri*, *debri*, *deri*. Kanchhi liked it. She called him nothing. Never had to call him.

It was in April that he first brought up sex. When the sun was fierce and the forest floor was covered in dust and dry leaves. He did not talk about doing it, just mentioned it, tested the waters first.

'Have you heard of Osho?' he asked. They were at the *chautara* as usual but much earlier in the day, around noon, because classes let out early in summer from mid-March to mid-June.

'No,' Kanchhi said.

'He's a big *yogi*,' Jhalnath said. 'Has a big meditation ashram in Kathmandu. We should go there someday. It's a big, beautiful place in the middle of a forest like this. I went there once. They were holding a devotional gathering. It was very emotional. A lot of people were crying.'

'Why?' Kanchhi asked.

'Because he moves them. His philosophy, I mean. You know what he says?'

'What?'

'He says, "Do whatever you want. Indulge yourself, indulge your senses. You want to drink liquor, drink all you want. You want to smoke *ganja*, smoke away. You want to have sex, go ahead. Let yourself free, and when you realize that pleasure does not lead you to freedom, come back and meditate. You'll enter the state of *samadhi* then."'

'*Samadhi*?'

'Yeah, a state of bliss, *nirvana*, *moksha*.'

'Really? How?'

'I don't know how. He's unconventional. Says sex is the best form of meditation.'

He said the word 'sex' in English. Both times.

A few days later, he touched her. Came up from behind and surprised her with a pat on her head. A little too hard of a pat. He had never touched her until then, not even accidentally. Kanchhi massaged the spot he had patted her and avoided him for two days. Then, he was at her house. On the eve of the Nepali New Year.

It was a warm night. A gentle breeze occasionally drifted in from the open window and the open door. Kanchhi, lying on her bed on her back, was reading the English grammar book that Dhan *didi* had given her. At the end was a glossary, with both the pronunciations and meanings of English words written in Nepali. Kanchhi was going through the words one by one, ticking those she wanted to remember – affection: *sneha*; amoebic dysentery: *aangu parnu*; conflagration: *dadhelo*; disregard: *bewasta*; emotion: *bhawana*; famine: *anikal*... She was at g for grudge: *ris* when she heard a knock on the window. At first, it sounded as if the breeze had blown off a seed and the seed had landed against a bar on the window.

Kanchhi sat up and listened closely.

Another knock came a few seconds later. It could have been a seed, but it was not the wind. Kanchhi grabbed the lamp and walked to the window. On the sill was nothing, but in the distance, beyond the field and the darkness, was a cigarette glow, and in that faint cigarette glow, a face. Jhalnath's. Just the tip of the nose and a thin line of mustache, but his.

Kanchhi slipped into a *lungi* and tiptoed out. The night was dense, darker than she had thought, and heavier. Kanchhi glanced at Maiju's door to see if the lamp in her room was still burning. It was not. She hurried to the crossroads, where Jhalnath, squatting low on the ground as if that would help him avoid detection, was waiting for her. When she got near, he stood up and told her to follow him. He was drunk and by himself.

He took her where she thought he would – to the abandoned house past Saru *didi*'s. The door was open, and he led her right through it up to the attic. There, when he finally turned on the flashlight that he had been carrying with him all along, Kanchhi focused on the state of the attic's abandonment – bugs and spiders, chipped floor and walls, tattered rags and random twigs and a few frayed, decaying mats. Jhalnath picked one of the mats up and gave it a shake. Nothing but dust and must flew out of it. Then, he spread it next to a wall and sat down, holding out a hand for Kanchhi as if she were on a field above.

Kanchhi took it and sat next to him. His hand was soft unlike Thirman's, the mat was damp, and the floor cool. Kanchhi reached for a twig in front of her and began snapping it into pieces.

'Kanchhi,' Jhalnath murmured.

Kanchhi did not look up at him. Jhalnath turned off the light and then turned it back on. It cast a weak, orange light and lit up only a tiny cone of space between them.

'Kanchhi,' Jhalnath murmured again. This time, Kanchhi turned her face towards him. He put her hand on the nape of her neck and leaned in.

25

November 13, 2005

BACK IN THE HOUSE, MAIJU SPREADS THE MILLET fingers plucked that morning and the day before out in the yard and lets them dry. She also brings the rice bean shrubs down to the yard. The shrubs are light and brittle, and they crackle when dropped. She will thresh the pods later that afternoon, Maiju tells herself.

This season has been good to her. The millet already covers two mats worth of space in the yard. There is more to harvest. And the grains are a beautiful brown, hanging on to the ear-heads like bees in a hive. Maiju looks up at the sky to make sure that it will not rain. It won't. The sky is as clear as a marble. Maiju gathers her *patuka* around her and tightens it. She does the same with a shawl around her head.

From the shed, the buffalo bellows. Maiju picks up a bundle of freshly cut millet stalks and walks towards the shed. Half of it is for the buffalo. It likes the green stalks and begins to chew them. The other half is for the goat, still in its pen on the side of the shed. Maiju lets it out and ties it to a stake next to the buffalo. The chickens too are in the shed, in the back, resting by the slope, grooming themselves. They follow Maiju back to the house. Maiju gets a handful of ground corn kernels from the kitchen and throws them in the yard. She saves a little for the sick chick inside the coop. The chick is still the same, still motionless, and now crouching down, unexcited by Maiju or the corn. If it does not walk by late afternoon, Maiju will have to gift it to the little boys.

'Kaki, eh, Kaki,' someone calls her.

Maiju turns around. A group of young men steps into the yard, banging a stick against an old aluminium plate. They are here to ask for money for the hamlet youth club. One of them has just been back from Waling and passes Maiju a steel glass that she had ordered. From the change he returns, Maiju donates twenty rupees to the club. The boys do not fuss about it. She is an 'old' woman who lives by herself.

As they leave, the school bell rings.

'Ka'lai ekkan 'ka'
'Ka'lai kannani 'ka'
'Ka'lai bayematra 'ki'
'Ka'lai daine 'kee'

('Ka' by itself is /k/
'Ka' with a macron is /kā/
'Ka' with /i/ is /ki/
'Ka' with /i:/ is /ki:/)

26

AFTER THAT NIGHT, JHALNATH CAME OVER EVERY other night, threw a pebble on Kanchhi's window and she tiptoed out, following him to different locations, first back to the abandoned house. She brought a *chadar* with her this time, and they fucked on top of it on the ground floor. Two nights later, they stopped at the abandoned shed, which they realized was not really abandoned. There was a pair of oxen at the bottom, and the loft upstairs was full of straws. The straws made the rendezvous noisier but also more comfortable. They spread them thick to create some bedding, and he finished on them. The next meet was outside, in the other direction, on a small field below Chiuridanda, a field that was yet to be ploughed. Oddly enough, Kanchhi felt more secure out in the open. If anyone saw them, she thought, she would run away before she could be recognized, and she would run away from Torikhola, towards another hamlet. On the fifth night, Maiju heard the pebble on the window.

'Kanchhi,' she shouted from her room. 'What's that sound? Go check on it.'

'What sound?' Kanchhi said, opening her door.

'I don't know. Go check on it. Seems like the buffalo is in distress. Shine some light around and holler. If it's a leopard, it will run away.'

The buffalo had just given birth, and Maiju thought a leopard had come for the calf. The sound, she assumed, was the buffalo knocking its horn against a stake.

Of course, there was no leopard. Kanchhi took her time looking for a flashlight and its battery and then walked out to the shed. There, the mother buffalo was up and standing, chewing on dried straws. The calf was safe in the goat room, along with the goat. Kanchhi smiled at the mother buffalo and shouted to Maiju that there was nothing to worry about. Maiju, from her room next to the shed, shouted back, 'Bolt your door tight.'

Kanchhi walked back and past her own room to the field where Jhalnath was waiting.

'I can't come out tonight,' she said. '*Ama*'s still awake.'

'She's not going to get up again,' Jhalnath told her.

'How do you know?'

'Nine o'clock and everyone in every hamlet falls asleep.'

'No, she's still up. Didn't you hear her? I can't come out tonight.'

'Go back in then. I'll finish this cigarette and go,' Jhalnath said.

Kanchhi didn't move.

'I said go,' Jhalnath said a little loudly.

'Shh,' Kanchhi said.

Jhalnath exhaled, and if it were not dark, Kanchhi would have seen him pouting like a sullen child. He did that sometimes, and back then, she found it endearing.

'All right, you can come in,' she said. 'But no noise.'

He stood where he was.

'Ready?' Kanchhi asked.

'Ready.'

'Take off your boots first.'

'What? No.'

'You have to take them off. I'm not risking anything.'

'They won't make any sound.'

'They will. And she will hear it.'

'No, she won't.'

'Yes, she will. You're not coming in otherwise.'

Jhalnath took a long puff and waited. When he realized that she was serious, 'All right,' he said.

'Okay, I'll go in first. You walk in a few minutes later,' Kanchhi said and walked back to her room.

A little later, Jhalnath snuck in with stinking feet. That explained why he was hesitant to take off his boots.

'Chhi,' Kanchhi said.

Jhalnath suppressed a laugh. Kanchhi shushed him.

'I've tried everything. Nothing works,' he whispered and then dropped the boots by the door. The door, double-panelled, creaked when he shut it.

'Put the bar across too,' Kanchhi said.

'Anything else, madam?' he asked.

'No,' Kanchhi said and hung a *chadar* across the window, covering it like a curtain. Jhalnath sat on the bed and took off his backpack. Inside was a bottle, a two-litre Coca-Cola bottle filled with millet liquor. He opened the cap and sniffed it, then offered it to her. Kanchhi, without any hesitation, took it. This was the first night in over a week that she had felt calm and unafraid, and she wanted to celebrate. Ironically, the reason, of all the reasons, was his being inside her room. Out in the abandoned house or on open fields, Kanchhi had to constantly worry about the whole hamlet running into them. Here, it was just Maiju, and Maiju, she thought, she could handle.

Soon, they both got drunk and fucked twice as quietly as they could. The bed took it well, surprisingly well. Did not creak at all. In between and at the end, Jhalnath lit a cigarette. It was clear that he did not just smoke sometimes.

'Is it fun smoking?' Kanchhi asked.

'Fun? Nobody smokes for fun,' Jhalnath said.

'Why smoke then?'

'Addiction.' Jhalnath got off the bed and put on his pants. Track pants with three long lines that ran vertically along the length on the sides. He hated his legs. Said they were too skinny. But he was proud of his upper body. It was big, broad and taut.

Jhalnath threw on his T-shirt and started tying his boots.

'I'll come again in a few days,' he said.

'When?'

'Friday?' Jhalnath counted the days in his fingers. 'Yes, Friday.'

'Should we meet only on Fridays from now on?' Kanchhi asked.

'Why? You don't want to see me anymore?'

'No, I'm just saying I'm in tenth grade now. I don't want to stay up too late every night.'

Jhalnath put on the track jacket and reached for his backpack. 'That's true,' he said. 'How about Tuesdays and Fridays? I'll leave early on Tuesdays, I promise.'

'Will you?'

'I will. I promise.'

Kanchhi chewed on her thumbnail and thought about it for a second. 'Okay, then,' she said.

'Keep this under your bed,' Jhalnath said and gave her the Coca-Cola bottle of liquor, half finished. Before leaving, he kissed her on the forehead.

He said he used to come first in class too but then, one day, one of his uncles burnt his books and he could not sit for the ninth-grade exams. He had to drop out.

'Why did they burn your books?' Kanchhi asked.

'Envy,' he said. 'They wanted me weak, wanted me unable to mount any legal fights when it came to property rights someday.'

'Did you ever get your share of the property then?'

'No, not yet, but I'll get it soon. Don't worry.'

He then told her of the fields he would inherit one day: rows and rows of them by a creek, all of them rice fields. He would also inherit a whole jungle in the east, he said, and since Kanchhi loved wheat bread, he would try to get hold of a few fields just for that. The house, he said, his uncles could keep it. He would build her a new one. As for work, if she wanted to, she could teach at a local school there. He had connections, he said.

'What makes you think I want to marry you?' Kanchhi asked.

'You don't have to. If you want to go to college instead, we can do that too. Wherever you want. Intermediate, bachelor's, master's, whatever you want. I'll pay for it.'

'They all say that.'

'Who says that?'

'Everyone.'

'Well, don't listen to them.'

Kanchhi laughed.

—

Sex was interesting. Definitely. A little bit of pain, a little bit of pleasure and a whole lot of awkward, self-conscious moments. Ultimately, though, an act of penetration, and therefore just as uninteresting. It was the stories in the aftermath that Kanchhi found better. The world of men astonished her, and their stories mesmerised her. Here was a man from Baglung who had at first tried to be in the British army but failed because his chest was not wide enough, who had then travelled to Gorakhpur in India to enlist in the Indian army but his bad luck – they were not open for recruitment. It would be the Nepal army then, he thought, and stood in line outside the gates of an army barracks in Pokhara, but his hair then was too long, and an army man disqualified him on the spot. The only upside to all of this, he said, was that by the time he made the rounds for the Nepal police, he knew what they wanted. It still cost him a jar of ghee and ten thousand rupees, but he got in.

'Didn't you want to be someone else?' Kanchhi asked.

'No,' he said. All his uncles were in the Indian army and his grandfather had been in the British. 'He died in Malaysia,' he said. 'We think he did, anyway, unless he had another family there and just stayed behind. He never came back.'

'What about you?'

'What about me?'

'Aren't you married?'

'No.'

'How come?'

'I don't know. Never did.'

Kanchhi did not believe him.

Jhalnath swore on his life and then on Kanchhi's, placing his hand on her head.

'On my mother's life too,' he said, pinching his neck

with his fingers. 'I'm just one of those men who never bothered to get married.'

'Don't worry,' Kanchhi said. 'I'm not trying to get married to you and lay a claim on your property.'

'You already have – on this heart at least.'

Kanchhi laughed.

'Marry me, Kanchhi, and I'll keep you happy,' Jhalnath said.

'No.'

'Why not?'

'I need to go to Pokhara first.'

'So? I can take you there.'

'I need to get a job there.'

'I can get you one. I know a lot of people there.'

Kanchhi paused and thought about it for a second.

'No, I need to look after my *ama*,' she said.

'Let me help.'

'No.'

'I'll get transferred to Pokhara then.'

'No.'

'You say "no" a lot.'

'No, I don't.'

'See.'

Kanchhi smiled.

'Well, we're almost like a married couple, anyway,' Jhalnath said.

'What do you mean?'

'You know with sex and all.'

'That means nothing.'

'*Nisthuri bhunti.*' A heartless little one.

Two months passed that way. Jhalnath came over twice a week, on Tuesdays and Fridays, and they fucked, they talked, and he walked down at around midnight. The rendezvous in the *chautara* stopped. If they saw each other during the daytime, they avoided eye contact, did not acknowledge each other. On the days he would come over, Kanchhi bathed, usually right after school, but if the chores kept her busy, she did so after dark, even if the water felt cold as ice and Maiju shrieked that it might give her pneumonia. There would be a certain spright to her gait then. A twang of excitement and fear. At around nine, Maiju would go to bed, and soon afterwards, Jhalnath would come in, without knocking. Since that night when Maiju heard the pebble, they had put up another communication system in place. If Kanchhi placed a lamp on the window, he could come in. If not, he would have to wait. Maybe she was still in the kitchen, maybe someone was over, or maybe Maiju simply was not in bed yet. Almost always, he drank. On some Fridays, she joined him as well. When drunk, they would play fight – she tore one of his vests once – and then fuck, usually twice. Once, when he was not able to visit one week, they did it seven times. Kanchhi came down with a urinary tract infection. The next day, Jhalnath walked to the only medical store in the area, on the way to Setibeni, and got her an alkalizing solution. Almost always, he came outside her, on her stomach, and she wiped it off with a petticoat. Later, he bought her a bandana. One Friday, though, he came inside her. Said it was too good, he could not help it. But after Kanchhi began to cry, he walked to Waling the next day and bought her Gulaf birth control pills. Swallow twenty-one of them right away, he said. She did. In the middle of the night, hours later, Kanchhi hunched over the yard and threw up. Maiju thought it was from too much buttermilk.

One night, after they had fucked and he had come, Jhalnath pulled her close to his chest and confessed that he did not understand why he felt the way he did. 'Huh, Kanchhi, why do I feel so deeply about you?'

'I don't know,' Kanchhi said.

'Don't you feel that way?'

'No.'

'Heartless woman,' he said and then kissed her, felt her body up and down, and when he reached her crotch, told her it was his. 'Whose is it?'

'Yours,' Kanchhi said.

'If I see you with someone else, I'll kill him,' he said.

Kanchhi laughed.

'For real,' he stressed, and when Kanchhi turned her body around and began to doodle on the wall, he asked her if she was not going to ask him the same.

'Ask what?'

'About my, you know.'

'Oh.' Kanchhi giggled. 'Whose is it?'

'Yours.'

'Yeah, right.'

'It is,' he said and kissed her forehead tenderly.. 'Only yours, *Kala*.'

Kanchhi smiled. He had fallen in love.

27

BY JULY, THE WHOLE MOUNTAIN WAS MATING. Insects fluttered in pairs, attached from end to end. Flies buzzed around and climbed on top of each other. Frogs croaked, mynahs cleared their throats and chirped, and jackfruits swelled like balloons. Everything in nature was mating and, if not mating, reproducing. Kanchhi's kitchen trellis, for instance, sprouted long, green vines with white and yellow flowers, and in the fields, the corn shot up tall with tassels and silk and cobs. That monsoon, Tara *bhauju* too gave birth. A son. And the next morning, Maiju asked Kanchhi who it was that was in her room the night before.

'What?' Kanchhi asked.

'Don't pretend you don't know what I'm talking about. I heard a man's voice in your room last night.'

'No, you didn't. Who told you they did?'

Maiju did not say anything. She was tired from the long night at Saili *didi*'s house and put Kanchhi's tea on the porch.

'Don't go around believing what other people say,'

Kanchhi said. 'You know how they are. They'll say anything.'

Three nights later, Kanchhi told Jhalnath what Maiju had said.

'Don't worry,' Jhalnath said, peeking out of the window. The corn plants were thick and high. If anyone was right outside the window, they would have heard them as well.

'No one's heard us,' Jhalnath said. 'She was just trying to see how you'd react.'

'Why would she do that?'

'That's just how people are.'

'Maybe you shouldn't come up for a while.'

'Don't be scared.'

'No, I mean it.'

'Well, I'll be gone in a few months, anyway.' Jhalnath sat on the bed. 'You'll then wish I'd come over every day.'

'Are you really leaving then?'

Jhalnath had told her that he was in Bagar for only a year and that he would have to go back to Mustang after *Dashain*.

'Yes, I told you,' Jhalnath said. 'It's only a ruse. This transfer. Mustang is a coveted place, you see. I can't be the only one who gets to be posted there for years. So, they lent me to this place for a while. But I can extend my stay here if you want me to. Do you want me to?'

'No,' Kanchhi said.

'Or better yet, you can come up to Mustang. They

have a lot of apples there. Apples and *jhwain khatte* liquor and—'

'And your wife who will come and grab me by my hair.'

'I told you I'm not married.'

'I don't believe you.'

'What are you doing with a married man then?'

Jhalnath did stop coming up for a while, but it was more the monsoon that made him do so than the chatter about them. It rained almost every day now, usually in the afternoon, but sometimes, all throughout the day and night. The paths were never dry then, but wet and slippery and too risky to walk up and down for hours, especially after dark. One wrong step and Jhalnath could tumble to his death or, worse, be paralysed. He spent the rest of the month down in Bagar then and Kanchhi up in Torikhola, harvesting corn and getting ready to plant millet.

One day, Tara *bhauju* came over, furious that someone had flattened her grass. Both Maiju and Kanchhi were in the yard, shucking corn.

'Grass?' Maiju asked.

'Yes, the grass. In the shed. Thought I'd move the oxen up to give them more space, but it's been nothing but a headache ever since I did that.'

It turned out that the two oxen in the abandoned shed belonged to Tara *bhauju*.

'When did you move them up?' Kanchhi asked.

Tara *bhauju* did not answer. She reached for a corn and began to husk it. 'First, the straws and now the grass. Couldn't they find another place to perform their act? Who wants to touch the grass with their shit all over it?'

'Are you sure it's the lovers?' Maiju asked. 'Maybe a dog slept on it.'

'It's not a dog. I know. Kanchhi, it's not you, is it?'

'What? No?'

'Do you have a boy?'

'No.'

'If you do, call him inside your room, okay? Don't go about rolling on somebody else's hard work. You know it's not easy to get grass and make straws.'

'I know,' Kanchhi said.

When they met again in mid-August, Kanchhi told Jhalnath what Tara *bhauju* had said. 'There's another couple loose in the village then,' was his response. 'Imagine running into them,' he said. 'But this is all good. Four of us makes it more confusing for them.'

It did not. The floodgates had opened. Every day, one woman or another, one man or another, began to come over and talk to Maiju about lovers on the loose.

Did you hear this?

Did you hear that?

How old is Kanchhi again?

Sixteen? That's an age there. An age to get married.

I know a young man who just got into the Indian army. Should I begin the conversation?

There's this other man – he isn't very educated, but he's healthy and can always find work and keep her alive.

What about the son of this woman I know in Tindhara? His father abandoned him too, but he's very industrious. Started a tangerine orchard all by himself.

One evening, while making dinner, Maiju buried her face in her *lungi* and cried.

'What's wrong?' Kanchhi asked. 'Why are you crying?'

Maiju did not say anything. She stayed bent into her *lungi*, sniffling, looking up only to throw some corn stalks into the fire.

'She'll talk,' Jhalnath said. 'Mothers are like that. You focus on your studies.'

By then, the schedule for the SLC preliminary exams had gone up. They would take place right after *Tihar*, in the last week of October. Jhalnath bought Kanchhi guess papers and past question sheets.

'Ready?' Jhalnath asked.

'For what?' Kanchhi asked.

'To top the board. I'll get you a wristwatch if you do,' Jhalnath said.

'Why don't you just get me one? I can't do that.'

'You'll have to wait then,' Jhalnath said and shone his flashlight around her room. Lately, Kanchhi had not been re-claying the walls or the floor as often as she used to, and cracks had begun to appear in the mud plaster. Jhalnath took a chip off of the wall and threw it on the floor. Then, he looked inside the alcove – Kanchhi's clothes, his watch, the liquor bottle and the ink bottle lamp.

'You're very organized. I like that,' Jhalnath said and stood on the bed, shining light on stacks of old textbooks and notebooks that were on top of the wall below the roof. That was where Kanchhi also kept her stash of *Tatyakatha*.

'*Tatyakatha*?' Jhalnath laughed. 'I didn't know you read them.'

He took one and flipped through the pages.

'I used to. I liked the crime stories there,' Kanchhi said. 'They taught me a lot.'

'Yeah? Like what?'

'Like abortion is illegal in this country.'

Jhalnath chuckled. 'Only to those who can't afford it,' he said.

'What do you mean?'

'I mean everyone in Pokhara and Kathmandu does it. It's nothing. You just gotta have some money.'

'How much?'

'Five to six thousand.'

'That's a lot of money,' Kanchhi said. The stories in Tatyakatha had never talked about money.

'I had to once take a senior officer's girlfriend to get it done,' Jhalnath said. 'Behind some hospital in Pokhara. She was young like you. Was sitting for her SLC exams as well.'

Kanchhi thought about asking where in Pokhara but kept quiet.

'Anyway,' Jhalnath said, putting the magazine back on top of the wall and rummaging through the rest of the stash. 'You know the stories aren't true, right?'

'They're not?' Kanchhi said.

'No, it's all fiction.'

'No, it's not.'

'Yes, it is. Some cops love it too. I don't know why. All it does is talk about sex and crime. It's written for unemployed men. You shouldn't read it.'

Jhalnath picked up another magazine. *Yuwamanch* – the one he had bought for her in Waling.

'You still have this?' he asked and opened it. Tucked in between the pages were the postcards Kanchhi had picked up in Bayakhola. 'Do you know who they are?'

Kanchhi did not.

'Sridevi, Divya Bharti, Raveena Tandon – all Hindi movie heroines. Do you know what Bombay means?'

'They aren't mine,' Kanchhi said.

'Whose are they then?'

Kanchhi shrugged.

Jhalnath put the magazine and the postcards back on top of the wall and asked again, 'Do you know what Bombay means?'

'No.'

'Beware of many boys around you,' Jhalnath said in English.

'What?'

'Beware of many boys around you,' he said in Nepali. 'Guess why?'

'Why?'

'Because they'll take you to Bombay and sell you.'

'No, they won't.'

'Yes, they will.'

'What about you?'

'What about me?'

'You're a boy too.'

'I'm not a boy.'

'You're not?'

'I'm a cop.'

'And cops are gods?'

'This one is.'

Kanchhi laughed. Jhalnath sat down and turned off the flashlight.

The next morning, he overslept.

'*Oye*, Kanchhi, don't you have to go to school?' Maiju's voice woke her up.

Immediately, Kanchhi realized what had gone wrong. On her left, with his head next to the alcove, was Jhalnath, blinking his eyes open.

'Don't panic,' he said, reaching for his watch. It must have been past six because slivers of sunlight filtered in through the slits on the door.

Maiju called again.

'Up, up, I'm up,' Kanchhi said and got into her *lungi*. Jhalnath too got off the bed and took his clothes off the rope.

'When you leave, close the door behind you,' he whispered. 'Don't bolt it, just shut it closed. Don't let anyone in.'

'But—'

'Get me a mat, and I'll hide under the bed. Let me out when no one's around.'

'What if she's here all morning?'

'Then, I'll have to stay here all morning.'

'No—'

'Does she ever come in here by herself?'

'No.'

'Then, don't panic. Just don't let anyone in.'

Kanchhi took the *chadar* off the window and threw it around her. Outside, the air was crisp and chilly. As usual, Maiju had left a glass of tea on the porch. Kanchhi picked it up and took a sip.

'Get ready to get some grass before school,' Maiju said, leaning an empty *doko* against the porch. 'Tara will be here soon.'

'Not now, I'm still waking up,' Kanchhi said.

'Who told you to sleep until this late?'

Kanchhi yawned loudly. Maiju walked to the sink and started to pour water out of a large basin into a small bucket. The latrine bucket.

'Is that for me or you?' Kanchhi asked.

'Do you have to go?'

'Not now.'

'It's for me then,' Maiju said.

Kanchhi stretched her arms and yawned one more time. Maiju lifted the bucket and put it down in the yard. Then, she walked to the porch and slipped into her flip-flops.

'Take Tara to the fields in Gairabari,' Maiju said. 'Let her get as much grass as she wants. Saili *didi* helped a lot with planting millet this season.'

'Okay,' Kanchhi said.

'Be careful, though. The paths must still be slippery.'

'Okay.'

Maiju walked back to the bucket and lifted it again. Some of the water spilled on to the yard and wetted the floor. Maiju ignored it. She scrunched up her *lungi* and descended a set of stairs to the field below. Kanchhi walked to the sink as if to wash her face and watched Maiju from there. Maiju had now reached the manure heap and was walking past it to another set of stairs. The latrine was right below, its roof made of branches and leaves visible to Kanchhi from where she was. When Maiju disappeared behind it, Kanchhi checked to see whether Tara *bhauju* had left Saili *didi*'s house. She had not.

Kanchhi bolted to her room and shouted, 'Out, out,' as fast as she could without being loud. Jhalnath was on the bed, about to doze off.

'Where did she go?' he whispered.

'Down to the latrine. You have to go now. She doesn't take long.'

'Are you sure?' Jhalnath got up and threw on his backpack.

'Yes, yes. Now. You have to go now.'

Kanchhi opened the door and walked back out. There was no sign of Maiju below the fields, no sign of Tara *bhauju* on the paths and no Thapa Nani *didi* or her family up above her. Kanchhi ran past the tangerines and looked down at Saili *didi*'s house one more time just to be surer. Clear.

Kanchhi signalled Jhalnath to come out. Jhalnath tiptoed up until the crossroads and then sprinted towards Saru *didi*'s house. The fields this time were covered in millet, and they were too short to hide him.

The first person he said he saw was Saru *didi*. She was out in her yard, throwing water out of a pot. They talked briefly. He said he was not worried about her. She was a Magar too. But the second person he ran into was Tara *bhauju* on her way back from the spring on that side of the hamlet. And her, he was not so sure about. Jhalnath said he told her he was walking down from Balakot after spending the night at the dwelling of a distant relative. Tara *bhauju* must not have believed him because, on their way to Gairabari later, she talked about him with Kanchhi.

'I'm sure he was in this hamlet,' Tara *bhauju* said.

'How do you know? He could have been walking down from Balakot like he said,' Kanchhi said.

'No. He looked like he'd just woken up,' Tara *bhauju* said.

'Maybe he got drunk and spent the night passed out somewhere around.'

'That might be true.' Tara *bhauju* thought about it for a second. 'But I doubt it,' she added. 'Thapa Nani *didi* says she's been seeing a light at the top of the woods every night.'

'Every night?' Kanchhi asked.

'Yeah, every night around midnight.'

'What is she doing up in the middle of the night?'

'Maybe she's a witch.' Tara *bhauju* laughed.

That same evening, Saili *didi* came up to Kanchhi and told her that cops could not be trusted. 'They have wives wherever they go,' she said. And when *Dashain* came and went, but Jhalnath was still in Bagar, she added, 'Don't squander your future away, Kanchhi. You are someone who can go to Pokhara, study further and make something of your life.'

'Why do you want to marry a Magar man, anyway?' Ramesh's mother said. 'You know how different they are?'

'This is what happens when you have a house without any men,' Bir Bahadur *dai* said.

A few days later, Maiju woke up in the middle of the night and began grinding corn right outside Kanchhi's room.

'I did everything I could,' she said. 'They said "sit" and I sat. They said "stand up," and I stood up. "Get going" and I got going, and still, I'm the one who never gets to be happy. Where did I go wrong that I'm being punished like this, huh? Where did I go wrong? First, the husband leaves, and now, the daughter wants to be kicked out.'

By then, Kanchhi was up and aware of why Maiju was babbling. Jhalnath, sitting upright and looking at his watch, had slept beyond midnight once again.

Kanchhi poked his arm.

'Go back to sleep,' he whispered.

'What time is it?' Kanchhi whispered too. There was no light coming in this time, only the sound of Maiju grinding corn and now talking about honour and reputation.

'Three,' Jhalnath answered.

Kanchhi lay back down and wondered how Maiju knew Jhalnath was in her room. Did he snore? Did he talk in his sleep?

'*Ama*,' Kanchhi shouted. 'What are you doing this late in the night? Go back to sleep.'

Maiju continued to grind. Kanchhi could hear her bangles clang against each other.

'*Kulankini*,' Maiju said.

'*Oof*,' Kanchhi sighed and rested her head back on the pillow. That word killed any desire she had to talk to Maiju and placate her.

'Go back to sleep,' Jhalnath whispered again. 'I'll wait for her to sleep too and leave.'

Kanchhi nodded in the dark and closed her eyes. It did not take long for her to fall back asleep.

When she woke up again, someone was banging on the door.

'Kanchhi, *eh*, Kanchhi. Open the door, daughter.'

It was Bir Bahadur *dai*'s older brother, with a loud but coaxing voice. He must have been knocking for a while because he stopped and told someone that he did not think the door was opening any time soon.

'Are they dead inside or what?' a woman asked.

'Kanchhi, open the door, daughter,' someone else spoke this time. Bir Bahadur *dai*.

By now, Kanchhi was completely awake, with her heart dropped to her stomach. The room was as bright as a sieve, and on the bed, by her feet, was Jhalnath, fully clothed. He too had dozed off.

'Kanchhi, open the door, *Nani*,' Bir Bahadur *dai* said again. He was kind and polite, but suddenly, a surge of anger swelled up inside Kanchhi, and she burst aloud, 'No. Go away, *Buwa*.'

'Kanchhi, don't say that. Just open the door,' Bir Bahadur *dai* said.

'No.'

'Kanchhi. *Nani*.'

'I'll open it only if *Ama* says it. Where is she?' Kanchhi asked, slipping into her clothes.

'Your mother's been crying all morning. She can't talk,' Bir Bahadur *dai* said.

'I'm not opening it until she says so. Why are you here? Go back to your own houses. Everyone, go.'

'She's telling us to go,' someone said, bemused by Kanchhi's audacity.

Jhalnath put his finger on his mouth and told Kanchhi to shush. So far, Maiju had not said a word.

'I'll go out and see what they want,' Jhalnath said.

'But—'

'Well, they know now. There's no point in hiding in here. Don't worry. They're not going to kill us. This is just how they react.'

Jhalnath took a cigarette out of its packet but did not light it. He smoothed his pants instead and kissed Kanchhi on her forehead. 'I'll close the door behind me,' he said and opened the door.

The crowd fell silent when they saw Jhalnath. Kanchhi, who had followed him to the door, stayed close to it.

'Jhalnath *bhai*.' Thapa Maila *dai* was the first to talk this time. '*Bhai*, please don't take it the wrong way, but we need to talk. As you can see, this is about a hamlet and its norms.'

Jhalnath did not say anything, but Kanchhi could tell Thapa Maila *dai* was taking him down to the yard.

'You can't just come in and do this, you know that, *Bhai*,' Thapa Maila *dai* went on. 'Policeman or not, you have to respect us. You have to respect our hamlet and our values. What you are doing here is setting a terrible example for our young men and women. What will they learn if we let this happen unchecked?'

'I understand,' Jhalnath said. 'And with your blessings, I'm ready to marry her.'

'That's not an excuse,' Bir Bahadur *dai* said. 'What if we hadn't caught you two together? Would you have still married her?'

'Yes,' Jhalnath said.

Bir Bahadur *dai* must not have expected that answer. He went quiet.

'If that's the case,' Thapa Maila *dai* said. 'Let's get them married, right, Bir Bahadur *dai*? The caste does not match, but he's a Magar, our own brother. Age too is only what? Twenty-five, twenty-six. Not too old. Not too young. And he has a good job. She won't starve. If he's already married, then let's make sure this marriage is registered so that Kanchhi can claim her share later.'

'Should we ask Kanchhi too?' Jhalnath asked.

'What's the point?' Bir Bahadur *dai* said. 'She didn't ask for our permission, did she?'

'Are you already married?' Thapa Maila *dai* asked.

'No,' Jhalnath replied.

'If you are, let us know right away.'

'If he is, it doesn't matter,' Bir Bahadur *dai* said. 'She's made her choice. If she's fated to be a second wife, she's fated to be a second wife.'

Jhalnath kept quiet for a while. Then, he said, 'Let me send a message to my mother. As soon as she gets here, we can get married.'

'No, we can't wait that long,' Bir Bahadur *dai* said.

'Why? Don't you trust me?'

'It's not about trust, sir. You are a policeman. You must have dealt with a lot of cases like this. A boy and a girl get together, the girl gets pregnant, and the boy leaves. What are we to do if you vanish and Kanchhi turns out to be pregnant? Who's going to look after the child? We can't keep a girl like that around, can we? Kanchhi, *eh*, Kanchhi!'

Kanchhi did not answer.

'Let me go talk to her,' Jhalnath said.

'Yes, bring her out. She can't hide in there all day.'

Jhalnath knocked on the door. 'It's me,' he said.

Kanchhi opened the door and walked back to the bed.

'I can't get married,' she said as soon as Jhalnath bolted the door and sat next to her.

'They only want us engaged,' he said.

'I don't want that either.'

'I know, but they won't let us off without it.'

'What will they do? They can't kill us, can they?'

'No, they can't, but you don't want them angry either. Let's cool them off first, and we can talk about what we'll do next.'

Kanchhi looked at the window in front. She could hear some children trying to peek in.

'So, we get engaged now?' she asked.

'It's just a formality. Will mean nothing.' Jhalnath lit the cigarette he had been holding all along.

'How do you know?' Kanchhi asked.

'I know. The government doesn't recognize any marriage that's not registered with the local administration.'

'But they talked about doing that.'

'They'll never do it. Nobody does it.'

'I don't want to go out.'

'Nothing will happen, Kanchhi. I'm right here. I've seen people like this everywhere. They just need to let their steam off.'

'I want them gone.'

'I do too.'

Kanchhi sat still for a second. 'I'm not going out there.'

Jhalnath looked at her and sighed, a little irritated.

'I can't go,' Kanchhi repeated.

'I know.'

'I've done nothing wrong.'

'I know.'

'Will we really talk about this later? Figure it out together?'

'Yes, we will. Let's send them home first, and we'll talk. You and me.'

'You promise?'

'I do. Let's go out now. I'll protect you, I promise.'

Kanchhi got up and reached for the *chadar*. She then threw it around her and followed Jhalnath out.

Outside, the entire hamlet had descended into her yard, and Maiju was already preparing a plate of *akshyata*.

'Do I need anything else?' she asked Bir Bahadur *dai*, sounding like a timid little child who Kanchhi could tell had been crying. Her eyes were red like tomatoes.

'Yes,' Bir Bahadur *dai* said to Maiju. 'A glass of water with some flowers in it. Are there any flowers here?' He looked around. There were some marigolds on the slopes below the yard and some hibiscus past the crossroads. Saili *didi* went to get the hibiscus. Bir Bahadur *dai* plucked the marigold.

When they got back, Thapa Maila *dai* said, '*La*, let's begin with Syani *bhauju*, then Bir Bahadur *dai* and Saili *didi* and the rest. Kanchhi, you sit—' He looked for a place for them to sit.

'Doesn't she need to wash her face first?' Saili *didi* asked. 'Kanchhi, come over here. You too, sir.'

Kanchhi and Jhalnath followed Saili *didi* out of the crowd towards the sink. There, Saili *didi* scooped water out of a washbasin and poured it first to Jhalnath and then to Kanchhi. None of them said anything to each other. Once done, Saili *didi* escorted them back.

On the porch, Thapa Maila *dai* had spread a mat. Jhalnath and Kanchhi sat down, their legs dangling towards the yard.

'Is that correct?' Bir Bahadur *dai* asked. 'Should we be facing east or west?'

'This is correct,' Thapa Maila *dai* said. 'They should be facing east. We should be facing west. Maybe turn a little to the left.'

Kanchhi and Jhalnath both turned slightly to their left. Maiju walked up and pasted a pinch of *akshyata* on Jhalnath's forehead and then on Kanchhi's. The ceremony had begun. One by one, the villagers came forward and did the same. A pinch of *akshyata* on the foreheads and then a pinch of petals on their hands. It took about twenty minutes to go through the crowd. In the end, Thapa Maila *dai* asked Jhalnath if he had any pieces of jewellery. Jhalnath had a gold necklace and a gold ring. He unhooked the necklace, which was woven like a chain without a pendant, and clasped it around Kanchhi's neck.

'Do you have anything like that to give to him?' Thapa Maila *dai* asked Maiju.

Maiju shook her head.

'We don't need it,' Bir Bahadur *dai* said.

'Okay, then, it's done and over,' Thapa Maila *dai* said. 'We'll set a date for the wedding soon. After that, Kanchhi is out of our hands and responsibility.'

Jhalnath lit another cigarette.

Ramesh's father fixed the wedding date for 17 November, about a month later, on the first day of Mangshir, as soon as the SLC prelim exams would be over. Astrologically, Kanchhi belonged to the human class, he said, and Jhalnath to the demon, but their compatibility score was still twenty-eight out of thirty-six. 'Agreeable,' he said. 'Best to do a tiny, simple wedding with gods and goddesses as the witnesses.' The village temple, then, would be the wedding venue.

Jhalnath told Kanchhi that they could leave afterwards, come back for the SLC exams and then leave again. The second time she would leave, he would drop her off wherever she wanted if she still wanted that. Kanchhi suggested that they leave only after the SLC exams because once she left, there was no knowing if or when she might be back. That was how it seemed to be. Her father, Thirman Thakuri, Bipana *bhauju*, even Laxmi and Dhan *didi*, everyone – once they left, they left. They did not come back.

'Where will you go?' Jhalnath asked.

'To my aunt's in Pokhara,' Kanchhi said.

'Where does she live there?'

'Chhorepatan. Have you been there?'

'Yeah, it's a little bazaar. A lot of Parbate there, for sure. What will you do there?'

Kanchhi shrugged.

Jhalnath laughed. 'Is getting married to me that bad?'

'No.'

'Is there anywhere else you can go if your aunt does not want you there?'

'Yes.'

'Where?'

'Dhan *didi*'s.'

'Who?'

'Laxmi's sister.'

'Oh. If she does not want you either, come to me, understand? You can stay with me for as long as you like.'

'Okay.'

'What will you tell your mother?'

'I don't know.'

'You should let her know. She'll worry otherwise.'

'I will.'

Kanchhi did not. Maiju had not said a word to her since that night, and Kanchhi thought it was worthless trying to convince her of anything. She put her head down and focused on the preliminary exams instead. The first was Nepali. Fittingly, one of the short-answer questions was: 'What does the saying *"Afnai chhori nakharmauli tannerilai dosh"* mean?' Literally and conventionally, it meant you cannot blame anyone if your own daughter is indecent. That morning, it took on a different meaning. What did it mean when your own can't blame anyone but you?

28

November 13, 2005

'IS NO ONE INSIDE?'

'Who is it?' Maiju asks from inside her room.

'A guest. Who else can it be?'

'Huh?' Maiju looks through her bedroom door, trying to see who it is without getting out. The voice does sound familiar, but she cannot tell for certain. The man's face is out of view; only his black pants and white sneakers are visible. Maiju finishes dabbing a dot of red powder on her forehead, right at the hairline, and walks out. It is Thapa Maila *dai*, wiping sweat off his face with a hat.

'*Oho*, Maila *bhai*, when did you get here?' Maiju asks.

'Just now,' Thapa Maila *dai* says.

Maiju chuckles. 'Of course, just now. Do you want some water?'

'Water? No. But I would like some buttermilk if you have it. Do you?' Thapa Maila *dai* asks, looking for a spot to sit.

'Here.' Maiju brings him a mat. Thapa Maila *dai* takes it and spreads it under the shade of the *badahar* tree. The shade is nominal. The tree has almost no branches, with the last of it lopped right before Maiju fell.

'The porch might be better,' Maiju says.

'No, it's good here. Once the sweat dries off, I'll want the sun again,' Thapa Maila *dai* says and takes off his backpack, making himself more comfortable.

Maiju goes inside the kitchen and gets Thapa Maila *dai* a glass of buttermilk. It is warm. Thapa Maila *dai* comments on it and then chugs it down.

'Missed it in Kathmandu,' he says and clicks his tongue in appreciation.

'You can't get it there?' Maiju asks.

'No, you can get everything else but not the things you want,' Thapa Maila *dai* says, returning the glass to Maiju.

'Do you want more?' Maiju asks.

Thapa Maila *dai* shakes his head and puts his hat back on. There is a thin line of buttermilk above his lips, and Maiju points at it. He wipes it off with the back of his hand and wipes that hand with the other.

'Did you meet Bir Bahadur *dai* on the way?' Maiju asks, walking to the sink to rinse the glass.

'No, but I heard he left for Pokhara this morning.'

'He did. Something to do with his son and land in Pokhara, Saili *didi* said.'

'Whatever it was, it could have waited.'

'I know.'

'I mean, my son isn't getting married again, is he? And who is to say when I might be back again?'

'Exactly.'

Maiju leaves the glass to dry out in the sun. 'How long will you stay this time?' she asks.

'I don't know,' Thapa Maila *dai* says and walks towards her. 'I have a week-long break, but I might stay longer.' Thapa Maila *dai* now works at a museum in Kathmandu, guarding ancient relics. He has been doing that for the last two years.

'Is it safe?' Maiju asks, meaning for him to be back in the hamlet. He's still on the Maoists' hit list, purportedly.

'Maybe,' Thapa Maila *dai* says, looking at the water pipes with interest. When he was in the village, the pipes had not been laid yet. In fact, the pipes were the last straw that got him evicted. The Maoists had charged him, among other things, with embezzling money meant for water in the villages. Water, electricity, schools. Every year, the charge sheet read, he was whisking money out of the village development budget and enriching himself. He, Bhime *dai* and the VDC chairperson – all members of the Nepali Congress party. Thapa Maila *dai* denied it all. Said if anyone was responsible, it was the VDC chairperson. He was just the secretary. The Maoists did not believe him, tied him to his office chair all night one night and then took him all the way to Mustang in the morning. A week later, they let him go. Thapa Maila *dai* knew he had to leave the hamlet. Only a Maoist spy could come out unscathed, the thinking went.

'Who helped to lay them?' Thapa Maila *dai* asks, walking around the millet drying in the yard to inspect the pipes over the sink.

'What? Them?' Maiju asks.

'Yes, these pipes.' Thapa Maila *dai* disconnects the one coming down from his house from the one going down to Saili *didi*'s. A little bit of water trickles out, and then nothing.

'They turn it off at nine,' Maiju says.

Thapa Maila *dai* looks inside the pipes, both of them. 'How many metres did it take?' he asks.

'I don't know. You'll have to ask Bir Bahadur *dai* about that. They told us to go down to Hatiya and carry the pipes up. That's all I did. Everything else was done by Bir Bahadur *dai* and the boys.'

'*Eh*, *eh*.' Thapa Maila *dai* connects the pipes again and starts to measure the one going up towards his house with his arm. He stops when he reaches the tangerine tree through which the pipe is threaded.

'Didn't they collect a thousand rupees each from every house? Looks like we overpaid,' he says.

Maiju does not say anything.

'Anyway,' Thapa Maila *dai* continues, 'I need to go. I haven't had anything but tea since this morning.'

'Really?' Maiju asks. 'I would have served you lunch, but I didn't cook today.'

'That's all right. My wife must have made something by now.' He hops over the millet and steps back into the yard. 'You are coming to the party tonight, aren't you?'

'Yes.'

'Good. We'll talk more later then. Oh, before I forget. I put Kanchhi's name down in the list of the disappeared.'

'The disappeared?'

'Yeah, those who disappeared during the war. Who knows what really happened? Maybe she didn't run away. Maybe she joined the Maoists. Maybe she got caught in between.'

'But—'

'I know,' Thapa Maila *dai* says. 'I know the war hadn't even begun then, but we should do whatever we can whenever we can. We don't know the whole truth. Maybe this will bring it out.'

Thapa Maila *dai* picks up his backpack and turns around. '*La*, we'll talk more later. See what else we can do. I need to go and eat now. I'll die otherwise.'

He begins to walk up. Maiju watches him until he disappears by a tap next to his house. Someone is there.

'*Oho*, my little *natini*,' Thapa Maila *dai* says. It's his granddaughter. 'Look, your dress is all wet, and no one around knows.'

29

'I HEARD ABOUT YOUR MARRIAGE,' GOVINDA SIR said. 'I don't think it's a good idea. We had such high expectations from you.'

Kanchhi narrowed her eyes and focused on a group of children playing *chungi* on the ground in front.

'Is it the family?' Govinda sir asked. 'Are they pushing you to get married?'

Kanchhi shook her head.

'Girls,' Govinda sir said. 'No matter how hard you try, they slip through the cracks.'

'What was he saying?' Jhalnath asked.

'Nothing.'

'Is he your teacher?'

'Was.'

'Was?'

'He taught us up until the eighth grade.'

'*Eh*, *eh*. Want some tea?'

Kanchhi did not, but Jhalnath did not see her expression. '*Sahuni*,' he called a little girl at the teashop.

'Two cups of tea and two plates of chickpeas.'

'No,' Kanchhi said.

'No chickpeas?'

'No tea. No chickpeas.'

'Why?'

'I'm not hungry.'

'Tea, then?'

'I don't want it.'

Jhalnath cancelled both orders. 'Want to come to the station for a bit?'

Kanchhi shook her head.

Jhalnath looked at her for a bit and then said, 'Okay, then.'

Turned out it was Tauka Kanchha *dai* who had heard them outside Kanchhi's room that night and woken Maiju up. Of all the people, Tauka Kanchha *dai*. It was Dhan *didi* who told Kanchhi that. Saili *didi* told Dhan *didi*. Who told Saili *didi*, she did not say.

'What was he doing outside my room?' Kanchhi asked Maiju.

Maiju did not answer.

In the distance, a group of Kanchhi's girlfriends stood against a wall by a classroom and talked to a group of boys. The girls, originally thirty-two in number when they had begun fourth grade in Bagar, had dwindled to twelve, including Kanchhi, Jharana and Samjhana. The rest had simply dropped out like flies, and almost everyone who had dropped out had got married. Kanchhi would be the twentieth of them. Twentieth. A neither-here-nor-there number. The boys, on the other hand, most of them, including Shiva Shirish, Tara Prasad and Ranjan Kunwar, had shifted to a better school up in Lunkhu. That school had a better reputation and a better SLC graduation rate. The boys even stayed in Lunkhu, rented a room there and walked down only when needed to carry back food every now and then.

'What was the bigger draw?' the girls asked Kanchhi. 'Caste or the age difference?'

'How old is he again?'

'He's an uncle.'

'No, he's not. Why would you call someone's husband-to-be an uncle?'

'Don't forget to invite us to the wedding, hai.'

'At least we get to see your wedding too.'

Only Jharana told her that she might regret it later. 'Those who marry young are never happy,' she said.

'I can't get married.' Kanchhi stormed into the kitchen one evening and threw Jhalnath's gold necklace on the floor. The wedding was less than two weeks away.

Maiju looked at the necklace, picked it up and went back to serving herself dinner. Kanchhi had already had hers.

'I'm running away. You can't force me to get married,' Kanchhi said.

Maiju continued to scoop food onto her plate.

'Everyone's fucking everyone here, and I have to be the one they punish?'

Maiju coughed.

'It's true. Tell me who's not doing that.'

'Pour me some water,' Maiju said.

Startled, Kanchhi stood still for a second. Maiju had not spoken to her since that night more than two weeks ago. Kanchhi walked over to the water pots.

'Here.' She gave an ewer to Maiju and sat on a *pirka*.

Maiju put the ewer aside and began eating.

'Ama,' Kanchhi said, a little calm this time. 'Can you please get me Pokhara aunt's number from Bir Bahadur *buwa*? I'll do the rest.'

Maiju looked for a green chilli pepper on a plate full of them.

'If you get the number,' Kanchhi continued, 'I'll call her and tell her that you're forcing me to get married and so I ran away. They live in a city. They'll understand.'

'You think they don't know by now what you've done here?' Maiju asked.

'How will they know?'

'*How will they know*? Everyone everywhere knows. News like this travels faster than lightning. *Jathi*, you think you know everything.'

It was now Kanchhi's turn to go quiet. She hated all the words ever used to insult or scold girls – *jathi*, *nakkali*, *ukharmauli*, *uttauli*, *randi*, *nakachari*. People who prefaced their sentences with such words were never open to listening. Kanchhi would have to wait.

'Put this there.' Maiju gave her a spoon. The spoon had been used to take some ghee out of a jar. Kanchhi licked it first and then placed it in a cauldron.

It took a few more days of prodding – Kanchhi talked about the smell of a wet dead dog in the air, Saili *didi* enquired about the wedding preparations and Jhalnath walked up one evening with a bag of mutton and a bottle of millet liquor – but Maiju slowly began to open up again. A tinge of pain and disappointment was still audible in her voice, but she was talking again, however obliquely, to and around Kanchhi.

The evening Jhalnath walked up, he told Maiju not to cook anything that night because he was. Maiju protested at first, but Jhalnath would not hear any of it. He was the best mutton cook in his squad, he said, and would not let Maiju even start the fire. Maiju's job that evening was to sit outside and away and rest, drink from a glass if she wanted to. As for Kanchhi, she would have to help him make rice and tend the fire, he said.

'Okay, then,' Maiju said and sat out on the porch that evening.

At dinner, Jhalnath said, 'I know how you feel, *Ama*.' He had long stopped calling Maiju *didi*. 'I know you don't like me very much, but that's how you're supposed to feel.'

Maiju, who was back in front of the hearth serving Kanchhi and Jhalnath first, looked at Kanchhi.

'What are you saying?' Kanchhi asked Jhalnath.

'She's your only daughter,' Jhalnath explained. 'She's your investment, and now, when it's time to reap the returns, she's getting married.'

Maiju moved a little on her *pirka*.

'Investment?' Kanchhi asked.

'Yes, an investment. All children are investments,' Jhalnath said to Kanchhi and then looked back at Maiju. 'But I'll look after you both. You don't have to worry at all. Kanchhi's mother is also my mother. I have two mothers from now on. I understand what it is like to be without a father.'

'Are you drunk?' Kanchhi asked.

'No,' Jhalnath said.

'Here, your plate, *Babu*.' Maiju lifted Jhalnath's plate and placed it in front of him. Kanchhi's plate, she pushed it towards her.

In the morning, Jhalnath brought Kanchhi tea in her room and then splintered some wood, after which, despite Maiju's objections, he went ahead and lopped some *badahar* and *bello* branches. Once he was finished with that, he joined Kanchhi at the spring. There, he rubbed her back with a stone and then soaped it with a washcloth. Afterwards, the two sat on a slab of stone above a line of rice terraces and dried their hair. As the sun beamed down on them, Jhalnath smoked and Kanchhi played with a flatsedge grass. The flatsedge grass used to be a fun way of predicting the sex of an unborn child. Kanchhi and her friends, when younger, would think of an expectant mother, ask aloud whether she might be carrying a boy or a girl and then split the stem down to the middle.

'Here, hold this,' Kanchhi told Jhalnath after pinching off the grass's root and crown.

'Now,' she continued. 'I tear it from this end. You tear it from that end. Ready? Slowly.'

When the splits met in the middle, the thin strands that did not split all the way through formed an 'N' shape. A boy.

Kanchhi looked for another grass. The second time, the shape was rectangular. A girl.

'Do you have a boy or girl at home?' Kanchhi asked. 'You can tell me now.'

'I told you I'm not married.' Jhalnath threw a pebble down to a rice field. 'Once you leave this village, you'll see that there are a lot of people who don't marry as soon as they turn sixteen or seventeen.'

'But you're not a city boy.'

'No, I'm not, but I went to a city when I was seventeen.'

'It's not the same.'

'Well, you can come to Baglung and see for yourself.'

'No,' Kanchhi said.

Jhalnath reached out and swept her hair aside, exposing her bare neck.

'Oh, I got you something,' he said and opened his backpack.

It was a watch, a second-hand mechanical watch made by Hindustan Machine Tools and in need of a good winding.

'Try it on,' Jhalnath said.

Kanchhi did. It was big on her and slipped up, down and around her wrist freely.

'Let me see,' Jhalnath said and pinched the loose, hanging part of the band around Kanchhi's wrist.

'Two, two, four,' he counted the links. 'Do you have a pin?'

'Not here.'

'I'll get it fixed once we get back then,' Jhalnath said.

At home, Maiju had made some popcorn and tea. She brought them over when Kanchhi and Jhalnath walked back.

'Your mother's going to be alone after you leave,' Jhalnath said after Maiju left the room.

'For a while,' Kanchhi said.

'We can take her with us later.'

Kanchhi looked at him and shook her head.

'What?' he asked.

'Nothing. She'll get used to it,' Kanchhi said.

'You should definitely take her to Pokhara someday and show her the city. Has she ever been out of the village?'

'She's been to Waling.'

'Beyond that?'

'No.'

'You'll have to show her Pokhara then. She can come up to Mustang too if you want.'

Kanchhi shook her head again. Jhalnath was looking for a pin in his jacket. The pin attached a nameplate to his uniform and when he found it, Jhalnath unclipped it and sat down to open the links on the HMT watch. He was a nice man, Kanchhi thought. In another world, in another life, she might have married him.

'Are you going down after this?' Kanchhi asked.

'No,' Jhalnath said, yawning. 'I need a nap first. I feel very tired. That mutton and that shower have made me very sleepy. We should take a nap together. We've never done that before.'

When she woke up, it was early afternoon and Jhalnath was out in the yard, peeling a tangerine.

'Finally,' he said. 'Done napping?'

Maiju was by the shed, checking on a goat tied to a tree and left to graze by itself.

'I'm going to Waling soon,' Jhalnath said. 'Do you want me to get you anything?'

'No,' Kanchhi said.

'Sure?'

'Yes.'

'And your mother? Does she need anything?'

'*Ama*, do you need anything from Waling?' Kanchhi shouted.

'No,' Maiju shouted back from the shed.

'Okay, then. I should get going,' Jhalnath said and walked back to Kanchhi's room to pack his bag.

'I'll get you a new *chadar*,' he said. 'A red one. Or should I get you *Tatyakatha*?'

Kanchhi laughed.

'Walk me out?' Jhalnath asked.

'Yes,' Kanchhi said.

She did not go too far, only up to the crossroads. There, Jhalnath kissed her on her forehead as usual, and for the first time since they had started seeing each other, he walked down via Saili *didi*'s house. Kanchhi herself walked to the end of the terrace field past the tangerine trees and watched Jhalnath leave from there. At the junction to Saili *didi*'s house, Bhime *dai* joined Jhalnath, and the two made their way down together. When they reached a gooseberry tree halfway to the primary school, Jhalnath turned around and waved. Kanchhi waved back. She could imagine him smiling and telling her to turn around, but he did so first and continued on in the shadow of the slopes. He had the gait of a self-assured man, and Kanchhi thought he was probably telling Bhime *dai* a story from his adventures as a cop.

At the primary school, Bhime *dai* turned right and vanished behind the school. Jhalnath continued forward.

Kanchhi expected him to turn around at the *chautara* before the woods, but he did not. He kept walking and disappeared from sight.

Kanchhi never saw him again.

30

November 13, 2005

SWAI, SWAI IS THE SOUND OF A STICK GLIDING through the air before it hits the rice beans. When it does, the sound is a mix of a crackle and a thud. The crackle comes when the pods break, the leaves detach and the twigs snap. The thuds when the stick comes to a stop. Once the shrubs are thoroughly beaten, Maiju lifts them up and out of the way. Underneath, on one of the twigs, is a cricket smashed into a pulp. Maiju picks up the twig. Everything, apart from the cricket's antennae, is a mess.

Maiju tosses the branch towards the chicken coop. The mother hen immediately sees it and scampers towards it. One of her chicks follows her, and when the mother hen points at the cricket with her beak, the crickety pulp disappears.

'*Kaki.*' A little boy comes up with two of his friends. All are about four to five years old. The one who called her *kaki* is Surya *dai*'s youngest son. The other two are his cousins.

'What is it?' Maiju asks.

'Grandma wants to know if you can come down and help her thresh millet.'

'Thresh millet?'

'Yes.'

Maiju looks down at the beans scattered in front of her and then over at her own spread of millet in the corner. 'When? Right now?' she asks.

'In a bit,' the boy says.

'Tell her I'll be down,' Maiju says.

The boys turn around to leave.

'Wait,' Maiju shouts. 'Do you kids want chicken?'

'Chicken?'

'Yes.'

Maiju gets up and goes to the coop. The sick chick is no longer on its feet but on the side, with its head crawled up inside its wing as if asleep. Maiju grabs it and takes it to the boys. They look at it with suspicion.

'Don't worry. It's dead, but you can eat it. Don't eat the innards, just the limbs and the breast.'

Maiju gives the chick to one of the boys, but they still look unsure.

'Don't worry,' Maiju repeats. 'You can eat it. It just died naturally. Here, let me throw the guts out and roast it for you. I would eat it myself if I hadn't raised it. Now, who here knows how to start a fire?'

'I do,' Surya *dai*'s son says.

Maiju asks him to gather firewood then and start a fire.

31

THE WIND CAME FIRST, FAST AND FIERCE, AS IF ON orders from the spirits. In the distance, high above the mountains, the lightning struck, and the sky thundered as if being ripped apart. Soon, a dark pillar of rain rushed through an invisible trail and splashed on Maiju's yard, spilling hail as big as a bird's poo. It did not take long for the branches to break then and for the millets to go prostrate. The storm was here to devastate, and it did. Both crops and plans. Kanchhi was supposed to leave in two days.

The next day too it rained. Continuously. No lightning or thunder this time. Just rain, steady like a heartbeat. In the afternoon, Saili *didi* came over, holding a plastic cone over her head, and told Maiju that one of the walls of the abandoned house had caved in. The left one. A tree by its side had collapsed too, on its right. Across the gorge, the mountains bore more signs of destruction – gashes from fresh landslides, mini and large, patches of red in a sea of green. Maiju, sitting on the porch picking over lentils, shook her head in disbelief.

'Here,' Saili *didi* said, taking a scrap of paper out of her blouse. It had the number Maiju had asked her to get from Bir Bahadur *dai*. Kanchhi's aunt's number in Pokhara: +61-460—.

—

'*Didi*,' Maiju shouted from the edge of the terrace field. 'Saili *didi*, have you seen Kanchhi?'

'What do you mean?' Saili *didi* asked. She had just dumped a *doko* of grass by her shed and was scratching her back with the tip of a sickle. Saili *didi* was the first person Maiju asked about Kanchhi that day.

'I can't find Kanchhi,' Maiju said, trying to keep her voice as calm as possible. By then, the sun had reached its zenith, and Maiju was certain Kanchhi had reached Bayarghari.

'Well, maybe she was too eager to get married and ran away,' Saili *didi* joked.

Maiju pretended to be irritated.

The pretence continued throughout the day.

After five, Thapa Maila *dai* walked up from Bagar and hollered from afar, 'Syani, everything all right?' Maiju waited for him to mention Kanchhi. He did not. He did not even ask how Kanchhi was, let alone say anything about her calling the shop in Hatiya and leaving a message. That was when a sliver of doubt first crept into Maiju's heart, but she dismissed it. A lack of message from Thapa Maila *dai* did not affirm anything, she told herself. Maybe Kanchhi had called and the phone line was busy. Maybe she called and nobody picked up the phone. Or maybe someone did pick up the phone and Kanchhi left a message, but Thapa Maila *dai* did not get it.

An hour later, the search began. Maiju, continuing the pretence, looked in the direction of the abandoned house and beyond with Saili didi. Tara *bhauju* and Thapa Nani *didi* went in the other direction: towards the spring and Harichaur. Thapa Maila *dai* and his sons searched the top of the hamlet, and Bir Bahadur *dai* and Bhime *dai* the bottom.

'Did you check the pillow?' Saili *didi* asked, referring to a note. Kanchhi, of course, had not left one.

'Pokhara,' Bir Bahadur *dai* said when everyone reconvened in Maiju's yard. 'Didn't I give you that number?' He turned to Saili *didi*.

'Yes, and I gave it to Syani. She must have taken it from her,' Saili *didi* said.

'Couldn't you have been a little careful?'

'Who knew she would use it to run away?' Saili *didi* said.

'What a fool,' Bir Bahadur *dai* said. 'We'll have to go to Pokhara now.'

'Right now?' Saili *didi* asked.

'Yes. Does she know that that number is not even her aunt's?'

'What?' Maiju asked.

'It's the number for a shop around the corner. It's not hers,' Bir Bahadur *dai* said.

'But the shopkeeper will get her if asked?' Maiju asked.

'If he knows who you're talking about. You can't just say, "Get my aunt," over the phone. Young people these days, they think they know everything. Did she not say anything to you? How could you not know?'

Maiju began to cry. Saili *didi*, who was standing by her side, put her arms around her and rubbed her back.

'These women,' Bir Bahadur *dai* said. 'Should have thought about it all before giving her the number. Let's go to Bagar now, unless Jhalnath's coming up tonight. Is he?'

Maiju did not know.

'Useless women.' Bir Bahadur *dai* turned to Thapa Maila *dai*. '*Dai*, you'll have to come with us. We'll have to go to Bagar and back.'

'Right now?' Thapa Maila *dai* asked.

'Yes, down to Bagar and back.'

'I say, we wait and walk down first thing in the morning. There's no point in going down now only to come back up and then go down again in the morning. We'll just tire ourselves out for no reason.'

Bhime *dai* agreed. So did the other people gathered in the yard.

'Let's stay here tonight and figure out who will go with us all the way to Pokhara,' Thapa Maila *dai* said.

'It'll be you, me and Bhime. Better to keep the team small,' Bir Bahadur *dai* said.

'Agreed,' Thapa Maila *dai* said. 'Jhalnath can come with us too if he wants.'

The next morning, Maiju, Bir Bahadur *dai*, Bhime *dai* and Thapa Maila *dai* walked down to the police station. The station, a small, once-abandoned hut, did not get any sun until after noon. Still, at 7 a.m., Jhalnath was out in the front yard, sitting on a stool drinking his tea.

'*Oho*, namaste, sirs. Namaste, *Ama*,' he said. 'Want some tea?'

'No, no, we're good,' Thapa Maila *dai* said and, after everyone sat on chairs that Jhalnath offered, got straight to the point.

'Pokhara?' Jhalnath asked. 'That sounds about right. Chhorepatan. That's where she always said she would go.'

'We're not wrong then?' Bir Bahadur *dai* said, a little relieved. 'We'll just have to go and get her back now.'

'I say, leave her there,' Jhalnath said. 'She never wanted to get married. We can't force her, not in this day and age.'

'That is true,' Thapa Maila *dai* said. 'But we still have to go and make sure she's all right.'

Jhalnath agreed. 'When are you leaving? I'll come with you.'

'We're leaving right now. Right after we're done here.'

'Right now? *Ama*, are you going too?'

'No, she's not,' Bir Bahadur *dai* said.

'I just walked back from Waling yesterday,' Jhalnath said.

'Waling? And you didn't see her there?'

'No, I didn't realize I had to look for her. Did she even go via Waling? We could check the ticket counters there.'

'Could she have gone via Bayarghari?' Thapa Maila *dai* turned to Bir Bahadur *dai*.

'Does she even know that route?' Bhime *dai* asked.

'Why wouldn't she?' Bir Bahadur *dai* turned to him. 'Even if she didn't, she could just ask people along the way. It's just one straight path up and then down.'

'I'm sure she didn't go through Waling,' Jhalnath said. 'But it's a big bazaar. I could have just not seen her.'

'Sir, don't you have a phone here?' Bhime *dai* asked, looking around at the station.

They did not. 'But we do have a walkie-talkie,' Jhalnath said. 'Only the ASI *sa'ab* is allowed to use it, though, and he's not here right now.'

Bhime *dai* suggested leaving him a message then. Everyone agreed.

In Hatiya, they stopped by a shop that had the only phone in the area. The solar rotary dial phone inside a wooden case. Bhime *dai* picked up the receiver.

'Nothing,' he said.

'Nothing?' Maiju asked and listened to the tone as well. Nothing at all.

'*Bhai*,' Maiju called a man brewing tea on the other side of the shop. '*Bhai*, has Kanchhi called?'

'The phone's been off for more than a month, *Didi*,' the shopkeeper said. 'I've been too busy to go and get it fixed. What happened?'

That night, Maiju dreamed that Kanchhi stood by the same riverbed past Bagar where Maiju had dropped her. She wore the same green *lungi* too and the same grey *chadar*. It was just as dark as well – the vast silhouettes, the creaking trees, the gurgling monsoon creek – but instead of a flashlight, Kanchhi had a matchbox in her hand, and she struggled to light it. Every time she struck a matchstick, the sparks would fizzle out in seconds. If they did not, a giant bamboo tree right behind her would do it – it would shake itself vigorously and put out the flame.

In the morning, Maiju lit a *diyo* in Kanchhi's room. The wick, dipped in ghee, sputtered at first but then glowed steadily. A long, yellow flame, with gentle sways and invisible smoke. Everything was fine, it said.

Two days later, Bir Bahadur *dai* and the team came back. When he licked his lips to soften the news, Maiju fainted.

Kanchhi never made it to her aunt's house.

32

November 13, 2005

AT FOUR, THE FINAL SCHOOL BELL RINGS. WITHIN seconds, little children run out like little ants. Maiju walks inside the staffroom and picks up a broom. The floor is an earthen one. Maiju covers her face with a shawl and begins to sweep. Dust flies everywhere.

Outside, a *simal* tree is in bloom. A little girl in school uniform picks up a few velvety, voluptuous flowers that have fallen to the ground and starts counting them.

Maiju flits from one classroom to another, sweeping the floors and then locking the doors behind her.

Just as she's done, a group of people walk up from the woods below – three young women and about ten young men in paramilitary gear, carrying rifles and pistols. It takes a minute for Maiju to notice that there is another man and woman in their midst. Their hands are tied with a rope, and the ropes are tied to each other. The man, probably in his thirties, has blood running down his thighs. He limps forward. The woman is in her fifties, about Maiju's age, and has no visible injury but is also limping forward. In fact, she is being dragged by two Maoist women.

'*Nani*,' Maiju calls the little girl, now picking pebbles on the ground in front. Frightened, the little girl runs to her. One of the young Maoist men looks at Maiju and the girl and then at a board above them. 'Saraswati Primary School, Torikhola,' it reads.

The villagers follow the crowd to the temple. Two of the Maoist women separate the woman from the man and tie her to the pole in the slaughter pit. Her head bobs just below the hilt of the *khukuri* painted on the pole. The man remains outside with the Maoists.

'No one touches her,' a man significantly older than the rest of them orders. 'She killed her own daughter-in-law. This is what she deserves.'

The third Maoist woman walks down to the pit and dumps the contents of a small plastic bag in front of the woman. The top half of a skull and a lot of tiny bones roll out.

'If she dies, no one burns her,' the older man continues. 'She gets what she gave.'

The villagers murmur, as if in agreement. The squad then abruptly turns around and walks out of the woods, taking the man with them. He is for another hamlet.

The party does not get cancelled. It starts early. People return from the temple and gather at Thapa Nani *didi*'s house. Saili *didi*, Ramesh's mother, Tauka Kanchha *dai* – each a victim of the war in their own ways. Ramesh, who joined the Maoists soon after the war crossed the Kali Gandaki River and reached the hamlet in the early 2000s, has been missing for over a year. Tauka Kanchha *dai*'s nephew, who was on the other side in the Nepal army, has also been missing for a year. No one knows what happened to either of them. There are only rumours, whispers and incidents like the one that just transpired at the temple to suggest what could have happened. Still, some say Torikhola is lucky – the list of the disappeared and the dead is longer in the villages around.

Thapa Maila *dai* walks back, relieved. He had gone into hiding as soon as the word reached him that the Maoists were in the hamlet. His oldest son is by him. His youngest, back from Afghanistan on a break, is with a group of men, all tense from what they had just witnessed. One of Thapa Maila *dai*'s grandsons begins to drum a *madal*. Tauka Kanchha *dai* motions him to stop, and the men talk. No one knows who the woman is or what they should do next, but all of them agree should she die, they should bury her below the temple.

'Times have changed,' they say to each other.

'I knew something like this would happen,' Saili *didi* says to Maiju. Her head had twitched that morning. 'It's an omen,' she adds.

'Isn't she the mother-in-law you mentioned?' Maiju asks.

'I don't know.' Saili *didi* shakes her head. 'I never met her. This one looked more like a Bahun woman, didn't she?'

Maiju turns around and looks in the direction of the temple. 'I don't know,' she says as well.

After dinner, Maiju throws a *chadar* around her, takes a flashlight and an ewer of water and walks back to the temple.

The woman is as she was before. Her legs are outstretched in front of her and her hands are tied around the pole behind her. Up close, Maiju can see that the woman's eyes are swollen shut, and the whole left side of her face is heavily bruised. Every time she breathes, blood trickles out of her mouth.

'What did you do?' Maiju asks, shining light on her face. The woman does not flinch. Maiju bends down, reaches for the rope behind her and begins to untie it. Then she lays the woman gently on her back. This makes her cough up blood.

'Bara,' Maiju says and begins to pour water in her mouth. The woman's lips only tremble. Most of the water spills out onto the ground. There is no hope for her. The woman will not survive the night.

Maiju unwraps her *chadar* and covers the woman with it. It is getting darker and colder.

'May your soul rest in peace,' Maiju says and gets up. Then, ready to head home, she takes a step back and on something that feels hard under her foot. Not a stone, not a stick, not a bone. But something brown and rusted, almost invisible among the pieces of bones and the dry leaves around. Maiju picks it up.

It's a razor blade. A blunt and chipped, handleless barber's blade.

Tyo jharile khar samatdai angan chhoyo, eh maiju
Dukha mutu kunaima rairahyo
Haaa – dukha, maiju, mutumai rairahyo

(That rain, my dear aunt, slid down the roof and touched the yard
But this ache stayed in a corner
My aunt, it's lodged deep in the heart)

33

KANCHHI REACHED BAYARGHARI WELL BEFORE noon. Like Waling, Bayarghari is a tiny bazaar along the Sunauli-Pokhara highway, and at that moment, it was quiet and deserted. No buses passed by as Kanchhi waited by the roadside.

'Where you headed, *Nani*?' an old man in his sixties asked. He was smoking a cigarette nearby.

'Is this where the bus to Pokhara stops, *Dai*?' Kanchhi asked him.

'Pokhara?' The man looked at her and then around as if for her parents. 'You have to cross that bridge for that. Where're you coming from?'

Kanchhi didn't answer. She craned her neck to see the bridge he was talking about. There seemed to be one in the distance. 'What time does the bus arrive, *Dai*?' she asked.

'There's no fixed time, *Nani*,' the old man said. 'Buses don't depart from here. Wait here, and you'll catch one that comes from the south.'

'Wait here?'

'No, across the bridge.'

'Oh.' Kanchhi picked up her bags and started walking towards the bridge.

'Have you eaten?' the old man asked.

'No,' Kanchhi said. 'I'm not hungry.'

'Eat something before you go. It's a long journey. Here, I know a place where you can sit and eat while you wait. I'll show you.' The old man got up and started walking ahead of her.

Kanchhi hesitated.

'Don't be afraid. It's my niece's place right where the bus stops,' the old man said and took her to a small eatery by a narrow side alley. Like the one in Waling that Kanchhi frequented with Maiju, this eatery too did not have a name but just two tables and a counter with a woman sitting behind it. One of the tables was already occupied by a group of men eating *dal*, *bhat*, curry. Kanchhi stood by the other.

'Bhanji.' The old man turned to the woman behind the counter. 'This *nani* here needs a place to sit and wait for the bus. Let her sit and wait, all right? Seems like she's been walking all morning.'

'You can sit all you want but only if you order something,' the woman said.

'Tea,' Kanchhi said.

'Tea is right there.' The woman pointed at a shack across the alley.

'What are you talking about?' the old man said. 'You can't send this girl there. That's no place for her.'

The shack across was full of men drinking tea from small glasses.

'You sit here,' the old man told Kanchhi. 'I'll order you a glass of tea. Milk or black?'

'Black.'

'What if someone wants to come and eat here?' the woman asked.

'Then, they'll sit right here.' The old man kicked a bench by him.

'What if they don't want to?'

'Who won't want to sit on an empty bench? Let her wait here. She'll go once a bus comes along.'

The woman didn't say anything. Kanchhi rested her bags on a bench in front of her and sat down.

The first bus arrived soon afterwards while Kanchhi was in the midst of drinking her tea, but it did not stop for any passengers. It honked and wheezed past like a breeze. The second one arrived much later, but it slowed down. The old man ran to get her. The bus was from Butwal, and it had one empty seat.

'Take it before others get to it,' the old man said, carrying the checkered bag for her. Kanchhi paid the teashop and ran after him.

He was right. There was only one seat left – the reason a couple who were there before her had let it go.

'How many people?' the bus conductor shouted at the old man.

'One,' the old man said.

'Any bags for the trunk?'

'No.'

'Follow me then.'

The old man followed him inside the bus. Kanchhi followed the old man.

'Didn't you say one?' the conductor shouted when he looked back and saw Kanchhi.

'I'm not going,' the old man said. The conductor looked at Kanchhi again and then led them all the way to the back of the bus. There was an empty seat in the back row, right in the middle of it, facing the aisle. On one side were two men and on the other was a couple with a child. Directly in front of the couple were two seats occupied by a young man and a woman as old as Maiju. The conductor tapped on the shoulder of the young man and asked him if he could exchange seats with Kanchhi. The young man looked at Kanchhi and then at the two men sitting at the back and reluctantly agreed.

'Do you vomit?' the conductor asked once Kanchhi had settled down.

Kanchhi didn't know.

'Have you ever been on a bus before?'

'No,' Kanchhi said.

'Sit by the window then,' he said. The woman as old as Maiju occupying that seat refused to give it up. She said she too suffered from motion sickness.

'You'll need to take turns throwing up out the window

then,' the old man, who was still standing by Kanchhi, said and laughed.

Kanchhi told the conductor she would be fine.

'No, you won't. I don't want my bus dirty,' he said and went to get plastic bags for her and the woman.

'Okay, then,' the old man said, patting the top of Kanchhi's bus seat. 'Don't forget that you have a bag here.' He pointed at the checkered bag under her seat. 'It might slide as the bus moves and brakes. Hold on to it.'

Kanchhi nodded, wondering how she should repay him. 'Want some tangerines, *Dai*?' she asked and reached down to get them.

'No, no, I'm fine. You'll need them along the way. Travel safe now. I'll tell the conductor to drop you off at Pokhara.'

Kanchhi nodded. The old man walked away.

Two and a half hours later, the conductor came and told her that the bus had reached Pokhara. Kanchhi was not asleep, but she was not wide awake either. The second the bus had moved, she had begun to vomit. First came out the tea. Then the lone tangerine she had had on the way. The woman, sitting by the window, had to give up her seat right away.

At Prithvi Chowk, Kanchhi held her head in her hands and stayed down on the pavement for a long time. She looked so sick no taxi driver bothered her. A few passers-by advised her to take a pill for motion sickness next time. Others just covered their noses and tried not to puke themselves. Some scolded her for throwing up in a public space.

Once she was able to lift her head, Kanchhi picked up her bags, slung them on each shoulder and began walking towards the roundabout. The streets here were much more crowded than in Bayarghari. The shops too were too many to count. They spilt onto the pavements as a footpath bazaar – shoes on tarpaulin, clothes on tarpaulin, jewellery on tarpaulin, herbs on tarpaulin and so on. Kanchhi avoided stepping on them and walked ahead. Across the roundabout, she stopped in front of a shop with a phone. A general store that sold a little bit of everything.

'*Dai*, I need to make a call,' she said.

A man leaning against a cabinet counter and swirling a bunch of keys around his finger looked at her. 'What's the number?' he asked.

Kanchhi rested the checkered bag down on the floor and looked for a notebook inside her orange bag. She showed the man the number.

'Is this a local number?' he asked.

'No, it's from Parbat.'

'Parbat? What's the area code for Parbat?'

'+67,' Kanchhi said.

The man did not believe her. He ran a finger down a piece of paper taped on the counter and looked for the area code for Parbat. Someone had written down all the districts and the corresponding area codes in a table.

'+67,' he said and unlocked the wooden case the phone was in. He dialled the number.

'Not connecting,' he said. 'Is this the right number?'

Kanchhi looked at the number. 'Yes.'

'Looks like the line's down.' He tried again, pressing the speaker button this time. Kanchhi heard a tone.

'Maybe it's busy,' Kanchhi said.

'No, that's a different tone. Any other number?'

'It's a solar phone. Maybe it didn't get enough sun today,' Kanchhi said.

'That could be it. Any other number?' The shopkeeper asked again, ready to lock the phone.

'Yes.' Kanchhi showed him her aunt's number. This time, someone picked up.

'Here, talk.' The shopkeeper passed her the handset.

'*Phupu*, namaste,' Kanchhi said.

'*Phupu*? Who *phupu*?' A man spoke.

'Oh, Uncle, namaste,' Kanchhi said.

'Who is this? Who are you calling your aunt and uncle?'

'Uncle, this is Kanchhi from Torikhola, Parbat. We haven't met, but—'

'Kanchhi? Parbat? Wrong number.' The man cut the call. Kanchhi looked at the shopkeeper a little shocked.

The shopkeeper looked at the time. Less than thirty seconds.

'What happened?' he asked.

'He says he's not my uncle.'

'Is that the right number?'

'Yes.' Kanchhi had memorized the number.

'Want to try again?' the man asked.

'Yes.'

The man dialled the number again.

'Namaste, *Dai*,' he spoke for her. 'Is this a house or a shop? A girl here is looking for her aunt. She has your number.'

The shopkeeper listened to the other end for a bit and then asked Kanchhi what the aunt's name was. Kanchhi didn't know.

'Where's your home?' he asked her.

'Torikhola, Parbat.'

'The girl is from Torikhola, Parbat. The aunt must be too.'

'*Dai*,' Kanchhi said to the shopkeeper. 'Can you ask him to tell her that I'll be there by tomorrow evening? That I'll call again in the morning?'

The shopkeeper relayed the message and after a '*La*' and a '*Hus*,' put the receiver down.

'The number belongs to a store,' he said. 'Your aunt will be informed. Where does she live?'

'Chhorepatan.'

'And you got off here? You should have gotten off there. The bus comes via Chhorepatan.'

'Oh, I didn't realize that,' Kanchhi said. 'How much was the call?'

'Give me five.'

Kanchhi paid the shopkeeper and then asked him if there was a pharmacy nearby. The man pointed her up the street.

Up the street were more houses and storefronts – a liquor store, an electronic store, a furniture showroom, more general stores and the pharmacy the shopkeeper had pointed to, but a man was behind the counter, and Kanchhi decided to look for another one with a woman in charge. It took her a while to find one. She had to walk past that pharmacy, turn around when there seemed to be none up ahead, walk back down past the same pharmacy and the phone store she had just been in and cross the roundabout. A line of storefronts later, she saw one where a woman was shelving boxes of medicine on a shelf. She was in a plain *kurta surwal* set with a cardigan on top, and Kanchhi thought she looked homely and compassionate.

'*Didi*,' Kanchhi said, climbing the first few steps that led to the store. 'Does a doctor come here as well?'

'Yes,' the woman said. 'But only in the evenings on Mondays. Come back at five.'

Kanchhi checked her watch. It was around 3 p.m. A young boy around ten years of age walked up past her and asked the woman for pills to stop diarrhoea.

'How is the stool?' The woman turned to him. 'How frequent is it?'

The boy said he had been to the toilet four times since that morning.

'How was it?' the woman asked.

'Very watery,' the boy answered.

'Nausea?'

'No.'

The woman reached for a box behind her and took out a pack of tablets. She also took out a packet of Jivanjal electrolytes. 'You know how to read, don't you?' she asked the boy.

'Yes,' the boy said.

'Then follow the instructions written here. This one, take it three times a day after some food.'

'Okay. How much is the total?' the boy asked.

The woman packed the medicine in a tiny plastic bag and hit the calculator. The boy unfolded the bills he was holding.

'I will be fine by tonight, won't I?' he asked before leaving.

'Yes. Might take a few more days too,' the woman said.

Kanchhi watched the boy walk down the steps. When she looked back up, the woman was staring at her. 'Do you need anything else?' she asked.

'No.' Kanchhi shook her head and pretended to read the writing on a pillar next to her. 'Available Services,' it said. 'Check-ups from an experienced doctor, Wound dressing and bandaging, Pressure check, Urine and stool test, Blood test, Three monthly Sangini Depo Provera injection. Clinic hours: M/W 5–7 p.m. Saturday 12–2 p.m. Ph. No. +61 44—'

Kanchhi looked for the clinic. It was on the other side of the room behind a green curtain. Above it were the words 'Examination Room.'

'*Didi*,' Kanchhi climbed up the rest of the steps to the pharmacy and stood directly in front of the counter. The woman, now sitting on a stool and writing something in a notebook, looked up.

'I have a question, *Didi*,' Kanchhi said, putting her bags down.

'What is it?' the woman asked.

Kanchhi looked around and then asked in a voice as calm as possible, 'Do you also check here to see if someone's pregnant?'

'Who needs to be checked?'

Kanchhi hesitated.

'Who?' the woman demanded.

'Me,' Kanchhi said in a low whisper.

The woman too looked around. Then, she finished writing in her notebook and shut it.

'When was your last period?' she asked.

'I don't remember. Five, six weeks ago.'

'Five or six?'

'Six. I don't remember.'

The woman didn't say anything for a while. She reached down for a bottle of water and took a few gulps. Then, she got up. 'You don't look married,' she said. 'Are you keeping it?'

Kanchhi only stared at her.

'Who are you with? Did you bring a friend?' the woman asked.

'No. I'm staying at my aunt's, but she's not here with me.'

'Does your aunt know?'

Kanchhi shook her head.

'Where are you from?'

'Parbat.'

'Where in Parbat?'

'Duktan.'

'Parents?'

'*Ama*'s there.'

'Does she know?'

Kanchhi shook her head again.

The woman sat back down on the stool. 'And who told you to come and ask here?'

'Nobody. I'd heard clinics do it.'

The woman shook her head as if she could not believe the audacity. She reached for a phone under the counter that Kanchhi had not noticed before and started dialling it. A little girl walked up the stairs and asked if she could use the phone. The woman pointed her towards the next shop. The girl walked away.

No one answered the phone.

'What can I say? You should have been careful. A young woman like you. A world like this. You know it's illegal, right? You can't just take care of things like that.'

Kanchhi began to well up.

'Don't cry now.'

'Can you do something about it, *Didi*? Can you please help me?'

The woman watched Kanchhi for a bit. Then, she told her to follow her to a quieter place. She stopped by the green curtain and whispered, 'It's not cheap. Cases like this are very expensive. Do you have the money?'

'I have a little. How much does it cost?'

'I don't know for sure, but it won't be less than four. At the least three.'

'Three thousand?'

'Thousand, yes, not hundred.'

Kanchhi had no choice.

The woman began to walk back to the counter. 'Come back again a little after six,' she said. 'Where does your aunt stay?'

'Chhorepatan.'

'You can't go there tonight. Get a room at a hotel, and don't say anything to anyone.'

Kanchhi looked out at the street.

'All those buildings.' The woman pointed at a line of them across the street. 'They are all hotels and lodges. There's more behind them.'

'How much do they charge, *Didi*?'

'Hundred to two hundred a night. Here, let me show you.' The woman walked to the top of the steps and pointed at a blue building up towards the roundabout across the street.

'See that building over there?' she said. 'There's a side street right by it. Take that street and look for a hotel named Putalibazaar Lodging and Fooding. Tell them the *didi* from Pokhara Medical Store sent you. Say you're my cousin. They'll give you a discount.'

Kanchhi picked up her bags.

'When you come back, come see me directly.'

Kanchhi nodded and walked out.

At Putalibazaar Lodging and Fooding, Kanchhi stood in front of its open shutter door and looked around for the manager or owner. The owner, a man in his forties, was at a table in the dining area, chatting with another man. When he saw her, he asked, without getting up, what she wanted.

'The manager of the hotel, *Dai*, or the owner. Where is he?' Kanchhi asked.

'I am the manager. What do you want? A room?'

'Yes.'

'For how many?'

'Two. My mother will join me later.'

The man got up reluctantly and waddled to the counter. Just then, a young boy walked in with a big sack of rice on his shoulder.

'Kanchha,' the man called him. 'Once you're done with that, show her room number nine.'

The boy lifted one of his eyebrows and jerked his head to say 'yes' and continued walking.

The room was on the third floor, immediately to the left of a set of stairs. Not too big, not too small. It had two single beds separated by a small tea table.

Kanchhi dropped her bags on the table and walked to the window to look out at the alley she had just come from.

'What's that smell?' Kanchhi asked, running her hands through the curtains and sniffing them.

'What smell?' the boy asked.

Kanchhi sniffed the air. 'I don't know. Something in here smells. Wet and rotten.'

The boy shrugged.

'How much is the room? Kanchhi asked.

'Four hundred.'

'Four hundred? The sister there told me it would be two.'

'Sister where?'

'A sister at Pokhara Medical Store.'

'You'll have to talk to the owner about that. I know nothing about it.'

Kanchhi looked around at the room once again. The bathroom, with its wooden door swollen from dampness and moisture, was at the other end. 'Let's go down then,' Kanchhi said.

It took some back and forth. First, the owner said that four hundred was already a reduced price and then that two hundred would not even get her a spot on the pavement, but he eventually agreed to lower the charge. Kanchhi entered her name in the registry as Laxmi. Number of people: 2. Destination: Kathmandu. Advance: Rs100.

For the next few hours, Kanchhi stayed in the room, thinking how smoothly things had gone before reading a paper she had picked up from the counter and eventually falling asleep. When she woke up, it was ten minutes before six. She lightened her orange bag, keeping only the essentials like the notebook and the razor blade, and walked to the medical store.

To her surprise, there was a long line of patients waiting outside, spilling on to the stairs. Somehow, she had thought she would be the only patient and that she would just walk in, get checked up, get the deed done and be out in fifteen minutes.

Kanchhi walked up to the woman she had talked to earlier. The woman was sitting on a stool right outside the green curtain, holding a stack of patient books in her hands. Patients who had just walked in would go up to her and give her their books. The woman would then call them up one at a time when their turns came to see the doctor. From the door that was slightly ajar, Kanchhi could hear him talking to a patient inside.

'*Didi*,' Kanchhi said to the woman.

'Come back in an hour,' the woman promptly said.

Kanchhi nodded and walked back out. But she did not go anywhere. She stayed on the steps and waited.

It was 7:30 p.m. when the doctor was done with the last patient and the woman came to collect Kanchhi. She immediately took her behind the building and past a small courtyard with bricks and sand dumped for construction. The street here narrowed into a lane, and the lane narrowed further into a grassy path. At the end of that path was an adobe house with a tiny wooden door. The woman asked a young boy playing outside to go tell his mother to boil a pot of water. She then opened the door to the adobe house and climbed a dark ladder. Kanchhi followed her. On the second floor was a room that was part storage for the pharmacy and part a clinic ward.

'Did you bring the money?' the woman asked.

Kanchhi reached for the pouch inside her *cholo* pocket and took three thousand out. Every rupee she had ever saved in her life. Money from *Dashain*, from *Tihar*, from *Deusi-bhailo* programmes and from Maiju and Jhalnath.

'Additional thirty for the pads,' the woman said. 'Put your bag on the floor and sit on the bed.'

Kanchhi gave her thirty rupees more and did as told. The bed was a single, metal one with a very thin mattress, often seen in health posts and clinics. That reassured Kanchhi.

The woman pulled a curtain around the bed and disappeared. The curtain and the bed sheet were both green. So was the wall and the tint on the poster of Mt. Machhapuchhre on it. The mountain, with its head slighltly twisted, appeared as if it was trying to take one last look at Kanchhi. Someone, somewhere near, fried cumin.

The pot of water came in first. Five minutes later, the doctor. Kanchhi stood up when he slid the curtain open. He had a mask on. No white coat.

'Sit, sit,' he said. 'Everything ready?' he asked the woman.

The woman walked in with a mobile tray. She too had a mask on.

'Where's the ultrasound report?' the doctor asked her.

The woman told him Kanchhi had not done it. The doctor shook his head. 'Okay, then. Give her the pills and get ready.' He walked out.

The woman gave Kanchhi two pills and a bottle of water. Kanchhi did not ask what they were for.

The woman spread a plastic sheet on top of the green sheet.

'Lie down and pull up your *lungi*,' She said. 'If you are wearing an underwear, take it off.'

Kanchhi took off her underwear and lay down. 'Does it hurt?' she asked the woman.

'No, you won't feel a thing,' the woman said.

Kanchhi took a deep breath in and out and looked at the ceiling. It was like any other ceiling in an adobe house, unpainted and wooden, with rows of beams sticking out. A light bulb hung from one of the beams.

'Roll up your sleeve,' the woman said. She had a rubber band in her hand.

The sleeve was too tight. Kanchhi untied the *cholo* strings and took an arm out. The woman looked for a vein.

'Count until ten,' she said.

Kanchhi looked back at the ceiling and began counting. By three, she was out.

It was a muscle relaxant. Fifteen minutes later, her heart stopped beating.

34

IF KAL EVER FOUND OUT ABOUT KANCHHI'S disappearance, Maiju never knew. She never heard from him or the aunt. On the fourth day, Jhalnath filed a missing person's report and sent a copy each to Waling, Bayarghari and Kushma police stations. They had already filed one in Chhorepatan, Pokhara. A day later, Jhalnath joined Maiju in her search for Kanchhi. They looked in the woods above the riverbed where Maiju had last seen her, went around a tea house three hours up and then around a *chautara* at the top of the mountain. They asked everyone they met along the way, searched around every landslide, but no one had seen Kanchhi, or if they had, they did not remember. Jhalnath told Maiju he would continue to look for Kanchhi even from Mustang and left in the first week of December. For a month afterwards, Maiju continued the search alone. Then, it became less frequent – once every week and then once every month. A year later, she stopped.

November 13, 2005

People accuse Maiju of not looking hard enough for Kanchhi. She gave up too easily, they say. Ten years, and she still lives in the same ho use where Kanchhi was born and raised. If they were her, they would have overturned the whole Earth inside out until they had found her. Or they would have become a *sanyasi*, their faith in everyday living lost. Salvation, for them, would have lain only in eternal search – that of Kanchhi or *moksha*. Anything else would have been pure torture, they say, for the disappeared never disappear.

No, they don't. Maiju knows it. The disappeared do not disappear. Their memories drape the yard like a fog. Their dreams hang like dew from every corner. Kanchhi sits on the porch and sings, '*Basa basa re basundhara baini.*' She stands in the yard and announces, 'Namaste, this is Radio Torikhola, *khulera bola*.' She looks out far across the gorge, forlorn, like the spectre men are raised to fear. Young and slender, with waist-long hair and an urge to escape it all: the fields, the slopes, the poverty, the invisibility. The truth is: the war is eternal. It is here and now, never won, unwinnable. The war against the mountains, the war against memories and the war against the fact that ten years ago, Kanchhi disappeared and for nothing. Nothing at all. The truth is: Maiju knows what disappearance means. She knows Kanchhi did not just lose her way home. To confirm her suspicions, however, is to expose herself to unbearable grief, guilt and regret. Maiju won't survive it.

Maiju enters Kanchhi's bedroom.

It is a shrine, left as it was the day Kanchhi left. The bed is made the way it was, the ink bottle lamp is still on the windowsill, and the walls are bare except for some drawings, newspaper cut-outs, and a copy of the poem Kanchhi had written and submitted to *Gorkhapatra*. *'Maya dui aksharko...'* Love. Synonymous with memories and pain. The woman, the bones, the blade under the foot.

Euta diyo debilai balani
Shunya bhayo amako kakha ni

(Light a lamp for the goddess
The mother's lap is empty)

A melody rings out from Thapa Nani *didi*'s yard.

Someone jingles a tambourine.

Maiju lights a lamp.

The flame, feeding on mustard oil, sizzles at first and then unfurls like a fern, its dim glow reaching for a heart never to be pacified again.

Outside, the razor blade keeps watch.

Glossary

Abui	An expression of fear and surprise
Adharma aja unkai chha geet (Anyaya)	His songs are on my lips today (Injustice)
Aiya	An expression of pain
Akshyata	A mix of rice grains and red powder often used in Hindu rituals
Alachhini	Impure, unfortunate woman
Ama	Mother
Amaro	Nepali hog plum
Apsara	A female spirit in Hindu mythology
Astami	The eighth day in each of the two lunar phases
Ba	Father
Babai	An expression of surrender, defeat, disbelief, surprise
Babu	Little boy
Badahar	The lakoocha tree; monkey fruit
Bafre	An expression of surprise/disbelief
Baje	Grandfather; a man old enough to be a grandfather
Bakulla	Fava beans
Banjh	Unploughed; infertile
Banmara	An invasive weed species. Literal meaning: forest killer

Bara/Barai	An expression of pity
Basa basa re basundhara baini	Come sit, O' sister from Basundhara; a line from a popular nursery rhyme
Bauko gula	Father's dick
Bello	A fig species in Nepal
Bhagwan	God
Bhagya Rekha	The lines of fate
Bhanji	Niece
Bhauju	Sister-in-law
Bhooli gaye samjhanalai	To remind yourself if you forget me
Bhoto	Innerwear, with tie strings at the shoulders, often worn by children for warmth
Bhrun	Foetus
Bindi	A decorative sticker worn at the center of the forehead or in between the eyebrows by Hindu women
Birya	Sperm
Bokaharu	Male goats
Buhari	Daughter-in-law
Buwa	Father or someone as old as fathers would be
Chadar	A long and wide shawl often used by women for warmth in cold weather
Chautara	A resting place, often with stone benches carved around a big tree
Chha bhane maya chhapakkai laideu	If you love me, love me deeply.
Chhamchham nachideu niurera	Dance with your head bent
Chhi	An expression of disgust at something dirty
Chhuchchhi	Bitchy

Chhyak	An onomatopoeia imitating the sound of a knife slicing through flesh and bones
Chhyama	Aunt; mother's younger sister
Chilaune	Needlewood
Chiuri	A butter tree
Cholo	A wrap blouse
Chuchchi	Pointy
Chungi	A bunch of rubber bands tied together and kicked for fun and games
Dai	Older brother
Dakshina	Money given as a gift during festivals
Dal, bhat	A typical Nepali plate of rice, lentils, and curry
Dalli	Shortie
Dandi biyo	A children's game played with a stick and a wooden pin
Dankini	A female demon
Dashain	The ten-day long Hindu festival celebrated in autumn
Debri	Disobedient
Deri	Cross-eyed
Deusi Bhailo	A traditional song-and-dance event during the festival of *Tihar*
Devi	Goddess
Dhaka	Traditional handmade Nepali fabric and design
Dhanya Prabhu	Thank god
Dhat	An expression of frustration, irritation or dismissal
Dhaturo	Devil's trumpets

Dhedo	A meal made of ground millet, corn or barley flour cooked in boiling water
Didi	Older sister
Diwana	A passionate lover
Diyo	A lamp often made of clay or brass, with cotton wicks dipped in ghee or oil
Doko	A conical bamboo basket often carried on the back with a tumpline
Ekadashi	The eleventh day in each of the two lunar phases
Galkote raja, luto laija	The king of Galkot (in the district of Baglung in modern Nepal), take measles away
Gatti	A children's game played with an odd number of pebbles, often five
Ghanse	A grass-cutter; a song sung while cutting grass
Gitilahar	Literal meaning: song vines
Goriya	Light-skinned woman
Gunyu/fariya cholo	Traditional attire containing a cotton sari and a wrap blouse
Haina	No; often used as a segue into another topic
Hantakali	Someone who eats a lot
Happy bijaya Dashami and shuva Deepawali 2049	Happy victorious *Dashain* and auspicious Diwali 2049
Harhar	A shortened form of 'Hari, Hari,' invoking Lord Bishnu
Hoi	Yes, as in a response to a call
Hya	An expression of frustration
Ja	An expression of surprise or surprised frustration

Jaba rati taba budhi tati	'It's the dead of night and the woman wants it' Meaning: To procrastinate until the eleventh hour
Jamara	Ten-day-old barley (also corn and buckwheat) saplings planted for *Dashain*
Janti	A group of attendants on the groom's side
Jathi	A term often used to denigrate girls and women. Literal meaning: pubic hair
Jay	Victory; victory to
Jhwain khatte	Oil-fried barley seeds
Jhyaure	A particular kind of a folk melody
Ji	An honorific
Kaha timro mayalulai	Where did you... your lover
Kaki	Aunt; father's brother's wife
Kala	An endearing term for a dark-skinned person
Kali	Dark-skinned woman
Kanchhi, Kanchhi bhet bhako ghyampo jatro pet bhako/ Babari phulko bot	Kanchhi and Kanchhi met, and their tummy is now as big as a pot/the plant of basil
Kanyadan	The act of handing over daughters in marriage
Karani	Rape
Kasam	A promise
Kauda	A folk melody/song popular among the Magar communities of Nepal
Khaneu	A fig tree found in the mountains of Nepal

Kheer	Rice pudding
Khoi	An expression that could mean 'I don't know,' 'Let me,' or 'Where is it?' depending on the context
Khukuri	A large knife smaller than a *khunda*
Khulera bola	Talk freely
Khunda	A large knife bigger than a *khukuri*
Kina badhdaichha dhukdhuki mutuko (Mayalu)	Why is my heart beating faster? (Lover)
Kisanko rahar	A farmer's wish
Kukurni	A female dog
Kurta surwal	Traditional attire consisting of a long top, a pair of trousers and a shawl
Kusume rumal	A silk handkerchief
La, la	Ok, ok
La, ta	Okay, then
Laijau! Laijau! Laijau!	Take me! Take me! Take me!
Lau na ni	An expression of shock, despair, disbelief
Lehenga choli	Traditional attire consisting of a long skirt, a blouse and a shawl
Lungi	A sarong predominantly worn by women in the mountains of Nepal
Madal	A hand drum
Madhuparka	A sweet offering consisting of honey, ghee, sugar, milk and water
Maiya	A term of endearment meaning a little, loved girl
Mata	Mother goddess

Moda	A low stool (taller than a pirka) used to sit on
Moksha	Salvation
Murdar	An expression of disgust meaning weak or dead
Nakachari	A shameless girl/woman; a term often used to denigrate girls and women
Nakkali	A girl who likes to be made up
Nanglo	A bamboo tray
Nani	Little girl
Naramri	Ugly
Narsinga	A trumpet in the traditional set of five musical instruments (*Panche baja*)
Natho	Lover
Natini	Granddaughter
Nisthuri bhunti	A heartless little girl
Padyo bhane hagyo, hagyo bhane chheryo, ani chheryo bhane maryo.	'If you farted, you shat. If you shat, it was diarrhea. If you had diarrhea, you died.' Meaning: Gossips change meanings as they travel.
Panche baja	A set of five traditional musical instruments in Nepal
Papini	A sinner
Parameshwori	The supreme goddess
Pathi	4.5 Litre
Patuka	A long piece of cloth wrapped around the waist for support
Pau	200/250 grams
Phohori	A dirty girl/woman
Phuchchi	Tiny
Phupu	Aunt; father's sister
Pipal	The Bodhi tree

Pirka	An extremely low stool used to squat on
Pote	A beaded necklace worn by married women
Puja	Ceremonial worship
Rakshasni	A female demon/rakshas
Ram nam satya ho	The name of God is the truth; Ram is the truth.
Randi	An insult used for a sex worker
Ratyauli	A party organized to welcome a newly married daughter-in-law into the house, often takes place immediately after the wedding ceremony but could also take place much later
Roti	Bread; flatbread
Sa'ab	Sahab, from saheb/sahib, meaning sir/master
Sahuni	A female shopkeeper
Sal	The sal tree
Salaijo	A folk melody popular in western Nepal
Sangini song	A traditional song sung by women in eastern Nepal
Santan	Children; progeny
Sanyasi; sanyasa	A Hindu religious mendicant who has renounced worldly pleasures; the state of being a sanyasi
Satya	Truth; an expression conveying the truth/validity of the speaker's words
Selroti	A ring-shaped, deep fried rice bread
Silauto	A spice-grinding stone
Simal	A bombax tree; a silk cotton tree
Sindoor	A red or orange powder used by married Hindu women

Solti	A sister of the sister-in-law or brother-in-law; a term often used flirtatiously
Subol	Say sweet things; bring good news.
Suna suna mayalu jodi ho	Listen, listen, couples and lovers
Sworga	Heaven
Syani	Little one
Tait	An expression of frustration
Tapari	A plate made of leaves
Tatteri ki	An expression of frustration
Teejako rahara	The occasion of Teej
Thunse	A conical basket like a doko but with holes often sealed with mustard paste
Tihar	The five-day long Hindu festival celebrated soon after *Dashain*
Tiharai ayo	*Tihar* is here
Ukharmauli	An indecent girl/woman; a term often used to denigrate girls and women
Uttauli	An excited/aroused girl/woman; a term often used to denigrate girls and women
Uttis	Nepali alder
Venaju	Older brother-in-law
Yi woth timra muskan timrai (Kanchhi)	These lips are yours. This smile is yours. (The youngest one)
Yuwamanch	Literal translation: a stage for youths

ACKNOWLEDGEMENTS

Let me begin from the beginning. I would like to thank Professor Elizabeth Tallent and then–Stegner Fellow Stephanie Soileau of Stanford University for guiding me through, what I would now like to call, the pre-drafts of *Kanchhi*. I was just a rising senior then, with nothing but a sliver of an idea for a book and a desire to be published. Both Prof. Tallent and Stephanie, nonetheless, lent me their full support and expertise and encouraged me to keep writing. I would also like to thank the university itself, especially its Department of English, for awarding me the 2008 Creative Arts Grant and setting me off on a long journey of discovery and exploration.

My deep gratitude also goes to another academic institution – Cornell University. In particular, I'm beyond grateful to Prof. Helena María Viramontes and Prof. John Roberts Lennon, my MFA committee advisors, for their unwavering faith in *Kanchhi* and wise counsel and generosity of spirit. I'm also indebted to the rest of the creative writing faculty at Cornell (Stefanie Vaughn, Maureen McCoy and Ernesto Quiñonez), my MFA fiction cohort (Shakarean Hutchinson, Peter Gilbert, Neal Giannone and Hema Surendranathan), and the members of the cohorts before and after mine (Christopher Seiji Berardino, Rocio Anica, Shane Kowalksi, Leo Rios, Mario Giannone, Remy Barnes, Alice Louise Mercier, Charlotte Pattison and Nneoma Ike-Njoku). Thank you all for being patient with the atrocious drafts I submitted for workshop. Much gratitude also to the Mario Einaudi Center for International Studies at Cornell and its South Asia Program, as well as to the Cornell Department of Literatures in English for providing me financial support as I researched and wrote the novel.

Outside academia, I am forever indebted to Manjushree Thapa, Kanak Mani Dixit, Tiku Gauchan and Dewan Rai for all the love and support they have shown to the novel over the years. Special thanks to Manjushree, Buddhi Sagar and Narayan Wagle for providing blurbs at extremely short notice. Speaking of short notices and prompt replies – thank you, Kavita Sherchan, for allowing me, in a heartbeat, to include your late father Bhupi Sherchan's poem '*Chiso Ashtray*' in the novel.

To the people who were always there, quietly but firmly behind the novel – namely, Tina Zhang, Aunohita Mojumdar, Vidhyadhar Gadgil, Meher Ali, Ojashwi Thami, Kabita Parajuli, Prawin Adhikari, Rabindra Maharjan, Bijaya Babu Siwakoti, Seanie Civale, Sabrina Toppa, Marisa Turesky, Sampreety Gurung and Purnima Ghale – thank you for being out there, cheering on. I